"Jordy, I have powerful dreams of you still. Just last night—"

Jordan shook his head. "Don't tell me about dreams, Raine. I've had dreams of kissing you and come awake with stinging tears in my eyes, hurting so bad I could hardly stand it."

Suddenly Jordy caught her to him again. Holding her with one arm, he cupped her face with his thumb and fingers. "Raine, if you only knew . . ."

"Knew what, Jordy?"

"What I've been through without you."

"It wasn't any easier for me. Fate threw us a wicked curve."

Jordy kissed her long and hard, his tongue going into her mouth where hers caressed it. Then he furiously darted damp kisses over her face.

Raine grew dizzy with pleasure. His big hands pressed her body into his and she felt his hot kisses on her upper body.

Then he lifted his head and whispered, "I still love you. I won't crowd you, my darling. *Just know that I'm here for you . . .*"

FRANCINE CRAFT
PRAISE FOR HER PREVIOUS BOOKS

Tahiti is the perfect setting for this very romantic story. Ms. Craft's fans are in for a treat.
—*Rendezvous on* LYRICS OF LOVE

If it's romance you want, this is a book to read.
—*America Online,* WCRG
Hattie Boyd, LYRICS OF LOVE

In this book, Ms. Craft has compellingly recreated Reconstruction in New Orleans with an impressive line-up of characters that sweeps the reader into a story rich with culture, history and romance.
—*Romantic Times* on
THE BLACK PEARL

A winner that you will remember long after you have turned the last page.
—*Rendezvous* on DEVOTED

STILL IN LOVE

FRANCINE CRAFT

BET Publications, LLC

www.msbetbooks.com
www.arabesquebooks.com

ARABESQUE BOOKS are published by

BET Publications, LLC
C/o BET BOOKS
1900 W Place NE
Washington, D.C. 20018-1211

Copyright © 1999 by Francine Craft

All rights reserved. No part of this book may be reproduced, stored in a retrieval system, or transmitted in any form or by any means without the prior written consent of the Publisher.

If you purchased this book without a cover you should be aware that this book is stolen property. It was reported as "unsold and destroyed" to the Publisher and neither the Author nor the Publisher has received any payment for this "stripped book."

BET Books™ is a trademark of Black Entertainment Television, Inc. ARABESQUE, the ARABESQUE logo and the BET BOOKS logo are trademarks and registered trademarks.

First Printing: March, 1999
10 9 8 7 6 5 4 3 2 1

Printed in the United States of America

DEDICATION

This book is dedicated to the following people: Myles J.—the best of friends, Charlie K.—with much appreciation, June M. Bennett—a very good and helpful friend, Bruce Bennett—a helpful friend, Herschel and Mario Krause-Lee—who know what love means. You all know how wonderful you are.

ONE

Raine Gibson came awake reluctantly. A dream had begun and she pushed it back as too painful. But after a moment, her heart took over and she slipped back into her dream. The kiss was long and slow on Raine's lips, tender at first, more nuzzle than kiss. Then it built swiftly to fevered passion as she gasped, responding fervently the way she always did to Jordan Clymer's beloved kisses.

They were down by the crystal-clear two-acre pond on Challenger Farm, sitting on a big sun-warmed stone block that felt good against her bare legs.

"Jordy," she whispered. "We've got to stop!"

"I know," Jordan whispered in a half-groan, "Lord, I know!" Then, "We have to get married, Raine. There's no other way for us. We're about out of control."

"Then we'll have to find a way. You've got one more year of college and I have two. Your mother would never forgive me if I interfered with your realizing your dreams."

Jordan shrugged, taking her in his arms again. "You're my best dream, Ray," he said gently, calling her Ray, he said, for his special ray of sunshine. "Nature won't always wait for people in love the way we are. Can't say I blame her."

He was so intense. They both were, Raine thought. If they somehow got careless and she got pregnant, would he one day come to hate her?

"My love. My precious love," he said against her throat.

"We can get married and finish school and hold down part-time jobs."

"Come on, be real," Raine said. "We both want children too much for it not to happen. You need grad school. And your mother's ill with heart trouble."

"Which she uses to her advantage," Jordan said with a hint of bitterness.

"She loves you," Raine pointed out.

"And I love her, but my father taught me that my life is my own. My father was crazy about you. He thought I couldn't have chosen a better woman."

"Oh, Jordy, I was just a girl when he died."

"A womanly girl. I scare you with my passion, don't I? My father was a passionate man. My mother always thought he—and I—overdid it."

Raine laughed. "Well, mister, you've met your match in me. You don't scare me one bit."

"I'm glad. That means we've got a great future together. I love you, cupcake, really love you."

His words went echoing in Raine's mind: "Love you. Love you," and a few tears of joy came into her eyes before she could tell him she loved him.

She came awake to the radio alarm coming on with a Nancy Wilson song about loneliness and a lost love.

Raine turned over and buried her face in her pillow. She and Jordan Clymer had talked in the meadow years ago about love and marriage, about just about everything ten years ago when she had been eighteen to his twenty. It was a lifetime ago. Hugging her pillow, she wondered how all that passion could have ended, and sadly she knew that for her it never had.

A light tap sounded and to her response, her daughter, Kym, who was nine came flying into the room.

"Oh, Mom," she cried, "this time next week, school!"

"Uh-huh. I'm so glad you like school so much." A junior high school teacher, Raine usually wholly enjoyed teaching junior high school art. But this year she found her heart heavier than usual. There wasn't anybody in her romantic life. Dan was dead, and she had lost Jordy forever.

Kym, with her dark eyes and flyaway soft black hair, her beanpole straight figure, and walnut brown skin, was the love of her life. Precocious, a lovely and loving child, she said often what she said now. "I love you, Mom."

"And I love you," Raine said, as Kym threw her arms around her hugged her tightly.

"I don't think you feel so good this morning," the child said, lounging on the bed.

"What makes you say that?"

Kym shrugged. "Your eyes seem a little wet to me. And you look like you're sad."

"I am a little, but I'll get over it."

"And I'll help you," Kym said. "Miss Vi said for you to come on so we can have breakfast, and we've got to go pick up your art supplies and my school supplies. Can I have the red plaid jumper and the white blouse we saw? Can we afford it?"

Raine hugged her again. "May I, sweetie. Oh, I think we can manage."

Kym went out of the room, blowing her a kiss.

"Tell Miss Vi I'll be out as soon as I shower," Raine said.

Jordan Clymer swung his dark-blue Mercedes onto the road's shoulder and leaned against the steering wheel, pulling himself together. Thinking about Raine still hurt. After nine years, the pain just hadn't lessened enough.

Washington-Baltimore Parkway traffic whizzed by him as he sat breathing raggedly. He was a short distance away from Minden, Maryland, which lay halfway between Baltimore and Washington, D.C., which meant he was a short distance away from Raine. Raine. Jordan passed his hand over his crop of short thick black hair, thinking. The man she'd married after he left—his cousin, Dan Gibson—had been dead three years now. Dan and Raine had moved to New Orleans shortly after their marriage, and their kid had been born there. She had moved back just a year ago.

Jordan had everything set up to move his thriving security firm from Montreal to Washington, D.C. He couldn't take Montreal's stinging coldness anymore, not with the coldness of his second loss: his wife, Rita, leaving him for another man. Yes, he thought now, he was successful, but he was a loser in love.

He was sorry about Dan's death in a training accident in Spain, but he didn't kid himself that bad blood hadn't always existed between him and Dan. When he'd learned that Raine and Dan had married several months after he'd left, he'd been wild with grief. But he felt it as his own fault, too. He should have moved heaven and earth to keep in touch. But his mother had had a heart attack, and no sooner had she begun to recover than he had been wrongly diagnosed with rheumatic fever. Instead, he'd had a heart valve problem that required an operation. Something had gone wrong, and he had gone into a coma for over a month. Raine didn't need that burden. Her own father was dying of cancer. So the months had passed, and he had been too young to know the meaning of time.

Funny how soon Raine and Dan had gotten married after Jordan left. She'd been Dan's girl first, but Dan had messed up with running around with several girls, and Jordan had moved in. Well, the joke was on him, he thought with some anger—and pain. Maybe it had been Dan she loved after all.

Raine, he said to himself. "What can we put in store for us, now? We've both changed so much.

Okay, so he still felt lingering bitterness about her marrying Dan. My man, he said to himself. You'd hate anybody she married. He smiled for a moment thinking how he used to tell her, "Mom's not being crazy about you doesn't matter. Dan's not wanting to let you go doesn't matter. You're my fate. I was fated to love you, cupcake."

She would come into his arms, soft and smooth as silk, and lie with her heart beating against his and murmur, "We're fated to love each other."

Well, fate had dealt them both a cruel hand. So much for fate.

He was lucky to have Scott Williams as his second-in-command. Scott was a true friend and talking with him meant that at least he'd had someone to help ease his pain. Did Raine have someone else? He hadn't let himself think about that. As beautiful and wonderful as she was, he was sure she did.

He couldn't sit there all day mooning, he chided himself. Starting his engine purring, Jordan pulled out onto the road. Great parkway to drive on, with its hilly tree-covered banks. His heart kept lurching when he thought of Raine, and every inch of this road brought him closer—to what? A love that could sustain him all his life, or more of the heartbreak he'd known in the past?

Oh, God, he said to himself, please let her be free.

But in spite of his fervent wish, he admitted his bitterness at her marriage so soon after he'd left. Would he be able to put that aside? Then grimly he thought there could be added bitterness if she had found somebody else.

Aloud he said, "Dammit, Jordan, you're a security expert. You've been all over the world protecting people. You're top-flight security, find anybody anywhere. Why don't you know what her status is?" But he could never bring himself to track her life just to soothe himself. Don't lie, he said further to himself. You didn't want to know if she's gotten over you. He'd heard the news about Dan from a mutual friend.

Steeped in misery, anxiety, and desire that thoughts of Raine had brought up in him, he drove on steadily to the outskirts of Minden to a homey little country store with a great soda fountain. Must be the last one in America. There were plenty of parking spaces here. He wondered if the love and affection widowed Miss Elly lavished on her customers was still there.

Miss Elly would be a great person to ask about Raine. He had only to ask, and she'd give him full particulars. Miss Elly was one of the ones he'd talked with when he'd come back years ago to see Raine, only to find her married to Dan and moved away.

Raine stood in the country store, chatting with Miss Elly.

"Mom, aren't we going to have banana splits today?" Kym asked impatiently. "I've got enough supplies to last two years."

"Now, sweetheart, you mind your manners. Miss Elly and I were talking."

Kym looked disappointed for a moment, then brightened. "I'm sorry," she said. "It's just that the banana splits are so yummy."

"Mighty early in the morning to be eating banana splits," Miss Elly said, her eyes twinkling. "However, I could eat them at daybreak."

Raine patted her daughter's shoulder and glanced at her watch. "Well, it's a little past eleven, so a small one ought to be okay. You're one darling, delicate little stringbean. Now your mother's going to have to forgo banana splits for a while because I'm certainly no stringbean."

Kym blushed, reveling in the love of the two women.

"The kids say you've got a great figure," Kym said. "What's an hourglass, Mom?"

"When it refers to a woman, it's too big in the hips, honey," Raine said, laughing.

"Well, Jimmy said you had an hourglass figure."

Jimmy was one of Raine's fourteen-year-old students. The school supplies that Miss Elly had in stock packed, and the rest ordered to be in in a couple of days, Raine sat at a table with Kym as Miss Elly bustled about. Raine spoke to a man and a woman who'd come in. She kept glancing at her watch. Why was she in such a hurry? she wondered.

"Now don't be rushing away," Miss Elly said. "Plenty of people come in here, but there's nobody I enjoy more than you and Kym."

"The same certainly applies here," Raine said, thinking Miss Elly seemed as anxious as she was today. It wasn't like Miss Elly to be controlling, but she'd almost insisted that Raine come and pick up her supplies this morning. And the sprightly, really lovely older woman kept smoothing her hair and nervously glancing around.

"This is great, Miss Elly," Kym complimented her. "Now, Mom, let's go and pick up my jumper and blouse."

It would be cheaper to go shopping in Washington, and they were only thirty miles away, but the shops in Minden were quaint and catered to the town's customers. Faquita Fairley kept an excellent stock of women's wear.

"Oh, stay and indulge an old lady's loneliness," Miss Elly cajoled.

Raine laughed. "You lonely? Oh, Miss Elly, most of Minden would kill for a chance to talk with you. Your lunchtime crowd will soon be in."

Raine was sure now that Miss Elly was nervous about something. And by her own admission, she was trying to keep them there. Well, a little while longer couldn't hurt.

Raine got up to get a glass of water from the counter, turned back to her table, and nearly fainted when Jordan Clymer walked in. Time had only made him more attractive, made his craggy features more appealing.

Jordy was a tall man, over six feet and fit. He moved with lankily deliberate speed, and her heart turned over as her eyes met his. He'd gained a resolute attractiveness, and it made the hurt go deeper.

She told herself she'd have sworn she was over him, then

knew she'd deceived herself. What about the vivid dream she'd had just this morning? And the other dreams she'd never stopped having, even when she was married to Dan. She'd felt guilty about those dreams.

Miss Elly went to Jordan and they hugged. She took him by the hand and steered him to Raine's table.

"Hello, Raine," he said simply.

"Hello, Jordan," she answered, hardly trusting herself to speak. "Please sit down."

His eyes went over her with longing. She was such an attractive woman with a beauty that went far past the physical. A lush woman with cinnamon skin and long brown hair that she wore in a French twist, she'd be too heavy to be a reigning model, but she was beautifully stacked, he thought.

Looking at him, drawn nearly out of herself, Raine noted his close-cropped black hair, his dark olive skin, and dark eyes that were so caring and patient. He'd been so set on law enforcement. What had he become? After Dan's death when she'd gone to look him up, she found he was married. She hadn't trusted herself to find out anything more.

Looking at him levelly, her heart beating painfully, she saw into the depths of his brown-gray eyes that he still felt something for her. Love distilled to a gentle liking? No, his breath was nearly as ragged as her own. They had always been so comfortable with each other.

"We have to talk," she told him.

Jordan only nodded and freed his gaze to focus on Kym. What could she say? Darling, this is your father?

"Jordan, this is Kym, my daughter. Kym, Mr. Clymer."

Kym gave him her most careful scrutiny with her nine-year-old innocent gaze and stuck out her hand.

"I'm delighted to meet you, Mr. Clymer."

Jordan felt a lump in his throat. She was such a lovely child. He and Rita had had no children, and it had been a dinosaur-sized bone of contention between them. Flippantly Rita had always said, "Later, Jordy. Later. We've got a whole lot of living to do first. Then maybe." And she had fallen in love and left him before later could ever come.

Kym looked from one to the other of them, wondering why they were both so nervous.

A bustling Elly brought two cups of raspberry cappuccinos to the table, with a cup of sugar-free cocoa for Kym. "Ah, I'm a meddling old biddy," she said gaily, "but I remembered you like raspberry cappuccino, Jordy, and Raine gets it often enough."

"Thank you," they both said, and Jordan reached for his wallet. Miss Elly lightly slapped his hand. "Now put that back. This treat's on me. I can't tell you how glad I am to see you again."

"If you're a friend of Mom's," Kym said brightly, "will you be coming out to see us?"

"If your mom invites me, yes," Jordan said huskily, and turning to Raine, he continued. "I've got to go on to D.C. and meet with my associate, Scott Williams. We've got some new security contracts to work over, and it may take a while."

Was he running away from her again? Raine wondered.

"But I'd like to come back this evening and take you somewhere, if you're willing."

She hesitated for a moment, then said, "I'd like that."

His big hand covered hers. "It's a date then." Turning to Kym, he said, "If your mom okays it, next time I'll take the both of you out."

Kym's face lit up. "That'd be neat."

Jordan studied one of Raine's paintings that hung on the side wall. Exquisitely done in pastels, it was of a crystal-clear pond flanked by multicolored flowers and lush green weeping willow trees: impressionistic, and like the woman, incomparable. With any luck, Raine was going to be a noted painter. He looked back at her, smiling, some of the stress gone. That scene was of their pond on Challenger Farm.

"That painting's great, Raine. It brings back a lot of memories."

"I'm glad you like it."

He thought she sounded shy, and that was one facet of her. Loving her had been finding one lovely gem after another, uncovering an endless wealth. They were both silent, remembering.

Miss Elly and Kym looked from one to the other of them.

"I like the sound of what I'm hearing," Miss Elly said.

"So do I, so far," Jordan said, smiling, his hand still over Raine's.

For a long moment their gazes locked and held, drawn deeply into each other, then Raine blushed and took her hand from his.

"I couldn't be sorrier, but I've got to go now," Jordan said, standing up. "I'll see you tonight, Raine, you and Kym, although I may be late, and I'll call. Miss Elly, I'll see you tomorrow."

He bent and kissed the older woman's soft cheek as she smiled from ear to ear. "I'm going to hold you to that," she said, patting his cheek. "Don't disappoint me."

Raine's breath caught when Miss Elly said that. Talk about disappointment . . .

Miss Elly's eyes twinkled again. "He called me from his cell phone to tell me he was nearby. I told him you were here, and he asked me to keep you here until he came."

Raine laughed. "Miss Elly, you're an incurable romantic."

Overwhelmed with contract terms and points at his office in D.C., Jordan was late as he'd said he might be. Kym fell asleep, although she tried very hard to stay up.

The couple who helped her, Miss Violet and Uncle Prince

Thomas, were delighted that Jordan had returned. The three of them ran a berry and flower farm, which the older couple largely managed. The flowers and the berries and the lovely farm meant Raine had many models for her painting.

"How is Jordy these days?" Uncle Prince asked Raine when Kym excitedly told them that Jordan was back. "He was such a decent young man. Even as a boy he had a good bearing: kind, tenderhearted. He used to help me with my white rabbits and hamsters for the lab in D.C."

"He seems to be just fine," Raine said. "I think he's quite successful."

"I'd say so, too, knowing him," Miss Vi said.

Kym had an early dinner and sat drowsing, watching a TV sitcom. Raine walked over to her easel and picked up her palette, studying the painting she'd been working on— a seascape of the Chesapeake Bay. She picked up her sketchbook from the nearby table and began to sketch Jordan's face from memory and today. Kym came to watch her sketch, interrupting her TV watching.

"That's Mr. Clymer you're painting, Mom. Gee, it looks just like him. You're really good, you know."

"Thanks, sweetie. I hope I am."

"Know what I'm going to be when I grow up?"

"No, tell me."

"A rich tennis player. Like Tiger Woods is a golfer."

Raine smiled. "I'd much rather you be an *excellent* tennis player. I'd hate to see you pursue wealth for the sake of wealth."

"I'm gonna be both." Kym held her arms far above her head. "I'm going to be rich and excellent and famous."

Raine blinked. This child was so advanced for her age.

Raine and her daughter looked at each other, smiling, and Raine told her, "Relax, baby. You've got a bit of time ahead of you."

The phone rang and Raine answered.

"I couldn't be more sorry I'm running this late," Jordan's pleasantly husky voice said.

Raine glanced at her watch. "You said you might have to be late. Where're we going? Or do you want to stay here?"

Jordan thought a moment, looking at his ringless finger. "I'd rather go out with you if you're willing. Like you said, we need to talk. Can you get someone to sit with Kym?"

"Oh, the Thomases are still here," Raine said. "Remember them?"

"How could I forget that wonderful couple. Uncle Prince and my dad were good friends, you know. What if we drive back into D.C. and go someplace fabulous? I've got a place in mind I think you'll like, but I'll bow to your wishes."

Raine smiled. "I guess this means I'm going to have to gussie myself up and knock your eyes out," she said then added, "I keep kidding myself."

"You're not kidding. You'd knock my eyes out in ragged jeans."

"You flatter me."

"No. It's true. Dress as you want to. I'll be your slave, your captive tonight . . . anything you want."

The old feelings kept sweeping through them both as they awkwardly tried to hang up. Finally Raine said, "I've got to bathe and dress. I wasn't sure you'd call."

"Raine," he said, feeling a mixture of the old anger he'd felt when she'd married so shortly after he left. "Give me credit. I'd never disappoint you if I could help it."

"I'm sorry for that bit of snideness," Raine said.

"I was disappointed, too," he said, "when . . . Oh, hell, Raine, I'll pick you up within the hour. And we can talk then. I'd say we've got a whole lot to talk about."

"Yes," she murmured. "I'm really looking forward to talking with you."

She hung up. Why hadn't he come back for her?

* * *

STILL IN LOVE 19

After he hung up from talking with Raine, Jordan walked into the office adjoining his where his buddy and second-in-command, Scott Williams, leaned back in his chair.

"I think Clymer-Williams Security is going to be bigger here than in Montreal," Scott said. Then seeing Jordan's mind was elsewhere, he ventured, "Made your contacts, boss?" he asked, brown eyes crinkling in his florid face.

Jordan nodded.

"Well, you don't seem altogether happy about it."

"Consider what I'm facing and you'll know why."

"How'd the lady warm to you?"

Jordan paused, sighing. "She was pleasant—noncommittal. Yet there's still everything happening where she and I are concerned."

"You mean that in the good way."

"I'd like to think it could still be, but I . . . Hell, man, my cousin's dead, but maybe she's still grieving, and perhaps she's found someone else."

"We could have found out. We're among the best in the security business. I like to think that I'm one heck of a private investigator, and you sure are. But Raine's always been off-limits for investigation. Why, Jord?"

Jordan shrugged. "She'd hate me if I went snooping into her life. But it might have helped in the beginning when I nearly died from shock and heartbreak when I came back and found her married and moved away."

Scott got up, came around his desk, and briefly put his arms around Jordan, patting his back. Scott, Jordan thought, was one in a million. They were college friends after he'd transferred from Howard to McGill University. Later, together, they'd pooled savings and overtime from the Secret Service Department where both had met and become fast friends. With Max, Rita's father, they'd set up Clymer-Williams Security.

"That damned near killed you," Scott said, remembering how his friend had suffered.

"I couldn't go through it again. That's for sure."

"Yes, you could. You're a strong man, Jordy—the way you weathered the constant hell that was your marriage."

"Maybe you've got the right idea, Scott. Don't get hitched."

Scott's face got wistful. "Nowadays, I wine and dine them in numbers. It's safer that way. But old buddy, sometimes I don't feel as if I'm really living."

Jordan stood with his arms akimbo, rocking steadily. "Tonight I'll find out if I have a chance."

"You still hold it against her that she ran out on you?"

"She could have notified me, written, called, something."

It hit Jordan then like a brick, and he wondered why he was just facing it. Looking back at Kym today, he saw the feminine side of himself—and he didn't want to let himself believe it. He and Raine had made that child. There was little resemblance between Dan and his side of the family. Could he believe what he thought he'd found? That would explain her hasty marriage to Dan. God. His child when he wanted them so badly and had none. For a moment he felt as if his feet didn't touch the floor. Then he reminded himself that he could be wrong. He and Dan shared grandparents in common. Still—

He couldn't talk about this to Scott yet, so he continued the line of conversation they'd had before his flash of possible insight.

"Maybe she tried," Scott said.

"What got in her way?"

Scott sat down and threw up his hands. "Jordy, I don't know. Things happen. Maybe the wedding invitation got lost in the mail."

"Yeah. Maybe. You know Dan—the man she married—was my cousin. She was his girl first, and he was crazy about her. But Dan had a wild streak a mile wide. He and I were both only kids, but his parents spoiled him. A month never passed without him getting in some kind of scrape. On Pop's pay as a small-town deputy sheriff, we didn't have much, but Dan's parents were the rich side of the family. Owning a successful department store didn't make them really rich, but they sure were comfortable."

"Yeah," Scott said, "and if you told me the truth, they were a miserable bunch."

"Yeah." Jordan laughed. "Aunt Kettie didn't like men very much, and sometimes it seemed Uncle Henry didn't like women at all. They fought like the gingham dog and the calico cat."

"But they ran a successful store?"

"Yeah." Jordan chuckled. "They put it all aside when someone else came along. And both adored and spoiled Dan. Handsome Dan, they used to call him in high school."

"You hold your own in the looks department."

Jordan shrugged. "Not where Dan was concerned. And Raine preferred him in the end, didn't she?"

"She preferred you first."

"Dan was fooling around with other girls. She laid down the law; he bolted. Dan could be a bastard, but I don't want to speak ill of the dead.

"Three years next month. Look, Scott, I'd better be going. I'm dragging my feet because they're cold. I hope I don't come back with my tail feathers drooping."

Scott laughed. "Keep those tail feathers high, man. Pitch in there with everything you've got."

Saluting him, Jordan went out of the office and down the hall. They were on the fourteenth floor, and watching the dark blue small-tiled walls and the dark-blue carpet, he admired the beautiful new building where they'd leased a suite of offices. His business was booming. He was doing okay. Except, he thought, he got lonelier all the time.

* * *

In her bedroom Raine sprinkled in French lavender oil and began a leisurely bath. She lay back and let the soft, seductive odor wash over her. Jordan. They had grown up together, with Dan. Jordan's family had lost its money in a business venture that failed. Dan's parents had prospered until they'd sold their store and had died within a year of each other, shortly before the telegram had come that Dan was dead.

Drying off, she wrapped herself in a sheet-sized deep rose towel and for the first time in ages studied her body: firm, deeply curved, healthy. Hourglass, indeed. Years ago Jordy had said to her, "You're my favorite timepiece." Seeing her puzzled face, he'd explained, "You've got an hourglass figure, honey." And today Kym told her that Jimmy had commented along that same line.

Her cinnamon-colored face with its long black lashes and almond-shaped light brown eyes was very attractive, she knew, and close to beautiful, but she was not in the least vain about it. Her lips were full, her nose nondescript, her cheeklines high. Did he still find her attractive? He'd been more than friendly in Miss Elly's, but that could mean nothing, just that life was treating him right and he was happy. Was he still married?

Throwing aside the towel, she gave herself one last glance, smoothed on French lavender-scented lotion and slipped into the clothes she'd laid out. She was certainly making a production of this, she thought: midnight-blue low-cut silk jersey dress that hugged her curves, midnight-blue sandals and a necklace of multistrands of tiny gold beads that came together like flowing water. She caught her breath. That had been Jordan's last gift to her before he went away. Perhaps she shouldn't. . . . She decided she would and firmly fastened the clasp.

Her dark hair, threaded through with darkest shades of henna, looked well, she thought. She jumped when the door chimes sounded, her heart thudding.

STILL IN LOVE

Uncle Prince and Miss Vi had retired to their cottage on the grounds, and Kym was with them. Raine got the door. For a very long moment, she and Jordan stared at one another. He spoke first, and his voice was tense with longing.

"Aren't you going to invite me in?"

"Oh, yes, Jordan, do come in. It's just been so long."

A smile tugged the corners of his mouth as he drawled, "Lovely necklace."

Raine blushed. "I've always loved it."

"Thank you for wearing it," he said.

He handed her a sheaf of red roses and a big box of Belgian chocolates from a very fancy D.C. store. "I'd have brought champagne, but there'll be plenty of that where I'm taking you."

Raine set the packages down, thinking she ought to get a vase for the flowers, but she didn't want to leave him. "I keep feeling I'm dreaming," she said.

"It's no dream," he said huskily. He couldn't keep himself from taking her in his arms, holding her for a time before he cupped her face in his hands and kissed her softly at first, then with increasing passion as he had done in the dream.

He was so intense, she thought. Well, what about herself?

"Raine," he groaned. "Why couldn't we have stayed together?"

Raine laughed hollowly. "The precious fate you used to talk about didn't allow it," she said. "Oh, I know neither of us believes in blind fate. So often, we make our own, but things happen, get out of hand. . . . How have you been, Jordy? How are you?"

Jordan thought a moment, ran his tongue over his bottom lip. "If I could just stop time in this minute, I'd say 'fine,' but I can't."

Quite bluntly she asked, "Did your wife come with you?"

"Hardly," he answered. "We're divorced."

Joy like music swept through her. Divorced? But that

didn't say he wanted her, Raine. Would he kiss her the way he just had if he had someone else? Had he changed from the straightforward, honest man he had been?

"Hadn't we better be going?" he asked her, then added, "I'd have liked to see Uncle Prince and Miss Vi, but I guess I'm a little late."

"Yes, they had to turn in early for an early start tomorrow. They wanted to see you, too."

"Well, I hope I'll be coming back often, if you say I can."

He seemed hesitant about something. Then he asked, "Kym's gone to bed, of course."

"She certainly tried to stay up. She took to you the way she takes to few people. She's with Uncle Prince and Miss Vi."

Jordan's breath came fast as he bluntly asked, "She's my kid, isn't she. Not Dan's? She looks like me."

A rush of feeling swept through Raine, but she wasn't going to lie. "Yes," she said simply. "She's yours and mine."

Cupping her face again, he asked her, "Why didn't you let me know?"

"I did. I wrote you a letter. I called. Your mother asked me not to call you again. She said you'd fallen in love with someone else."

"But you knew she didn't like you."

"Yes. I was distraught, Jordy—crazy with worry. Papa was dying, and I had no one else to turn to. Sure, neighbors were helpful, but they weren't Papa and they weren't you. I didn't think. I just acted."

"You married Dan."

"Yes—he begged me, never failed to tell me how much he loved me. His mother told me, too, that you were in love with someone else. Unlike your mother, Mrs. Gibson, Dan's mother, wanted me to marry Dan. She thought I could make him settle down. I was young, impressionable."

"I'm being a bastard for asking, but did you?"

"Make him settle down?"

"Yes."

Raine laughed shortly. "For the brief time we weren't married, he was all a woman could ask except that he wasn't you. After we were married, he became something of a monster: too much liquor, too many women—a few snorts of cocaine when the spirit moved him. You name it. Our life was very hard. He loved Kym, and he was kind to her, but he wasn't the role model I wanted for my daughter.

"We moved to New Orleans because he wanted to get away from his parents. They really wanted us to make a go of it."

"Then he went into the Army," Jordan said. "Died there."

"Yes." Then, "Jordan?"

"Yes, love." She looked so beautiful, standing there. Those long lashes lay on her cheeks as she closed her eyes, and he wanted to crush her to him.

"I was thinking that although I'm dressed for the bigtime, please don't drive back to D.C. to take me out, then back here to bring me back, then back to D.C. You've got to be tired after driving all the way from Montreal."

"What do you have in mind?"

"I want to drive out to the Bay. Walk along the shore, enjoy the water and the stars—the way we used to when we didn't have money to go out to fancy places."

Jordan looked delighted. "I'm game for that. You're still full of surprises. I've missed that in women. Do you want to change clothes?"

Raine shook her head. "I'm living out my fantasy of being with you again. Let me put your gorgeous flowers in a vase, and we can go."

While she was out of the room, Jordan spied the sketch she had done of him, picked it up and studied it. It was a damned good drawing, he thought, and thought, too, of the lake painting she had rendered so superbly that hung on Miss Elly's wall. His heart filled with joy that she still seemed to want him in her life.

TWO

Cameron Shore by Chesapeake Bay was beautiful in the night lights with the water sparkling like cut diamonds. The iron guardrails were still warm from that day's sun.

"We're crazy," Jordan said, "all dressed up and standing at the edge of the Bay."

Raine ran her hands over the smooth fabric of his dark blue raw-silk suit. With his blue and white diagonally striped silk tie, and his soft blue shirt, he looked like the successful man he was.

"I didn't want to share you," Raine said, beginning to laugh, but her voice caught on a light sob.

"Baby," Jordan said, taking her in his arms. "It's all right. The two of us . . . we'll be all right now."

They clung together, caught in a web of time and circumstance that neither one could break free of.

"Listen," he said urgently, "is there anybody else for you now?" He held his breath against her answer.

Raine laughed a little. "If there were, they'd get pushed out of the way. No, Jordy, there's no one but you." Then she added softly, "There never was."

"Do you really mean that?" He wanted to believe her implicitly, but he knew how much Dan had loved her. But Dan had hurt her, so she might be denying her love for him.

"I mean it," she said. "I told you I tried to contact you."

"Yeah," Jordan said. "It was all snarled. Mom must have

destroyed your letter. Then when I did get well enough to find you, you and Dan had married."

Raine placed her finger over his lips. "Jordy, don't," she begged him, pulling his face to hers, kissing the corners of his lips until he caught her to him, his hands caressing her back, bringing up fever and flaming desire in both of them.

He felt her draw away from him.

"What's wrong?" he asked.

"Jordy, when I thought you didn't want me anymore, I wanted to die, I hurt so bad. Loving you like that has made me scared to love you again."

Jordan held her at arm's length. "I'm sorry, Ray," he said gently. "I'd never hurt you if I could help it."

Groaning in the back of his throat, Jordan said huskily, "I'm going to take you somewhere in Minden. We can't stay out here like this. With Kym in the picture—and even if she weren't—I won't compromise you."

Raine thought wistfully that for once in her life she wouldn't mind being compromised, not if it were Jordy doing it. She smiled a bit at the thought, yet her heart was chilled with fear of loving him so much.

"We're adults," she said, her voice catching in her throat. "We can handle it. We came out here to talk."

"Talk?" he said slowly. "Out here, I don't want to just talk with you. I want to know you in the deepest Biblical sense. I want to strip the clothes from your body that seems to have just gotten lusher since I was last with you. It seems like yesterday."

"To me, too, Jordy—I have powerful dreams of you still. Just last night."

Jordan shook his head. "Don't tell me about dreams, Ray. I've had dreams of being deep inside you and came awake with stinging tears in my eyes, hurting so bad I could hardly stand it. If only I had known about Kym."

Raine was silent for a moment before she said, "Think back, Jordy. You ached with wanting to be something big in law enforcement, the way your father was deputy sheriff of the county. He died a broken man, cancer-riddled, too young.

"And you wanted to carry out his plans for a more law-abiding way of life, and it didn't have to be in Minden County—just somewhere. You can't do that these days without a good education. I didn't want to stand in your way."

"Your mom wanted to go home to Montreal, you know now to die, but she was as wrapped up in your dreams as you were, as your dad had been for you.

"Think, love, how you would have felt with a wife and a baby to support. I didn't have ultrasound, but Doc Tanner thought I might have twins. I was sick with despair. Mom always cautioned me to be a good girl, a sweet girl. Bearing a child out of wedlock wasn't in the picture.

"Dan was there for me. He dragged it out of me that I was pregnant and said he didn't mind supporting your child. And he wanted me. His mother and father urged us to marry."

"Because Dan was out of control, and they were depending on you to control him. They weren't doing you any favor."

Raine nodded. "I suspect you're right."

"Oh, Dan loved you," Jordan scoffed, "as much as he was capable of loving anyone." He added to himself, and I wonder how much you came to love Dan.

As if she'd read his mind, Raine told Jordan, "I cared about Dan. He got me out of a major bind, providing a name for Kym, and he was pretty decent to her until his demons started acting up and he went into the Army to get away."

"Did he mistreat you?"

Raine nodded. "At the end of the period just before he went into the Army, he was moody, irritable. He was abusing his body, but it hadn't caused him any physical problems at the time. Dan was a coach, and he was very healthy."

Images of her making love to the very healthy Dan made Jordan wince before he shut them out.

Abruptly he said, "Do you want to waste that beautiful dress standing out here on the waterfront?"

Another couple strolled by dressed in jeans and sweatshirts. A patrolman walked by, smiled, and touched his hat to them.

"I'm with you. The dress isn't wasted. I wanted to please you, vamp you."

Suddenly Jordan caught her to him again. Holding her with one arm, he cupped her face with his thumb and fingers of the other.

"You please me," he said, "just by being you. Raine, if you only knew . . ."

"Knew what, Jordy?"

"What I've been through without you."

"It wasn't any easier for me. Fate simply threw us a wicked curve."

He kissed her long and hard, his tongue going into her mouth where hers caressed it. Then his tongue was darting furiously damp kisses over her face, then her neck and upper breasts in the low-cut dress. Raine grew dizzy with pleasure. His big hands pressed her body into his so that she felt the hard swelling of his shaft and felt his hot kisses on her upper body. Then he lifted his head and whispered, "I still love you."

Flinging her arm around his neck, Raine cried, "And I still love you, but it scares me. You'll never know how much."

They clung together then, both aching with longing. He drew apart, his voice shaky. "I won't crowd you, my darling. Just know that I'm here for you."

Drawing her slowly to him, Jordan said tenderly, "I've got to be up early. What's on your plate?"

"Now that you're here, everything tasty," Raine said. "I've got the usual. Going to planning sessions for school that opens next week. Looking after the handful that goes by Kym's name . . ."

"Already I love that kid. And painting, always painting."

"Yes, I'm going to work on that sketch of you. I'm going to call it Warrior's Return."

"I'm not really the warrior type," Jordan said thoughtfully, "although I'm in law enforcement. Dan was the warrior type." Once he'd said it, he was sorry. Let sleeping or dead husbands lie.

"Oh, I don't know," Raine answered. "I don't know when I've felt so safe, so protected as when I'm with you. Yet as I've said, you scare me. What I feel for you scares me."

"I'm sorry about that. I don't want you to be scared of loving me. You don't need me to protect you," Jordan said. "You're one tough, smart, and altogether beautiful cookie. I'm only the icing on your cake."

Raine put her head to one side. "Thanks for the compliment. There're some who think the icing is the best part."

"You're the icing on my cake, too, and I'm one of the ones who think that's the best part. Let's have a nightcap, and I'll take you home before the trooper has to take me in for appropriating privileges that don't belong to me."

"You would ravish me?" Raine asked.

"I would want to, because you bring up old, old and new fevers, lady."

"You're too much of a gentleman for that."

"Lust, especially the loving lust I have for you, strikes gentlemen and those who don't care to be gentlemen alike."

"You know, one of the things I've missed is the way you bring me joy, the things you say: your openness."

"I want to please you in every way," he said hungrily, drinking her in, feasting on kisses from her mouth.

Raine stood close to him. Strange that with his presence, she would so vividly remember the pain of being without him.

"Let's get out of here," Jordan said. "I want to see your beautiful face more clearly."

Caleb's Inn was the rendezvous for Minden's younger set, and not a few of the middle-aged and older set.

Nestled back in a five-acre tract, there was plenty of parking, and the brick-and-glass building with its many flowering bushes and low-cut shrubbery made you want to explore its inner workings. It didn't disappoint you. Richly carpeted in deep burgundy with burgundy and rose decor, you felt comfortable there.

"Well," Jordan said, raising his eyebrows, "I'd never have guessed that Minden had something like this."

"Yes, it's quite lovely," Raine said. "I've come here only a couple of times with Caroline. A D.C. crowd comes out all the time."

"Caroline Lindsey? Or has she married?"

"No, Caroline hasn't married. She's had a couple of bum raps in the romance department. She runs an art gallery on Capitol Hill in D.C., and I must say we've both accommodated to the absence of romance in our lives—at least the romance that a man brings."

Jordan grinned. "You used to say just living was romantic."

"That was before you left," Raine said truthfully.

"If I could turn back time," Jordan answered her.

"I'm beginning to feel really good, Jordy," Raine said as the headwaiter seated them.

"Not as good as I feel. I love you, no matter what happens."

"Why did you say that?"

"No matter what happens?"

"Yes."

"Because no matter what happens, I'll find a way for us to be together."

"Old disappointing fate again."

"Me and fate. I'm putting this one together."

Seated to the side of each other, Jordan reached over and held her hand, and his touch sent electricity through her.

Raine nibbled at the warm and delicious cheese rolls from a warmer on the table. Fat pink candles under glass lighted her face, and her eyes were like stars.

"You're a beautiful woman, Ray, and you would be if you weren't physically beautiful at all. There's something about you that fills me. When I'm with you, I don't feel empty anymore."

"We're alike, Jordy, in so many ways."

He asked what she wanted to drink and ordered crème de cacao in small crystal glasses for them. He leaned toward her, his fingers stroking her face.

The deferential young waiter brought their drinks.

"I forgot I've had only a sandwich this afternoon," he said, feeling the crème de cocao hit his stomach. "We'd better order. What would you like?"

Raine studied the menu. "I'll take the seafood platter with a double lettuce salad. It's a real winner."

"I'll follow your lead." He gave the waiter their orders.

When the waiter had left, Jordan turned to her, stroking her face. "Would you like to dance?"

"Yes, I'd like to dance."

At this time of the night, the excellent small band played love songs—the old and the new—pop tunes that transcended age and class. The band was playing "That Old Black Magic" when they started dancing.

Her nearness was putting Jordan in a trance. Lord, she smelled wonderfully seductive as he hummed the tune to her.

"Raine."

"Yes, my love."

"You haven't changed."

"Oh, but I have changed," Raine said softly. "I was never afraid before.

"Tell me about Rita, your, ex-wife."

"There's not much to tell," he said slowly. "We were both lonely. I found out she was in love with someone else all the while. He didn't want to marry.

"Her father, Max, helped to set us up in business. I owe him a lot."

"Was he upset about the divorce?"

"Yes, but Rita was brought up motherless, and her dad has spoiled her terribly."

Jordan sighed. "Let's not waste the night talking about others."

But Raine was persistent. "Is she beautiful?"

"Definitely. Someone is forever looking at her and commenting on her beauty, but she isn't in your class."

"I'm not beautiful. Not really."

"Well, to me you are. And if you're not, you're the next best thing to beautiful. No, to me you're the most beautiful woman I've known."

Raine laughed. "We could spend the night arguing about beauty. Eye of the beholder, that kind of thing."

Jordan brought her closer to him, his face close to hers before he told her, "I said I wouldn't press you, but the next nights we spend for quite a while aren't going to be spent arguing over beauty, or over anything. I can guarantee you that."

"You were never a sex maniac," she teased.

"Make that love maniac," he returned.

THREE

Raine passed the next day in a happy daze. Jordan was due to have dinner with them, and by six o'clock that afternoon, preparations were under way full speed.

Miss Vi moved about with the energy of a teenager, belying her seventy years. Her pale-yellow face beamed with pleasure, and her short, silver-gray hair went into wispy curls that framed her maturely sweet face. Her husband, whom everyone called Uncle Prince, was silver haired and solid mahogany, with black eyes and a dourly loving mien. They were quite a pair, devoted to each other and to Raine and Kym.

As Raine sat at the table, making chocolate curls for the solid chocolate cake, Kym came to her.

"You like Mr. Clymer a lot, don't you, Mom?"

Raine looked at her keenly. "Yes, I do," she said quickly. "Don't you like him?"

Kym shrugged. "He's okay, I guess."

"You said you liked him."

Kym stood, her small body agitated. "You just seem different, Mom."

"Different how?"

"You haven't been listening to me for the past day or so."

Raine put the bowl aside and caught Kym to her.

"I'll always listen to you, sweetie—always. If you think I'm not listening, tell me."

Kym breathed a sigh of relief. Since Dan Gibson had

STILL IN LOVE 35

joined the Army, it had been Raine and her against the world.

With the dinner table set by Kym, and a sumptuous dinner prepared by the two women and Kym, Raine went outside to look at lovely Challenger Farm the way she often did, letting its beauty soothe her.

A flower and berry farm that supplied markets in Washington, the farm was well managed by the Thomases—Uncle Prince and Miss Vi. Now lavender, gold, bronze, white, and yellow chrysanthemums grew in sturdy profusion. Dahlias and gladioli grew in the small greenhouse. The blackberry, boysenberry, and blueberry bushes had been pruned and awaited another season. Wild plum trees had begun to turn in readiness for winter, then another season when Miss Vi would make jam from the tart wild plums.

Oh, they were lucky, Raine thought, to have this precious twenty-five acre farm. It had been in the family for over a hundred years. Thinking of her own farm brought memories of Jordan's family and the loss of their farm when his father had died of cancer and a broken heart. As a deputy sheriff, he was an upstanding figure until a teenaged boy had died in his custody. He swore he had nothing to do with it, that he had left the boy in the care of two county policemen and come back to find him dead. But both men said the boy was fine when they left and that they had seen the deputy sheriff strike the boy and grossly mishandle him.

Jordan's mother, never a strong woman, had gone nearly mad with grief. Lonely, she had taken over the life of her only child, Jordan. And from the beginning she had hated having him pair off in his late teens with Raine.

Raine's daughter's voice brought her back to the present. "Mom, you look so pretty, but you don't look happy." Kym, bathed and fresh in a blue ruffled dress, where she lived in jeans, came outside.

Raine bent to hug her. One day soon she was going to have to know that Jordan was her father.

Now Kym said, "It's hard for me, not having a dad when all the other kids do."

Raine smiled to herself. Now Kym was being her age. She wanted a father, but she wasn't yet willing to share her mother. No precociousness here.

"I know, sweetheart, but not all the other children do have dads. There're a fair number of single-parent families in our school."

"I know, and they're all sad, too," Kym said wistfully, hugging her mother.

Hearing the back screen door slam, Raine looked around to see Miss Vi come out, wiping her hands on her apron. She glanced at her watch. "Hadn't you better get dressed up, missy?" she asked Raine.

Miss Vi called her "missy" and Kym "little missy."

"You're right," Raine murmured. She looked at Miss Vi, her eyes shining. "Know what I'm thinking?" she told the older woman, who was like a mother to her.

Eyes twinkling, Miss Vi said, "I don't know what you're thinking, but I can sure guess who you're thinking about."

"Over nine years just slipped away, Miss Vi. It was just as if he'd never left at all."

Then Raine thought, no, that wasn't quite true. She hadn't known this deep fear when they'd been very young and in love. She hadn't had the truly sad experience of her broken heart without him.

"Yes," Miss Vi said. "Uncle Prince and I were two of the ones rooting for you when you stopped dating Dan and took up with Jordy. I love that boy like he's the child we never had. I guess I never really cared that much for Dan. Something about him didn't sit right with me."

Raine nodded. She had learned not to care much for Dan, too, but it had taken a while for that to happen. After

STILL IN LOVE 37

all, he had rescued her when she was desperate and carrying Jordan's child.

Lounging in the tub she had scented with jasmine oil, Raine closed her eyes as the night before filled her heart. Letting the warm water lull her, she found herself daydreaming: Jordan's touch, Jordan's kisses, Jordan's love. He was so sure they still belonged together. There was no one else for her. If only they could be together for eternity. She still loved him so.

Drying off on the huge rose towel-sheet, Raine stood in front of the full-length bedroom mirror and frankly appraised her body. All shapely with the wide hips and moderately full breasts, the swanlike neck and round face with its wide-spaced eyes, straight eyebrows, full lips, and her nose that was a bit too large. Well, she drawled to herself, she'd always passed Jordy's inspection in the old days. And it seemed that still held true.

Padding nude across the wine-red carpet, she went to the closet and selected a rose silk jersey wraparound, a bit too dressy for an informal dinner, but it flattered her immensely. After donning her special Victoria's Secret rose satin lingerie, she swept her moderately cut and chemically straightened hair back from her face and placed a wide barrette of rose velvet across the front. Slipping into the wraparound rose dress, she slid into transparent-topped, flat-heeled sandals. There, she was ready!

Kym, Uncle Prince, and Miss Vi made a fuss over her when she joined them.

"Mom, you look great!" Kym cried.

Uncle Prince chuckled. "That boy ain't got a chance with all this beauty around." Miss Vi put her hands on her hips. "You go girl," she said, picking up the language of far younger people.

"You know," Uncle Prince said, "you look so much like

your mama, but you're really the female spit of your grandpa, my friend Frank. Lord, he'd be so happy if he could see you now."

His face looked suddenly somber. "You've made yourself into a woman and a mother to be proud of, Raine."

"Thank you," Raine said simply, going to the large vase which held the roses Jordan had brought the night before.

They were a merry group that a nervous Jordan came into that night. He held an exquisitely wrapped box and a baker's box from the D.C. West End bakery.

He kissed Raine briefly on her lips, shook hands with the Thomases, kissing Miss Vi's cheek.

"Man, you're a sight for sore eyes," Uncle Prince said, hugging Jordan. "One day when you've got enough time, we'll have to go fishing. You used to go along with your dad and me back when you wasn't kneehigh to a grasshopper." He paused, chuckling. "Raine tells me you're coming back to these parts."

Jordan nodded, a lump in his throat at the mention of his father. Seeing his expression, Raine touched his arm.

Kym came into the room, suddenly bashful. "Hello, Mr. Clymer," she said shyly.

"Hello there," Jordan answered, handing her the package. "This is for you."

With a little gasp of pleased surprise, the child took the package, asking her mother, "May I open it now?"

"By all means," Raine said.

Eager fingers untied the bow and removed the wrappings and then opened the box to reveal a lacquered black music box with stenciled pink flowers and gold motifs.

"Oh, it's beautiful!" Kym cried. "Mr. Clymer, thank you so much."

At that moment she sounded like her mother, Jordan thought.

Kym lifted the lid, and the music box played "Londonderry Air" as Kym listened in awe.

"What's the tune?" she asked, and Jordan told her.

"I'd have gotten you one with music that you're more familiar with, but there just weren't any."

"Oh, I like that tune very much," Kym said, playing it again.

"It's also called Danny Boy," Raine said, and her words set Jordan to wondering. He'd been in a hurry to buy that music box, and he'd liked the design and those colors. It was the only one they'd had left. Londonderry Air . . . Danny Boy . . . Dan. But his adversary, his nemesis, Dan Gibson, was dead. Why beat a dead horse? Jordan cleared his throat.

"I had something in mind for you," Jordan told Raine, "but it wasn't ready. I think you'll like it."

Raine threw up her hands in a little gesture of surprise. "Even when we were courting, you always gave me presents, Jordy. You haven't changed."

"You're quite a present giver yourself," he said, pointing out the gold nugget cufflinks she'd taken a part-time job to get him for their last Christmas together.

Miss Vi came back into the room with a silver tray displaying the solid chocolate cake Jordan had brought. "You see," he said, "I remembered how much Uncle Prince and, well, we all like solid chocolate. It's not in the class with your chocolate cakes, Miss Vi, but I wanted you to have a rest from making them."

Miss Vi laughed delightedly. "You always did the kind thing, Jordy," Miss Vi said. "I can't tell you how much I thank you." She came to him and kissed his cheek, not telling him about the solid chocolate cake they'd made. Raine thought they'd send that cake home with Jordan. "Welcome home, son," Miss Vi said. "I wish I had words to tell you how welcome."

Jordan took her small hands, soft in spite of a heavy workload, and squeezed them gently.

"I'm glad to be back," he said.

They were in the middle of the baked ham, fried catfish, fried chicken, collard greens, sweet potato pudding, wild rice, and the big salad of various greens and raw vegetables.

"I made the vanilla bean ice cream you were so crazy about, Jordy," Miss Vi said. "Only this time we've got an electric freezer that goes into the fridge freezer."

"Thank you. You're making my mouth water," Jordan said, "and it was already doing that with this scrumptious meal you've whipped up here."

Jordan glanced around him at the bay windows of the dining room, the old-fashioned mahogany furniture, and the cream linen appliqued tablecloth. Miss Vi and Raine knew how to set a wonderfully appealing table, right down to the low-cut purple and pink dahlia and fern flower arrangement.

Jordan kept smiling. "I'm thinking food hasn't tasted this good to me in many a moon," he said.

"You eat, son," Uncle Prince said. "You're just a mite too thin for my taste."

Jordan laughed. "Doctors these days want you to be skin and bones."

"What do they know?" Uncle Prince grumped.

When the doorbell chimed, Raine got up to answer it and found her best friend, Caroline Lindsay, standing there.

"Can you welcome a weary traveler?" Caroline asked, then speaking behind her hand, "He is here, isn't he? Oh, never mind answering, I can see by the glee on your face. Take me to him."

By then Jordan had excused himself and was out of his chair and across the room, giving Caroline a bear hug.

"Ca'line, Ca'line," he said happily. "My old friend."

Nobody except Raine and Jordan ever called her Ca'line, shortening the name the way Jordan had done as a lisping child.

STILL IN LOVE 41

"You look wonderful, Jordy," Caroline said. "Something's going right in your life."

"Yeah," Jordan said, laughing. "As of yesterday—when I went into an ice cream parlor in Minden and found certain people I know there. That's where my happiness began."

"It's great to have you back."

Jordan glanced around him, feeling absolutely comfortable and at loving ease with these people. Caroline had gained some weight, but it became her. She was ginger to Raine's cinnamon, with reddish-brown close-cropped hair, and a sculpted attractive face.

"How's your art gallery coming along?" Jordan asked Caroline.

"It's beginning to zoom," Caroline began when Miss Vi came into the living room.

"Now I'm not taking no for an answer, Caroline," Miss Vi said. "We've got a right good dinner here, and Jordy's brought a chocolate cake that just might rival mine. I've set you a place. Matter of fact, I had it all laid out on the buffet."

"You talked me into it," Caroline said immediately. "I haven't had time to feed myself properly today. But you'll have a lot to answer for, Miss Vi, if you insist I eat that chocolate cake."

"If she doesn't insist, I will," Uncle Prince said, getting up to seat Caroline. "You see, I even remember my manners for ladies when you come around. You eat," Uncle Prince said. "You're a fine-looking woman. I just want to see you stay that way."

"Thank you," Caroline said. "I wish the men in my age group were as gallant as you and other men in your age group are."

"I'm gallant," Jordan said. "How many times have I told you you're a fine specimen of a woman."

"You're taken," Caroline said impishly. "And you always have been. Even in high school."

Jordan shrugged. "Some of us just find what we want

early." His face went somber. "But sometimes we lose what we've found."

"Mom, do you and Mr. Clymer know each other?" Kym asked.

"We go back a very long way, honey," Jordan answered her, "a very long way. I'm hoping we can tell you a lot about that soon."

"Yes, love," Raine amended. "Soon we'll have a lot of talking, you and I. But just now set it aside for future reference."

"Okay," Kym said, giggling. "It's hard for me to wait."

"It's hard for all of us to wait," Jordan told her. "It's especially hard for me at times."

"You know," Caroline said, "I'm about to forget to mention that someone is very interested in one of your paintings of your pond. I set a higher than average price, and they didn't quaver. It was a couple from New York. I think he's an art dealer. Raine—either that or he knows an awful lot about paintings."

"He's welcome to it," Raine said. "That makes me happy."

"Congratulations," Jordan told her. "I can use a couple for my office and Scott's. He's admired the old one I have in my apartment and expressed a desire to own one."

Raine's face warmed. She couldn't remember when she had felt so good.

"I gather this man Scott's your—what, partner? Deputy?" Caroline asked.

"Yeah, he's my partner, and he's as wrapped up in the security business as I am. He's a great guy."

"Did you hate leaving the Secret Service?" Raine asked.

Jordan thought a moment before he answered slowly. "I really liked the Secret Service and most of the people I guarded. But I've always wanted my own corner of the earth. Now I feel like I'm on top of my mountain. Except for one thing: getting the woman I want by my side."

STILL IN LOVE 43

He took Raine's hand.

"You're divorced, then?" Caroline asked.

"Yes," he answered.

"I can hear the wedding march from here." Caroline couldn't help smiling at her two friends. Uncle Prince and Miss Vi gave each other a loving glance.

"Wedding march?" Kym asked, her heart beating faster. "Mom, are you and Mr. Clymer getting married? But he just came here."

Jordan reached over and patted her hand. "Remember, little one, I said we go a long way back."

"Believe me, sweetie, you'll be lucky to get him for a da—ah, stepfather."

Kym's eyes were wide with shock and wonder.

"Listen, sweetheart," Raine assured her. "I'll let you in on everything, and you and I will be a special pair for a while longer."

Kym's eyes lit up as Raine said the words. Then Raine looked at Jordan and saw that he understood.

When they were done with the dinner, including the delicious solid chocolate cake, Caroline said she had to go.

"No rest for the weary," Caroline said. "I've got paintings to sort for another hour."

Raine turned to Jordan. "Caroline's having a weekend show three weeks from now. The New York galleries are paying a lot of attention to us now."

"Are you going to get enough rest with your teaching and all?" Jordan asked Raine, who shrugged.

"Sometimes it seems that painting gives me more energy than it takes away. But thanks for being interested."

"That's only the beginning of my interest where you're concerned." His glance at Raine was a vivid caress.

Later with Kym in bed, Caroline gone, and Miss Vi and Uncle Prince insisting on putting the dishes in the dishwasher, Jordan turned to Raine.

"Speaking of the pond and painting, could we walk out there now?"

He sounded wistful, and Raine looked at him sharply. "I'll get a wrap," she said. "It's turned much cooler."

Going to the hall closet, she chose a mulberry lightweight shawl that went well with her rose wraparound.

"I like that dress on you," he said. "It sets off your figure."

"Thank you," Raine said quietly.

"Does this ever bring back memories," Jordan said as they walked down the pathway to the pond that was lighted at night by a couple of electric lanterns. The water was clear in the large pond, planted to catfish, a few turtles, and water lilies, with weeping willows swaying in the breeze. Along with the pond, the whole expanse of Challenger Farm surrounded them.

Jordan stopped and, taking Raine in his arms, pulled her hard against his rock-solid body.

Raine said breathlessly, "You aren't making this any easier."

"You see that three-quarter moon up there?" he said, his head thrown back as he looked at the silvery moon.

"Yes, I see it. It's beautiful, as usual."

"Well, it's waxing, not waning, and it's sending me messages to make love to you. It doesn't want to take no for an answer."

"What if it has to?"

Jordan kissed the corner of her mouth. "I was a fool to bring you out here. Why torture myself?"

"And me. Oh, Jordy, how I wish—but you understand."

"You know I do. We'll get it right this time. We've got to. We have a child together."

Three large black cats came ambling up from Miss Vi's.

"We looked at Chesapeake Bay last night," Jordan said. "Tonight it's the pond where we spent so many wonderful hours. Raine, everything's going to work for us this time. I'm going to see to it."

Raine nodded. "We're both going to see to it. But, Jordy, it isn't going to be easy for me. You haven't mentioned children."

"Luckily Rita and I had none. Rita always said later. I think you've done a terrific job with Kym."

"Thank you. She's jealous that you're in my life."

Jordan took a deep breath. "I'm sorry she feels that way, but I'll try to help her get over that jealousy—the way I'm going to fight to help you get over your fear. Speaking of kids, I love Kym already."

"You should, since she's yours."

"When do we tell her? She ought to know."

"I don't know, Jordy. Kym's life hasn't been easy. She's talked often about having a father."

"I'm hers for the asking, but I'll take my time. How could I have possibly been back such a short while?"

As they circled the pond and walked back toward the fieldstone cottage in the moonlight, a few catfish leapt and the weeping willows looked silvery green. Yellow, purple, and rose water lilies made Raine think of Monet and other artists of the impressionistic school in Paris, where she'd always longed to go.

"Jordy?"

"Yes, love."

"I'd like to see Paris with you one day."

"I'll take you anywhere you want to go, love."

"You're a sweet man. Pinch me to show me I'm not dreaming."

"I don't want to hurt you."

"And I don't want to hurt you. I don't want you to leave."

"You know I don't want to, but I've got to be up early, and you've got school meetings all day tomorrow, all week, in fact. Let's both keep our fingers crossed that nothing goes wrong."

As they neared the house, Raine stopped. "Come in for a nightcap. I've got your favorite cognac."

"Later," Jordan said, sounding a bit grim. He opened the back screen, and they climbed the steps up to the porch and stood awkwardly facing each other.

"Jordy," Raine said huskily. "We never did know how to say good-bye to each other."

"That's because we both know in our hearts we shouldn't be saying good-bye."

"I love you," she said. "I always have. I always will."

"Raine, my darling woman," he said softly. "This time I won't rest until we're together and married." He stroked her face lovingly and kissed her eyelids.

"When I first got to Montreal, I used to look in a jeweler's shop I passed daily, and I picked out your engagement ring. I couldn't buy it, but I wanted to. Then I got sick, and Mama and I had my illness to deal with as well as her bad heart."

"Are you okay now?"

"The doctors don't find anything wrong. An operation restored my heart valve. Thank God, it wasn't rheumatic fever. Yes, I do seem perfectly all right now."

"I'm glad, Jordy. People like you should live forever."

She walked him through the house, and they stood on the front porch, looking at the moon. His Mercedes waited in the driveway. She walked with him to the car, and he began to kiss her, then stopped.

"What're you thinking about?" she asked when he stood there so silent.

"About us and how much I love you."

Raine placed a hand on each side of his face. "Now stop that, or I'll be begging you to take me home with you."

"Would you like that? I'd get you back very early."

His voice was warm, eager, bringing out all the love she felt for him.

She shook her head. "No. Kym would be afraid if she

woke up and found I wasn't home. Besides, Jordy, I think we should wait until—well, until . . ."

"Until you can trust me again. Okay, sweetheart, that's what it'll be."

He got into the car, drove down the driveway, and stood in the road in front of the house until Raine went inside. Then he leaned against the steering wheel as he had on the Washington-Baltimore Parkway the day before, mulling it all over.

It had sure been a wonderful two days, he thought. Restarting his motor, he drove the short distance to the highway, then full speed ahead toward D.C.

By the time he parked his car in the parking lot of his building's garage, Jordan was tired, but he felt so good he decided to stay up awhile longer. As he put his key in the lock, startled, he heard water running, but it stopped when he opened the door. He stood on the threshold a moment. Hadn't he cut the lights off? Sure he had. Then what was going on?

A woman with long light brown silken hair and a lightly tanned body came into the room with a towel wrapped around her. She looked at Jordan and burst into laughter.

"Oh, Jordy," she trilled. "You look so shocked!"

"What the hell are you doing here, Rita, and how'd you get in?"

"My old wedding ring, my license to wed you, which I was savvy enough to bring, and any concierge would let me in, don't you think? I'm your ex-wife, and I need you for a few days. Ah, Jordy, once you and I were—"

"Stop it, Rita! I won't stand for this. I came home expecting my apartment to be empty. You're going to have to leave tonight."

"Mike's walked out on me. I came down to see him. He

called me a vicious flirt, can you imagine? You never seemed to mind."

"Maybe I wasn't as in love with you as he is."

"Now you're being mean."

Rita's light green eyes grew opaque. "Anyway, here I am, without my new love. Once you loved me, Jordan. I'm sure of that." She glanced at him slyly. "Been to see your precious Raine?" She toyed with Raine's name, and it infuriated him.

"Your hated cousin's wife," Rita reminded him. "She sure didn't wait long after you left to marry him, did she?"

Once he would have been drawn to her nakedness under the towel. She would have brought up strong feelings. Now he saw her only in terms of her rotten, poisonous heart.

"You can't stay here," he said thickly, determined.

Rita's laughter trilled again. "Very well. You could let me spend the night. You owe my father a lot."

Jordan clenched his teeth. "Very well. You take over the damned apartment. I'll go someplace else."

"To Mrs. Gibson's, perhaps? As a matter of fact, you do look happier than I've seen you in ages. Believe me, I don't like raining on your parade."

A furious Jordan told her, "You're not going to rain on my parade, Rita. Raine and I . . ." He stopped, unwilling to discuss any aspect of his life with Raine with his ex-wife.

"Be nice to me, Jordy. I don't care if you love Raine—now. You loved me once. So you've got a new affair cooking."

Jordan went toward her, fists clenched, but she knew him as the peaceable man he was.

"Now, Jordy, cool down."

"I won't have you cheapening what Raine and I have," he told her.

Rita shifted the towel around on her body, exposing more of her bosom.

"Okay, Rita, stay the night, and as I said, I'll go elsewhere, but I want you out of here tomorrow."

"Afraid of me?"

"You know I'm not."

"Where will you go?"

"That's not your business."

Rita sighed. "Back to Raine's, I suppose."

Jordan was silent, pulling down an overnight valise and gathering clothes to go into it. He was going to call Scott and ask if he could spend the night there. Scott had two bedrooms. But he wasn't going to call here where Rita could hear. She'd think nothing of picking up the phone in another room. He'd call Scott from the concierge's desk. And he'd call Raine from there, too.

Suddenly his head began to pound. He didn't have time for an aspirin or a Tylenol. He had to get out of there and quickly.

FOUR

After Jordan left, Raine stood at the window a long while, looking out at the starlit night, idly wondering how many golden clustered stars lit up a night like this. She went in and slowly undressed, feeling Jordy's many glances as kisses on her bare skin.

She had expected to stay awake until he called her as he'd done the night before, but she fell fast asleep, and the deep dreams of foreplay and making love to him came again. They were by the pond, hidden by the weeping willows, breathless with glorious passion. She came awake suddenly and looked at the luminous clock radio dial. Twelve o'clock. He'd had plenty of time to get home. Had something happened? Her heart raced a bit with anxiety.

No need to be so antsy, she thought. He might have stopped by Scott Williams, his sidekick's apartment. Still, it was plain she wasn't going to get any sleep until she spoke with him.

Wide awake now, she dialed his number, and a woman picked up on the second ring with a throatily sexy "Jordan Clymer's apartment. Mrs. Clymer speaking."

Raine nearly dropped the phone. Rita was there.

Displaying a cool steadiness she certainly didn't feel, Raine asked, "Is he there? And may I speak with him?"

"Is this Mrs. Raine Gibson?"

"Yes, it is. Is he there?"

"My, aren't we anxious tonight. No, Raine, Jordy isn't here just now. I thought he was with you."

"He was, but he left. Are you expecting him?"

Rita laughed a little nastily, "Sweetie, I'm just hoping he returns tonight because I have plans for him, but I doubt it. He left here in a huff. Maybe he's on his way back to you."

"Thank you," Raine said, and before she could hang up the receiver, Rita's voice gone harsh brought her back.

"Good luck on your affair with Jordan," she said. "I wish you well."

"Thank you," Raine said evenly and hung up. She sat on the edge of her bed, thinking. Why was Jordan's ex-wife there? And where was he?

A half hour later Jordy called and explained to her what had happened. Raine told him about her conversation with Rita.

"I'm sorry about that," Jordy said, "but Rita is a sadist. She gets a big charge out of hurting people. I waited to call until I could get to Scott's apartment. I'm in Alexandria with him. Let me give you this number. As long as Rita's here, I won't be going back to my apartment except to see that she's out."

Dully Raine wrote down Scott's number.

Jordan laughed bitterly. "Rita's spoiled rotten, remember I told you. She's got the body of a woman, the mind of a child." He paused a minute before he asked, "Raine, how are you taking this?"

"Not too well. It hurts. I've been having big dreams about you and me since yesterday. Still, having you here eases some of the pain, and like you said about yourself, I'm not so empty anymore. Good luck with putting Rita out, Jordan."

"I'm sorry this had to happen, love, but like I said, I've got a few aces up my sleeve. I hope we both can get some sleep now, and Raine?"

"Yes, Jordy."
"I love you as much as a man can love a woman."
"Thank you, sweetheart. That goes double for me."
"Goodnight, my love."
"Goodnight."

Raine placed the ivory phone in its cradle, sighing. She didn't expect to sleep, but after tossing about for fifteen or so minutes, she fell into a deep and troubled sleep in which she stood alone, tossed by the same Chesapeake Bay waves they had watched the night before. A beautiful woman stood on the opposite shore, laughing at her and crying out, "I won't stay away from him, Raine. Not yet! Not yet!" and the voice kept echoing across the water, as Raine struggled to swim ashore. She was going under as the beautiful shrew on the shore laughed merrily and kept repeating, "Not yet!"

When she came awake from the dream, Raine got out of bed, went downstairs, and padded across the floor barefooted to the dining room and her easel with the sketch of Jordy tacked to it. She sat at the easel, filling in the drawing. It was almost as if he were there. Paintings had soul, she had long ago discovered. Andy White, her favorite art teacher at Pratt Institute in New York, had made her know that when she had painted a picture of a woman grieving. He had said abruptly, "A grieving woman and a serene landscape. Everything has a soul, Raine, every raindrop, every blade of grass. Let the landscape grieve with the woman."

Raine leaned back and put out her hand, caressing Jordy's face in the painting. Jordy's wife sounded cruel, vindictive, but she also sounded far younger than Jordy had said she was. Spoiled meant getting what you wanted. But

STILL IN LOVE 53

she had divorced Jordy. Now she wanted—no, intended, to come back to him.

She paced the floor with her heart aching the way she had thought she knew how to stop it from hurting. She wanted to call him again, but what would she say? It crept like poison to mind that Jordy might still love this woman. After all, she had left him. That might have hurt too much for him to acknowledge loving her.

In many ways she felt as she had felt when she couldn't get in touch with Jordy when he'd first moved to Montreal. The pain had been crushing then, and it was little less now. But there was a difference. She had Kym to look after now as well as herself.

Raine got up at first dawn and made coffee. The weather had turned even chillier than the day before. They used an old-fashioned percolator, and within minutes the smell of Colombian coffee filled the room and wafted through the house.

She unlocked the door as Miss Vi inserted her key, came in, and hugged her, frowning.

"See here," Miss Vi said. "You look like you've been dragged by a herd of wild horses." She came close and took Raine in her arms. "It's got to be about Jordy if it makes you hurt like this."

Raine nodded quickly. "His ex-wife has come back."

"Oh, Lord. That's a dirty trick. He doesn't love her. I saw the way he looked at you last night."

"I keep thinking that he might. She left him. He might not have wanted her to leave."

Miss Vi patted Raine's back. "If that's the way it is, he'd have told you so. Jordan's about the most honest and straightforward person I know. You can count on him."

"I hope so," Raine said, "I love him so."

"You two are going to find a way to be together. I just

know it." Picking up Raine's coffee cup, she took the cup over to the sink where she poured out the small amount of coffee down the drain and came back with the dregs in the bottom of the cup.

Sitting down as Raine sat opposite her, Miss Vi said, "Now we know I'm no conjure woman, but my uncle was a conjure man, and he taught me to read the coffee grounds and a few other things." She raised her hand for silence, narrowed her eyes, and sent herself into a mild trance, breathing deeply.

"There is trouble ahead, Raine," she said, "No doubt about it. Now this surprises me. There is more trouble on your side than on Jordy's, although there's trouble on his. I don't know if the coffee grounds are telling me this or if it's just coming into my head the way things do.

"Maybe I oughtn't to tell you, but I had a dream of a storm blowing through, and it hit this house, but lightly. Please be careful and tell Jordy to be careful. Something's going to happen, missy. Something's going to happen. I just feel it in my bones."

FIVE

A week later classes at the junior high school where Raine taught art were fully under way. Jimmy Coles, her star pupil, sat at his easel in her classroom, looking distraught. Raine placed a slender hand on his shoulder.

"How's your painting coming along?" she asked. The attractive, dark mocha-skinned boy shrugged.

"There's somethin' I'm not gettin' right," he said.

Raine studied the canvas. At fourteen, he was painting deep grief photographs of classmates and schoolmates who had been injured, and who had died in the past years of turmoil in the city. He was gifted enough to be headed for the Ellington School of the Arts.

"I see something I'd like you to consider," she said quietly. "The boy is grieving his dead friend, but your landscape is altogether serene. It doesn't follow through. Put some erosion there, let the rocks be sharper, more jagged, the sky more threatened. I have a hunch that will work."

She was repeating her teacher's words when she studied at Pratt. Now proudly she thought, she was the teacher.

Jimmy scrunched his shoulders up, then expelled a hard sigh, grinning.

"When you come up with something like that," he said expansively, "I know I'm lucky to have you for a teacher."

Raine flushed. "Oh, I'm glad you feel like that," she said, "because I think you're going to go far."

School was out for the day, and only Jimmy and she remained in her classroom. The boy took up his painting with a new resolve, and Raine went back to her desk, musing. She had seen Jordan every night since he had come to town.

A light tap sounded on the door. When she went and opened it, a tall and beautiful, pale-skinned, light brown-haired woman stood there, unsmiling. She was perhaps two inches taller than Raine, fashionably thin and exquisitely dressed in a beige designer suit. Her manner was cold, mocking, derisive.

"May I help you?" Raine asked, wondering.

"Yes, I hope you can. I'm the ex-Mrs. Jordan Clymer."

"I see," Raine said evenly. "I'm glad to meet you, Rita. I've talked with you only by phone."

Rita nodded. "May I come in?"

"Oh, of course." Once inside the room, Rita looked about her, taking in the students' painting, the big drafty apple-green room—and most of all, Raine.

"Won't you have a seat?"

Both women sat down and Jimmy got up. "I guess I'll work on this again t'morrow," he said gruffly. "See you then, Miz Gibson."

He gathered his things and went out, with a pleased expression on his face about his picture. Raine turned to Rita. "What brings you here?"

Rita shrugged. "As you say, we've talked by phone—only by phone, and briefly. I'll be blunt. I miss Jordan. I made a mistake getting a divorce. I want him back. Somehow you seem to me like a woman who likes to win, what little I see of you here. Am I right?"

Raine shifted in the hard-bottomed chair. "That's really too vague a question to answer. We can't always win, but often we can."

"My father's money took Jordan to where he is. Did you know that?"

"He told me your father helped him. But Jordy would go up with or without your father. He's his own man."

STILL IN LOVE 57

"Oh, my husband's a charmer, all right. Jordan has high school and college photographs of you and him. I think he said your husband died in an accident overseas."

"That's right." She wasn't going to discuss Dan with this woman.

"That was several years ago. I guess you must get lonely. D.C. isn't a great town for women and love, I hear."

"For some, it's a great town. For others, it isn't."

"Nicely put." Rita smiled, exposing a model's teeth. "You're an attractive woman, Raine. There must be other men for you. Because of his relationship with my father, our fates are enmeshed in ways you can't possibly understand."

"You surely don't expect me to answer that."

Rita's voice dropped, quickly became almost a snarl. "I warn you. I'm going to try to get him back."

Raine was silent, pondering, when Rita attacked again.

Rita leaned back in her chair. "I hope you listen to what I'm saying, because I don't fight fair. I fight to win. And as I said, I want him back. I will hurt you if you keep seeing Jordan."

"Do you mean physically hurt me?"

Rita laughed merrily. "Oh, Lord, no. That would be too tacky. There are many ways—"

Raine got up. "I'm afraid I have to cut this short. I'm meeting someone." She glanced at her watch.

"Very well." Rita looked around again. "I see you're advertising already for a Winter Wonderland Fair. I'm impressed with what I see here."

Shocked, Raine noted that Rita had changed like a chameleon from threatening to pleasant in a few seconds.

"Thank you," she said as the other woman rose.

"You will consider what I've said."

Raine breathed deeply. "Rita, I'm going to continue seeing Jordan. If I felt that even in small part he wanted to go back with you, I wouldn't see him at all. But he's happy out of this marriage."

"You and Jordy have just come back into each other's lives, may I remind you."

Raine nodded. "That's true."

"A man changes," Rita said. "The Jordan you knew might not be the man who exists now. Jordan is charming, Raine, but he's scheming. Those traits take him far in his work, but believe me, being married to him is no heaven."

"Then why do you want him back?"

Rita didn't skip a beat. "Because I liked being married to him, and I handled the situation with him very well. My father's money being so deeply tied up in this makes me feel more secure." She laughed harshly. "Surely you don't believe you're the first woman he's taken to and bedded."

Raine started to say that she and Jordan hadn't slept together since he'd been back, but she clamped her mouth shut. This was none of Rita's damned business. She was his ex-wife. In every other way, he was hers, Raine's. But a small voice chided her: Perhaps you don't know him anymore. Perhaps, like Rita says, he's changed.

Jordan's partner, Scott, and Caroline arrived a little late at Caleb's Inn which Raine and Caroline frequented, and where Jordan and Raine had gone the first night.

Goldfish leapt in the quartz pond in front of the restaurant-club and, watching the big black, gold, and white fish, Raine felt happy in spite of Rita's visit. Dressed in off-white silk crepe with a matching band around her hair and gold strap sandals, she thought she compared at least favorably with the beauteous Rita.

As they went inside, Jordan drew her a little aside and whistled long and low as Raine blushed. "You're very quiet," he said softly.

"With reason. Rita came by to see me at school this afternoon."

"I'm not surprised. I'm also not pleased."

"Jordy, she asked me not to see you again. She asked me to remember that you're not the young man I knew. She wants you back."

Jordan's mouth set in a grim line. "She's right, I'm not the man I was a while ago. I'm not even the man she divorced. But for you, Ray, I'm the same guy who fell in love with you back then. Believe me."

And looking at the serious expression on his face, she did believe him. And yet . . . Dan had said he adored her before they were married, and in spite of his perfidy while they were courting, she'd believed him. She had learned to her bitter dismay that many men could say one thing and mean another. But surely not Jordan.

"I'm not going to stop seeing you, Ray," he said urgently. "I'll park on your doorstep with only the dogs, Ripley and Lilac to keep me company if I have to. I love you, sweetheart, and I'm not giving you up again."

"I'm glad," Raine said simply, "because I don't want to give you up."

Jordan took her hand and squeezed it tightly, reveling in her soft flesh and in her nearness.

"You're lovely tonight," he whispered. "But then you're always lovely. The symphony-in-browns lady." His eyes caressed her, missing nothing. He couldn't believe the urgency his body knew these days, where he had been completely enmeshed in his work from the time Rita had asked for a divorce and when he'd seen Raine again. And even before Rita had asked for a divorce, the romantic side of him had lain dormant for a while.

"How's my daughter?"

Raine sighed. "I want to tell her so badly that you're her father, but she's not ready for it."

"We'll take it slow and prepare her," he said. "I want Rita

to leave, but she intends to badger me for a while. When Mike comes back to her, she'll settle down."

"Won't Rita and Mike be getting married?"

Jordan pondered her question.

"Maybe, but I found Mike had promised to marry her and dumped her before we were married. He's never been married, so I don't know."

"Were there other women for you?" Raine asked hesitantly.

"She told you that?"

"Yes."

"Did she name names?"

"No."

"There was one woman. A friend, Carla—a lovely woman, but we never got off the ground. When she saw Rita wasn't going through with a new marriage, she broke off. Other than that, I was faithful to Rita, and she's lying when she says I wasn't. Obviously if she was leaving me for another man, she wasn't entirely faithful." Jordan stopped and ran his hand over his brow. "Nobody ever said that Rita fights fair. Not even Rita."

"Yes, she also told me that."

Scott and Caroline came up. Jordan introduced Scott to Raine, and Caroline and Jordan renewed their old friendship with a bear hug. They were happy to see one another. Scott was a different story. He seemed a bit edgy and kept giving Caroline oblique glances.

As the waiter came to seat them, Caroline said she wanted to go to the powder room, and Raine said she'd go with her.

"You two come in often enough to know the menu by heart," Jordan said. "In case you get lost in the powder room, what're you having?"

"I'll take surf and turf," Caroline told him, "and a piña colada."

"And I'll celebrate our first night here and have the sauteed shrimp and oysters, and red wine."

Jordan took her hand, bent and kissed it. "Ah, madame knows what pleasures ze heart. You doll."

Scott still looked a bit unhappy as she and Caroline walked away.

The men were seated as Raine and Caroline went into the nicely appointed rose-colored powder room.

"My dear, you do look lovely," Raine said, "but a wee bit unhappy. What's da matter, girlfriend?"

Caroline thought a moment. "I guess it's this Scott creature. He's a hunk, I think, and maybe I haven't had a date in so long, I came on too strong: chirping, twittering. You know how it goes when I'm nervous. He was friendly enough at first, but no more than ten minutes into our relationship he got quiet, and everybody's been quiet ever since. Did I say something wrong? Do something wrong? Do I look like Gravel Gertie? You look great, girlfriend. Give me some tips."

Raine looked at her friend somberly. "You don't need tips, Caroline. You're a babe and you've got to know it." Her glance quickly swept over the aquamarine lace top and white jersey harem trousers Caroline wore.

"You say," Raine ventured, "that he seemed to like you at first. Well, I'll let you in on a little secret. Your boy was savaged in love by his ex-wife, and he doesn't like it one bit, Jordan says, when he feels he's getting close to a woman."

"My guess is you wouldn't be so rattled and upset by his not seeming to like you very much if you didn't like him."

"What an intricate mind you have," Caroline said, raising her eyebrows.

"But I'll bet I'm right."

Caroline sighed. "You could be."

"Just go out there and be your sweet, charming self. Knock him dead in the waters of love."

"You know, you're some kind of matchmaker."

"I try, love. Oh, how I try."

Raine told Caroline about Rita's visit that afternoon, and Caroline was agreeably outraged.

"How dare she do that to you, ask that of you?" Caroline said.

"Well, wife Rita is nothing if not daring," Raine said, sighing. "Even if she struck the first blow in asking for a divorce, she changed her mind, and now swears she's going to fight to get Jordan back."

On the way home that night, sitting beside Jordan as they rode along, Raine felt close to him and happy in spite of Rita's visit.

"Penny for your thoughts," Jordan said.

Raine sighed. "I seem to always be thinking of you and me long ago."

"Think about us now. I love you even more, if that's possible. Lord, Kym's a wonderful kid. I want both of you securely in my life."

"We are in your life. Kym admires you, I think, and you know how I feel. Give us both a little time."

"I'd give anything, do anything for you and her."

Raine pressed his arm. "That's sweet, Jordy. But then you always were a sweet guy."

Jordan turned to look at her, smiling. "I'm glad you think so. I've come to the conclusion that you're my angel. The only one I'll ever need."

"I like that, but what if Rita pulls out all the stops in getting you back?"

"Good question. But I happen to know Rita. She wants Mike, not me. I've got a good living, but Mike is rich and the heir of a wealthy family that owns a food conglomerate. I don't rate compared to him. She'll leave me alone, all right. She'll give me up if she can inveigle him to come running again."

"What a miserable way to live."

"Yeah. I'll take our way any time. Love and honor. All that good stuff."

The seed embedded itself in Raine's mind that Jordan must surely be a bit bitter about Rita just walking out on him, ditching him for another man, not to mention waltzing back in after their divorce.

"Were you very hurt when she asked for a divorce?"

Jordan thought a long time before he answered. "Well, for me, the bloom came off the rose in our marriage a little more than a year after we were married, but I had my work. Rita was a good hostess and always said one day she wanted children. You had married Dan before I got married. I'm a big one for families, and I wanted one."

Jordan stopped again, then continued. "I'm not biting the bullet, am I? Yeah, I was hurt. I told myself I'd settle for half a loaf, and Rita would settle down once she had kids."

"She's such a beautiful woman."

"Until you come to know her. You're far more beautiful. Rita's cruel. It's a part of her makeup I don't like. I came up with your loving ways, and I've gotten spoiled."

"Life can be rotten sometimes."

"Yeah, and it can be really good, the way it was with us as teenagers."

"The moon and stars we watched at night," Raine said. "Not to mention the sunrises and sunsets. Jordy, what if that's all there is for us?"

Jordan groaned. "Don't say that, Ray. We're going to spend the rest of our lives together, if we have to take Kym and run away to do it."

"You're too solid for that, and although I'm an artist and more flighty, maybe I am, too."

"Don't place any heavy bets on it. I'd never have thought I could get so desperate in a little over a week. Do you have any idea what you mean to me?"

"I think I do, and you know you mean even more to me. I think in both our hearts we were meant for each other."

Jordan drew up onto a shoulder of the road.

"Care to neck?" he asked, laughing.

"The cocktails've gone to your head."

"No. You've gone to my head. I'm in need of a few choice kisses to tide me over."

"You're greedy. We've exchanged so many kisses since you've come back."

"And I'm good for uncountable more. Raine, we've got to find somewhere to be alone." He shifted a bit. "Just stop me when I move too fast. I'm paying a lot of attention to what you said about being hurt when I left, and I'm willing to wait."

She didn't tell Jordan about Rita's veiled threats to her. He had enough problems.

Jordan drew her close and buried his face in the hollows of her throat. "I'm all tangled up with you. We're talking about my heart and my soul. We're talking about my life here."

"I know. I feel the same way."

Jordan turned the side of his face to listen to her steady heartbeat. The gardenia fragrance she wore was light and heady, and it drove him a little mad. And Jordan thought, hell, without any fragrance, her own sweet, loving, natural fragrance made his heart race.

Raine laughed shakily. "We've got to stop meeting like this."

Jordan chuckled as she stroked the sturdy smooth strands of his thick, close-cropped black hair and lightly massaged his shoulder.

"If I were a cat, I'd purr for you," Jordan said.

"You're a tiger, love, and I'd say you're doing a pretty good job of purring. You're breathing heavily. We need to go home. Each to his own, that is. We're dangerous together."

STILL IN LOVE

"If we're dangerous together, then that's what I want my life to be: dangerous."

When he was silent so long, Raine asked, "Are you asleep?"

"No. I guess I was thinking about us—about your being married to Dan and how crazy it made me when I found out. I almost couldn't take the pain. I felt you were mine, God's own special gift to me and I to you, and Dan had no right to interfere."

"But I was pregnant."

He placed a finger on her lips. "I know, love. I know that now, but I was just a callow kid then. I didn't know you were pregnant. I felt betrayed. I'm not sure how any of us gets past adolescence."

"Have you got it straight now?" Raine asked. "At least in your head?"

"Yeah, I have. Raine?"

"Yes, love."

"We have to be together. Get to know each other again."

"Meaning in the Biblical sense."

"Yes, love. Yes. I'm coming apart with wanting you."

Raine sat up straighter. "We're both having a hard time with wanting each other, but I've got a hard day ahead tomorrow and with things being the way they are, Jordy. Don't let's make it harder for ourselves."

"Loving you is pushing the hell out of me."

Raine laughed throatily. "And love for you is pulling me the same way. Okay, you win. We'll find a way."

Jordan started the car again and let it idle a few moments.

"I want everything to be right for us," Raine told him, hating the disappointment they both felt.

"What I'm feeling is that I'm dying with wanting you," he said.

"That makes two of us, but we're doing the right thing to wait until a better time."

Jordan stroked her thigh, feeling the firm flesh under

the softly crisp silk crepe. He leaned over and kissed her again, long and deep.

"Let's wrap it up for tonight, tiger," Raine whispered, remembering how they had often parked in this same spot in their high school days, just for a few stolen kisses before she was home and under the watchful eyes of her loving parents.

SIX

At Raine's house Jordan opened the car door for her, helped her out.

"Do you want to come in for a nightcap?"

"That would mean you were trusting me when I don't trust myself."

"Jordan," she said softly, "I love you and love you over again."

"Hush. You're revving my motor even more."

They were on her screened front porch then, with its porch swing and pale blue ceiling.

"I'll see you in.' "

"No, I want to sit out here for a few moments to cool down and pull myself together. My heart'll stop pounding once it's not around you anymore. Oh, Jordy, our bodies are often so wise."

"You're telling me. I don't want to go, but I'll just say good night and walk away."

But he didn't walk away. He took her in his arms and his mouth against hers was searing. Sweet fire swept like honey through her veins. They kissed until both were gasping for breath. Every pore of her being craved him and they both could have wept with wanting each other. It was Raine who drew apart.

Reluctantly, Jordan let her go, drew her close again in a quick embrace, released her and turned away.

"Good-night, sweetheart," he said.

"Good-night, my love, she answered, emotionally clinging to him.

After he had left, with her watching his car until it was out of sight, Raine sat down on the porch swing. Every cell of her being seemed to be alive and singing. The night had never seemed more beautiful with its hanging clusters of stars and its brilliant silvery moonlight.

The night was made for love. Why weren't she and Jordan in each other's arms out in this moonlight, gazing at those stars?

Challenger Farm was lovely tonight, its boarded fences across the front sparkling white from a new painting by Uncle Prince. The fieldstone house fitted into the landscape of low hills and valleys. In her mind's eye, she could see the big catfish pond out back where she and Jordy had spent so much time studying and being together as teenagers.

Challenger was her maiden name. She was the only daughter of Kitty and Joe Challenger. Her mother had died early, and at times she still longed for the sweet-faced, soft-spoken woman. They would have adored Kym, she thought now. Her father had lived until she was in college before he died of cancer. Her father had loved Jordan and disliked Dan, whom he regarded as a rascal.

She and Dan hadn't spent too much time here. They had quickly moved to New Orleans after their marriage. Dan had been open about his envy of his cousin, Jordan.

"The sooner we shake the dust of this place off our feet," he'd said, "the sooner you'll get over Jordan."

Hurt and believing Jordan had left her, she had been happy to agree. With her parents dead, she had sold Challenger Farm, but the new owner had kept Uncle Prince and Miss Vi on to manage it for him. Getting rid of the farm had hurt, but Dan had been insistent.

STILL IN LOVE 69

"I want to stifle all the memories you've got of Jordan," Dan had said. "I think this'll help do it."

Her heart had cried out then that no matter what Dan did or what she did, the memories she and Jordy had shared were inlaid emotional gold and precious gems deep in her heart. But Dan didn't have to know that.

After Dan's death the family that had bought Challenger Farm had wanted to move west to Montana and had sold the farm back to Raine. Her paintings had been popular in New Orleans, she had taught part time in a private high school, and there had been Dan's insurance money. While they lived there, Dan coached at a local high school. She smiled a bit grimly. Dan would have been furious to know that his money had helped to buy back what he had been so intent on getting rid of.

Now Jordy was back in her life. Gloriously back! With an ex-wife who had suddenly decided she wanted him back.

Ripley and Lilac began to bark suddenly, growling and snapping as if they didn't like what they saw one bit. She would normally have told them to pipe down, but her own blood had suddenly cooled.

"Ripley, Lilac," she called softly, before she saw the bulky figure of a man at the corner of the porch. He had evidently come up the side path from the back.

"Evening, Raine," the man said in an easy drawl she'd have sworn she recognized.

She got up to latch the front screen door, angry with herself that she hadn't done so before.

"Who are you?" she asked.

"It's Dan, Raine. Your ever-loving husband," he answered as he pulled the door open.

By then the bearded man was two feet away from her, and he reached out and took her hand.

"A kiss would be the natural thing to do," he drawled.

"No, don't," she rasped, willing herself to be calm. "Who are you?"

"It really is me—Dan," he said. "Your husband. Turn on the light."

No, she thought, the front door was locked, so he couldn't get inside, and the light switch was inside.

"No, I won't turn on the light, and I want you to leave."

There was a cellular phone in her purse, but how was she going to get to it?

"You don't believe me," he said. "I guess it's the beard. You couldn't know."

"Dan's dead," she said flatly. Maybe that would let this fool know how he was coming across.

"No. I'm not dead," he said, chuckling. "You've thought I was. The Army thought I was. But I'm very much alive."

"Dan Gibson died in Spain in an accident three years ago. They found his gear, but never his body," she said slowly.

When the man continued to stare at her, breathing heavily, she said with a note of hysteria creeping into her voice, "Mister, I don't know what your game is, but I want you to leave now."

"Hell, I'm not dead, I tell you," the man said, his voice harsher now. "I waited until my cousin Jordan left tonight, and I'd guess from the way he was kissing you up, you'd just as soon I was dead. But you wait a minute."

The beefy man fished a penlight out of his jacket pocket, raised his shirtsleeve, and shined a penknife on a long scar that Dan had gotten on his forearm from Ripley years before. Raine would never forget that scar. The dog had bitten Dan when he kicked it.

"Oh, my God," she said raggedly. This man was the same height and build as Dan, but heavier than she remembered him. If it was Dan, the sun had tanned him the color of molasses where he had been the color of maple syrup.

His chuckle seemed more threatening this time. "You're making me go like a broken record, sweetie. I'm your ever-loving husband, Dan. And maybe I will have that kiss."

"No," she began, but he grabbed her and held her stiff and unyielding body against his, forcing his tongue past her lips only to meet with the solid resistance of her teeth.

His laugh was ugly as he drew back. "You sure were hot enough with my cousin Jordy. You were all over him."

"Jordy and I love each other," she said heatedly. "We have a right to passion."

"But you're my wife, Raine, and don't you forget it."

"We had grown apart, Dan. That's one of the reasons you went into the Army. You wanted to travel, you said, to get away."

Dan shrugged. "I was wild and young. We all were. Listen, after Jordy ran out on you, I'd think you'd know better than to trust him. I picked up the slack. Gave you a name for Kym. How is the kid?"

"She's fine." Her own voice sounded distant in her ears. Was this a nightmare . . . or truth? How could she handle this? Inside the house there was a phone where she could call police, but what would she tell them? That her husband had come back from the dead? Her body ached for Jordan. What if Dan attacked him? He had once when they were in college, and she had stopped dating Dan, whom she'd never been intimate with and fallen in love with Jordy.

Oh, Lord, what now? Dan was saying something, and she hadn't been listening.

"Wake up, sweetie," Dan said with a nasty laugh. "I didn't force myself on you, did I? And I won't. You cared about me once. I'll make you care again."

"Dan, please," she said softly. She meant for him to please leave, leave her alone.

"You didn't answer me about Jordy running out on you."

"He didn't know I was pregnant."

Dan's harsh laughter rang in her eyes. "Oh, I'll just bet. Ah, hell, let's sit down. You were all over Jordy tonight. I nearly got scorched from where I was standing."

"You watched us? Dan, that's so immature."

"I'm a coach, remember. It's my business to watch closely and keep track of what's going on."

"Spying is what it is."

"Well, I saw plenty. Yeah, I've watched you for a couple of nights, getting my bearings, finding out how to fight to get back what's mine."

Raine's brain began to frantically spin. Maybe he wasn't Dan. What if he were a friend who had some ax to grind, and he was faking the scar tissue on his forearm? Game shops had patches of plastic that looked like real scars.

"My beard threw you off," he said in a more pleasant voice. "I've had it a long time. Let's go inside, and I'll shave and you'll know it's me if the scar didn't convince you."

"No, I'm not going inside with you."

"You trusted me once to make good on a promise Jordy didn't keep."

"He couldn't."

"Stop defending him. In my book he's a louse for running out on you. Like I said, I picked up the slack."

Raine's throat nearly closed. "I'm grateful that you gave Kym your name. But the past is past, Dan. We have nothing going for us anymore."

"Maybe you don't. I do. I've been around a few days, tracking down what's been happening in your life."

"Yes, in a few years she can decide for herself. Dan, surely you haven't forgotten how outrageously mean you were before you left us and went into the Army."

"I've been sorry about that for a long time. Don't you want to know what happened to me?"

"Yes. I guess so."

He didn't need much urging. "I was in a training jeep that turned over, leaving me in a ditch. I struck my head on a large boulder, and it knocked me out. When I came to, I didn't know who I was."

"Didn't you have identification?"

"I was in the mountains of Spain, touring. When I came

STILL IN LOVE

to, I'd been stripped down to my underwear. My money, dog tags, wallet were all gone. Those Spanish mountain boys play rough. My mind was a total blank. I remembered going off the road, hurtling into space. And that was that."

"Oh, my God, how terrible. I'm sorry."

"Yeah, you always had the sympathy in the family. Well, after that I got lucky. A mountain family took me in. They didn't have much, but they were good to me. Someone stole the jeep before they found me. I lived with them until one day a month ago, my memory began to return."

"But you remembered being married?"

"Not until a few weeks ago."

"But shouldn't you have turned yourself in?"

"I did. In Torremolinos, Malaga. The Army checked me over there. Kept me a week as I remembered more and more every day. They gave me leave to visit here. I have to report to Fort Riley day after tomorrow. I'm getting out, Raine. The Army isn't for me."

What was for Dan? She couldn't remember a time when he hadn't been discontented, at least partially unhappy.

"I'm truly sorry for what happened to you," she said, "but please understand, Jordy and I are together again. Dan, please understand and let me go. It's so easy for you to find somebody else."

"You're the only one for me."

Raine shook her head. "There were other women for you in New Orleans, and here. There'll always be other women for you."

"I'll never love them the way I love you. Having other women is just a natural male reaction, sweetie. Come on, Raine. Don't be naive. It's just the nature of the beast for a man to run around."

Dan slapped his palm against the leg of his faded blue denims.

"Like I said, Jordan left you to have his kid alone. How can you trust him now?"

"It wasn't like that, I tell you."

"The hell it wasn't."

Raine couldn't believe it when Dan suddenly shifted his position and began to get up. He leaned over and kissed her on the cheek.

"If I want you back," he said, "it's plain I'm going to have to watch my step. And I do want you back." His fingers stroked the cheek he'd just kissed.

His voice was sober and apparently sincere. "I'm going to fight for you, Raine. You're all I've got. And yeah, you're right. We weren't on good terms when I left, and I intend to make it up to you."

He left then, walking down the curved walk and into the night. She wondered vaguely if he was driving and where he was staying—but panic set in quickly, and she dug her keys out of her purse, and with fingers trembling so badly she could hardly hold the keys, let herself in.

She willed herself to quiet her near hysteria as she threw her purse on the bed and dialed Jordan's number, talked with him, as best she could.

"You hold tight, sweetheart," Jordan said. "I'm coming back."

"No, darling," she told him. "It's all right. He's gone, and I don't think he'll return. I'll see you tomorrow. I thought you should know about this."

"You're damned right, I should know. I'll be there in the shortest possible time."

"Jordy, be careful. I really am okay."

"No. You won't be okay until I'm there to hold you."

"Well, you're about right there."

She hung up and called Uncle Prince and Miss Vi, who were with her in a very short while. Miss Vi's lovely old face was blanched with fear and concern.

Uncle Prince shook his head when Raine had finished telling them what happened.

"That Dan's always been a strange one," he said. "His

ma and pa spoiled him rotten. Now he expects the world to be at his beck and call, and it ain't gonna happen."

"He didn't hurt you now?" Miss Vi asked.

"No," Raine said. "He just nearly frightened me to death."

"You called Jordan and told him."

"Yes. I didn't want him to, but he's coming back."

"It's a good thing. You need him now," Uncle Prince said.

Miss Vi rocked a bit on her feet as she hugged Raine. "There, lamb. Calm down. But then you're about as calm as a soul could be in the face of this. I never did like Dan Gibson. I know he's never been good enough for you. As a child he was a bad one for stoning dogs, and you'll remember Uncle Prince gave him a good tongue lashing for kicking old Ripley one day. He tried it again and Ripley bit him."

"People do change sometimes," Uncle Prince said, "but it seems Dan don't want to choose that road. Lord, it's gotten to be a cruel world we live in."

Raine closed the blinds of a window she usually left open and with the blinds open. She couldn't shake a feeling that Dan was watching somewhere in the dark night he'd gone into. The same night that had seemed indescribably beautiful to her, a short couple of hours before, now seemed blighted and dangerous.

She sat at the kitchen table with its cheerful yellow plastic covering and wanted to weep with tension. First Rita and her stated desire to get Jordy back. Now was it a dream—or a nightmare—that the unbeloved husband she had felt little for when she thought he was dead was back in her life and wanted to go on with her as before?

Soon the smell of New Orleans coffee and chicory filled the air. Raine usually drank it with cream and sugar, but tonight she took it black. They all did.

Miss Vi couldn't do enough for her. She got Tylenol from the medicine cabinet to still a pounding headache, drew a glass of warm tap water and handed it to Raine. Obediently swallowing the tablets, Raine's throat felt dry with fear.

"I knew a guy who had amnesia a long while," Uncle Prince ventured. "It was more'n a few years before he got his memory back. He had a lot to hide—like Dan. You reckon Dan was involved in somethin' over there in Spain he hadn't oughta been involved in?"

"Knowing Dan," Raine said, feeling empty, "anything is possible. It's hard to believe he wasn't involved in something he had no business being into."

"Lord, help us all," Miss Vi said.

Hers was a prayer that Raine repeated silently as she drank the black coffee, hardly waiting for it to cool.

Later, as they sat there, she heard Jordan's car door slam and was at the front door as he bounded up the steps.

"Oh, sweetheart," he said, pulling her close. "I wish I'd stayed longer. I hate having you face that monster alone. Did he hurt you in any way?"

Raine shook her head. "No, not physically, Jordy. But he wants me to stay married to him. He's been watching us—he said for a couple of nights, but who knows for how long."

Jordan swore. "That's just what I'd expect from Dan."

His eyes expressing all the love he felt for her, he examined her carefully for bruises and found one on her forearm she hadn't been aware of.

"Did this come courtesy of Dan?" he asked through clenched teeth.

"Yes, it must have. He caught my forearms a lot." She hesitated before she said it, wanting the whole mess out in the open.

"He said he's going to fight to stay married to me, Jordy. By law he's my husband."

Dan's bruising Raine infuriated Jordan.

"He doesn't know what fighting means if he wants you back from me. We used to laugh and say, cupcake, that fate put us together. Well, as far as I'm concerned, fate is going to see that we get back together for good."

Again, Miss Vi and Uncle Prince had retired to their house for the night, but at one in the morning, Raine and Jordan were still sitting in the kitchen.

"I hate Dan for shocking you like this and for bruising you," Jordan said finally, taking her hand as they sat at the table. "He could have called."

"It's vintage Dan."

"I haven't asked you questions about being married to him," Jordan said after a long pause. "It seems to me you tighten up when I mention his name."

"With good reason. There are things I haven't told you."

"I'd guessed as much. You don't ever have to tell me if you don't want to talk about it."

"A little later I want to. But let me get over the shock of this first."

When they had finished their coffee, Jordan got up, came around to her side of the table, and pulled her to her feet.

"I'm going to spend the rest of the night. I'll sleep on the sofa. Did Kym wake up? Kids have a way of coming awake at the very time you don't want them to."

"I let her stay with Miss Vi and Uncle Prince, remember? I decided to just let her spend the rest of the night."

"Good thing."

"I can sleep in her room and you take my bed."

"This isn't going to be easy for either of us. I won't be getting any sleep. Let me massage you a bit and relax you."

"Just my shoulders," she said. "I don't trust myself to let you take it any further."

Raine still felt a sense of numbness, of nearly total shock, but Jordan's closeness helped her to cope.

"Did my fool of a cousin say when he'd be back?"

"No, just that I'd see him again—that he would be back.

He's grown a beard, Jordy. A full beard. He looks like an angry bear."

"I don't like his bruising you one damned bit, but that's about his style. He didn't push you around when you two were courting in high school, did he? You never said."

Raine put a hand to each side of her head. She hated remembering her past with Dan. "No, he never did push me around in high school. And he did precious little of it after we were married. It was an emotional thing with Dan. He's verbally intimidating. And there were always other women for him, even in high school. I think he didn't push me around only because I wouldn't stand for it. There were those, I understand, that he did push around."

Raine's throat was suddenly tight with an excruciatingly painful memory she didn't want to talk about. "One day," she said, "I'll have to tell you what happened to tear us apart. I've only recently stopped hating him for that. Oh, Jordy, don't the bad things ever stop hurting?"

Jordan took her in his arms and held her. Her eyes were dry, but her face was tense, strained.

"Sweetheart," he said softly, massaging her entire back and her shoulders and neck, then cradling her head in his capable hands.

Jordan felt a sense of unreality, too. So Dan was back from the dead.

"What happened to have the Army declare him dead?"

"A jeep accident when he was touring in Spain, and he said amnesia."

"Sounds like you don't believe him."

Raine thought a moment. "He could be telling the truth. People do get amnesia, but Dan slides away from so much. There was constant trouble at the school in New Orleans where Dan coached. He got reported any number of times. He had an easy principal, but even he got tired of Dan's behavior. But he was a very good coach. His team won many awards."

"But he had to be a hell of a role model. Dan's spoiled beyond redemption. Look, Ray, you've got that haunted expression again. You get it when your mind goes deep when you're talking about Dan."

"One day I'll tell you what happened," Raine said softly. "Right now, I just want to sleep."

They had moved to Kym's bedroom. Raine removed her clothes in the bathroom, put on a gown with sleeves, and got into bed. Jordan sat on the side of the bed. "This has been one crazy night," he said. "And it began with us out for a perfectly great evening. Raine, my darling, try to relax, but I guess that's asking the impossible." His own heart hurt with sympathy.

"No, not with you here. I'm much more relaxed. Jordy, how are we going to work through the snarls we're in?"

Jordan took her hand and squeezed it gently. "By taking it one step at a time. We'll make it somehow. This is going to require a lot of thinking through on both our parts, but we're going to be together."

"If Rita's beloved Michael really is through with her, she'll hang on to you even though you're divorced."

Jordan shook his head. "You're right. Like Dan, Rita's incapable of behaving like an adult. I've always felt that because of my ties to her father, I'm not as adamant with her as I could be. I'll check up on myself there."

Raine was drifting off to sleep thinking Rita might not be such a problem after all. But Dan was not only back, her instincts told her Dan could be dangerous.

The dream came quickly as Jordan still stroked her back. Dan with his beard in full growth forced her close to him and kissed her long and hard, a hateful kiss, while she struggled to get away. He pinioned her arms, and she was helpless as she screamed beneath his savage onslaught.

"No-o-o-! Stop it! Do you hear me? Stop it!"

She came groggily awake as Jordan shook her gently, calling her name.

Raine sat up gasping for breath.

"You dreamed about Dan."

"Yes. He was kissing me and I hated it."

"Lord, this is getting next to me. Maybe I should just move in to protect you." He held her close.

Raine shook her head. "I'm not afraid of Dan, Jordy. I never have been. His hurt to me has always been to the heart."

"But that's pain, too, Ray, the worst kind. I don't want him hurting you on any level."

Raine's breathing slowed and became more even. Looking at his beloved face above her, his eyes as tender as his kisses, Raine swore she and Jordy would find a way out of this madness and a way to fully enjoy the deep love they bore each other.

SEVEN

Next morning, except for Raine, they were all up and about early. Raine came awake to the smell of freshly brewed coffee, Jordan running the shower, and Uncle Prince romping with the dogs. The minute she woke up, her heart felt heavy at the thought of Dan's return from the dead. At a little knock on the door, Raine called out, "Come in, love." It could only be Kym. She was glad Dan had come as late as he had. How was Kym going to take this?

"Mr. Clymer spent the night, Mom, and here you are in my room."

"Yes, honey."

Kym came and sat on the bed. She hugged and kissed Raine and patted her cheek.

"You look sad again, Mom. What's wrong? Today's Saturday and you can paint all day, unless Mr. Clymer's staying awhile."

Raine smoothed her daughter's soft black hair. How like Jordy she was. As if on cue, Jordan stepped from the shower wrapped in a one-size-fits-all white terry-cloth robe.

"I thought I heard a sweet little bird chirping," he said.

Kym smiled but clung to Raine's side. They should be together as a family, Raine thought with bitter longing.

"Oh, I forgot," Kym said. "Miss Vi told me to come right back. I'm to tell you that breakfast will soon be ready. Flapjacks and maple syrup. Sausage, eggs with mushrooms, and

I'm squeezing the orange juice. Tomorrow Miss Vi and I are making sourdough pancakes."

Kym was so happy today. When to tell her about Dan's return? She thought she should tell her later today before Dan came around again. Kym skipped from the room, and Jordan sat on the side of the bed.

"She's my kid, and I want her to know she is," Jordan said. "How are you feeling, love? I came to check on you several times. You tossed a lot."

"Thank you for being so sweet. I'm glad today is Saturday. I don't think I could make it otherwise. You're right. I want us to think about telling Kym. She's mature for her age."

"I'm thinking about something else," Jordan said. "I'm certain Dan will be back, and he's likely to say something to Kym about my being her father. Or he'll try like hell to convince her to take his side."

"You're right," Raine said.

Then Jordan's lips on hers were warm and fervent. His rippling muscles under her fingertips sent thrills through her hungry body.

"Jordy, I think we need to tell Kym that Dan is back. He helped her a lot, but he was mistreating her as well as everyone else when he left."

"It's been four years. Maybe she's largely forgotten."

Raine shook her head. "An elephant's memory is nothing compared to Kym's."

"It's the painful things we tend to forget."

Raine nodded. "You're right about that."

"Would you like me to run your bath water?"

"Thank you, but I need the sting of the shower to wake me up." She shuddered a bit. "What if you hadn't come back into town, Jordy? I don't think I could take this without your being here."

"I'm glad I'm here, but you're strong, Ray—strong and beautiful. We'll get through this. And we'll be together for good."

STILL IN LOVE

* * *

But they didn't get a chance to tell Kym about Dan. Raine, Kym, Jordan, Miss Vi, and Uncle Prince were deep in good conversation and delicious food when there was the sound of Ripley's snarl as someone knocked on the side door by the breakfast room.

"Now who could that be?" Uncle Prince wondered and got up to answer the door.

"I saw my cousin's car and thought I should come around again before he left," Dan said. Uncle Prince unlatched the screen door and a clean-shaven Dan came in.

His eyes went directly to Raine. "I guess I'm not as scary without the beard as with it, huh, Raine?"

Raine stiffened as he came to her and began to kiss her on the mouth. Averting his kiss so that it went onto her cheek, she shot him a furious glance. "It's not in the beard, Dan," she said evenly. "It's what's in the heart."

"Hey now, my heart is full of love for you and Kym anyway." He turned to Kym. "Got a kiss for your old dad," he said, seeking to win her over.

"But I don't know you," the girl said.

"I'm your dad."

"My dad was killed in an accident in Spain."

"Four little years," Dan said, "and you've forgotten all about me. Do you still run?"

"Yes. Sometimes."

"Good. Look, I don't want to slight anybody. How's it going, Miss Vi and Uncle Prince?"

Both older people nodded and spoke with no enthusiasm at all.

Jordan watched the whole show that was intended to make him the outsider. He bided his time until Dan got around to him.

"Cousin," Dan said sharply. "You're still crashing through boundaries where you shouldn't be."

"That's a matter of opinion—your opinion," Jordan said tautly. "At least I don't go where I'm not wanted."

Dan laughed harshly. "There was a time when Raine not only needed me, but wanted me. Am I right, girl?"

"Life changes," Raine said. "We can't live in the past."

"So Jordan has come back into your life. I gather you two are not married, or you wouldn't have left last night and had to come back. Hell, I've got nothing to hide. I've been here several days and I've asked questions."

"We thought you were dead, Dan. You know that. You could have notified me," Raine said heatedly.

"I wanted to surprise you. And I did just that, didn't I? But I got the bigger surprise: that you and Jordy were back together. Listen, be careful he doesn't desert you again. He did the last time."

Raine got up. Nobody had offered Dan breakfast and she certainly wasn't going to, not under these circumstances. She stood by Kym's chair.

"Darling, let's go outside. I want to tell you something."

Kym pursed her lips the way she did when she was nervous. "Sure, Mom." She looked wide-eyed at Dan, and unpleasant memories began to stir. "Excuse me," she said to her tablemates.

Outside in the soft and misty September air, Raine and Kym walked down to the pond.

"You said he was dead, Mom."

"And that's what I thought. He came by last night. Do you know what amnesia is, Kym?"

"No."

"Well, that's when a person's mind blanks out and they remember nothing about the past."

"Not even their name?"

"That's right."

"And that's what happened to—the man at our house?"

"Yes. He was hurt in a touring accident when he was in the Army in Spain. His memory just came back weeks ago."

"Wow! That's pretty scary. Does it happen to many people?"

"Rarely." Raine bent and hugged the girl. "I love you very much, Kym. And Jordan Clymer loves you, too."

In a small voice Kym asked, "Did he tell you he loves me?"

"Yes. Oh, Kym, there's so much I have to tell you, but please be patient. How much do you remember about Dan?"

"Do I have to call him Dad?" Kym burst out. "I don't think I'm going to like that."

Raine thought a moment. "No. Until you get accustomed to him again, you can call him Mr. Gibson."

"Thanks, Mom. You know, I remember he was mean sometimes, but at other times he was real nice. He was great teaching me to run. He used to say I could be a world-class runner if I tried hard enough."

"And you can if that's what you want to do."

Kym shook her head. "No, when I run I think about him and how he could be mean, I don't want to anymore. Maybe I'll be an artist like you or a sculptor. Or a blues singer."

"I'm going to leave that up to you. I'll provide the support."

"You're the greatest, Mom. Is Mr. Gibson still your husband? Is he my dad?"

"Yes and no. I'm afraid he's still my husband, but he's not your real dad."

"Is he going to move in with us?"

Raine's breath caught in her throat. She hadn't thought about that. "No, I don't think so. You see, sweetheart, Mr. Gibson's a proud man. I don't think he'd want to stay with us when we don't want him."

"But he said you were his wife and told Mr. Clymer to let you alone."

Chalk one up for Kym, Raine thought. She saw into things.

"I'm going to file for divorce, Kym."

"And marry Mr. Clymer?"

"Would you like that?"

"No. I want it to be you and me."

Raine smiled. "But darling, remember saying the other kids have dads and you don't?"

Kym flung her arms around Raine. "Oh, Mom, I don't know what I want anymore."

Raine felt an urgency to tell Kym, and it seemed to her the right time.

"Darling, Jordan Clymer is your real father. You'll understand this when you're older."

"My real . . ." Kym's breath came fast, and she looked puzzled.

Raine caught her child close.

"Everything's going to be all right, honey. You're going to be fine."

Back in the breakfast nook, Dan got up and looked out the window at Raine and Kym down by the pond.

"Makes a man feel good to come back to family," Dan said cheerfully.

"Cut it," Jordan grated. "Things weren't going too well with Raine and Kym when you left four years ago to join the Army. You've got a short memory."

"I was mixed up. I didn't know how much I love them. Weren't you mixed up when you walked away and left her pregnant, old buddy?"

"You know damned well I didn't know about that. My mother had a bad heart, and I had to nurse her until she died."

"How long does it take to pick up a phone."

"If you'll do me the courtesy to wait, Dan. I had a heart valve problem that made an operation necessary. When Raine found out and was coming to be with me, I wasn't going to let her sacrifice her life to a sick man, so I let my mom call and say I was in love with someone else. When it was all over and I knew I'd be able to live a normal life, I came unannounced just as you've done now, to see Raine and she was married to you. I left without seeing her. I never knew she was pregnant. When I knew she had a child, I assumed it was with you."

"I did the raising, the supporting, of that kid out there. I adopted her. By all rights I'm the father you sure as hell never were."

"Only because I didn't know. But I know now."

Dan laughed nastily. "You're going to have a mighty hard row to hoe, Jord, if you try to take her away again the way you did when we first went to college."

"My God, man, live in the present. Raine doesn't want you anymore."

"Well, I'm not divorcing Raine. And sympathy will be on my side. Army vet getting over amnesia comes home to find his wife in the arms of another man."

"Knock it off, Dan."

But Dan continued. "As a matter of fact, a man—if you can call him that—who'd deserted her years ago. You need to get your act together, cousin."

Dan came away from the window. "If no one'll offer me a cup of coffee, I'll get myself one. I guess I have some rights since I've got a wife living here."

Slowly and carefully he got a cup, saucer, and spoon from the cupboard, went to the counter and poured himself a cup of coffee, adding several lumps of sugar and thick cream. Bringing it back to the table, he sat down, sipped it and smiled. "You still make great coffee, Miss Vi."

Miss Vi sniffed. She wanted none of Dan Gibson's insincere compliments. She fixed him with a steady eye. "I guess I'm wondering why you turn up here now," she said testily.

"I guess I never was your chosen child," Dan said easily.

"I remember how you always favored Jord here. He did a lot of kissing up, and I never held with it."

"Well, you can call it 'kissing up' if you've a mind to," Uncle Prince said, "but I call it treating people the way a human's got a right to be treated."

"I'm going to join Ray and Kym," Jordan said, getting up abruptly.

"You do that," Dan said, "because I'm planning to exercise my rights as a husband, not to mention my conjugal rights."

Jordan laughed shortly, his heart thudding with anger. "You've been away awhile, Danny. More and more you'll find the courts in this country on the woman's side. If Raine doesn't want you anymore, you're going to have to settle for that."

Dan's face went ashen with anger. "You may be the one who finds himself settling for a lot of things," Dan said sourly. "She's mine until she can legally get away from me, and I don't plan to make any moves to get in the way of having her as mine until then."

EIGHT

The Quarles Junior High School Art Festival, which was held on the last Saturday in October, found Raine in a flustered mood. Her child was beginning to accept that Jordan was her father, and Raine kept her fingers crossed that the two of them would grow closer.

In the spacious auditorium, students from Raine's classes helped her monitor paintings, so many of which were excellent.

Kym and Raine wore mother-daughter outfits of navy jumpers and red and white diagonally striped jerseys. Kym was a normally happy child, but Raine thought now she would have moved heaven and earth to bring Jordan into her child's life if she had known the difference it would make, because Kym blossomed under Jordan's attention. The mistakes she and Jordy had made were the stuff of life. How lucky she was to have gotten a small part of it together. She shuddered a bit at the thought of Rita, and now Dan.

"Oh my, don't you two look wonderful."

That was Mrs. Quarles, her principal. The school had been named for Mrs. Quarles's husband's father and was a model school located in Minden.

"We're on top of the world today, aren't we?" Mrs. Quarles said to Kym.

Kym nodded heartily. "I have a lot on my mind."

The child sounded so adult that both women looked at each other.

"Well, it's best to have a mind well occupied," the older woman said. She bent to hug Kym, then walked away to greet a group of people from the community.

"Mom," Kym said, "when I look at these paintings, it makes me think I want to paint. Could I be a runner and paint, too?"

"Of course. You're a bright kid. The way I see it, the world's going to be your oyster."

"You say that all the time. What does it mean?"

Raine bent to hug the child. "It means you can gobble it all up. Be what you choose to be, as long as you're willing to pay your dues. Which means you study hard and work hard and be smart and learn to listen."

"You sound just like my teacher, Mrs. Marshall."

"Well, we both know how much you like her."

"Mom, we haven't seen Da—Mr. Gibson anymore. I know he's still here because when I went to play with Tricia, Tricia's mom, Tricia, and I went to the store, and we saw him there."

Raine's breath caught in her throat. "Did he speak to you?"

"Oh yes, he was very nice. He bought us a big box of chocolate chip cookies and told Tricia's mom how glad he was to be back."

Raine was annoyed that Ellen, Tricia's mother, hadn't mentioned that.

"Why didn't you tell me?"

"We had so much fun at Tricia's house, I forgot. Gee, Mom, I'm sorry."

"It's all right, love, but I'm going to sue for divorce, and I don't want you in the middle of this."

"I like Mr. Gibson okay, but I like my dad a lot better."

"And he loves you."

Jimmy Coles came up. "It looks, teach," he said, "as if we've got another winner on our hands."

Raine patted the young man on his shoulder. "Thank

STILL IN LOVE 91

you so much for all the help you've given me. I think you can count on getting a prize."

They moved along until they were at Jimmy's painting of a turbulent Potomac at Haines Point: stormy, dark, beautiful. Still the boy looked less than happy.

"Is everything all right with you, Jimmy?" Raine asked.

He nodded, then burst out, "My pop's left town again."

"I'm so sorry," Raine said gently. "It's rough for you when he leaves, isn't it?"

"Yeah. Mom's got arthritis bad. Pop works wherever he goes and he's a good mechanic. But he says now he needs to know computers to get a job, so he doesn't get top pay anymore. I don't fault him. He's hurtin', too.

"But Mom cries something awful when he leaves. I wish I was out of high school and college instead of graduating from Quarles."

Raine hesitated only a moment. "Jimmy, I may have things you could do around the farm, and I have a friend I'll introduce you to who's going to need errands run."

The auditorium was beginning to fill and, as if her thoughts brought him there, Jordan came up. Jimmy had moved away.

Jordan took her hand briefly. "See what self-control I've got? I didn't kiss you," he said.

"But you did," she answered him, laughing. "You kissed me with your eyes and I responded."

"I looked as I walked along, and I like what you've put together here."

"Thank you. A lot of the credit belongs to the students."

"You all ought to be proud of yourselves." He caught sight of Kym, and they waved at each other. "My woman and my girl look lovely today."

In his dark green tweed jacket and dark green pants and a natural cashmere pullover, Jordan looked relaxed, but a bit unhappy—the way they both looked nowadays.

"Where's Rita? After what she said the day she visited me, I half-expected her to show up and make a scene today."

Raine knocked on the wooden table behind her.

Jordan shrugged. "She called me to say she was flying back to Montreal, then coming back down to New York. If I can believe her, she won't be back here again for several weeks anyway."

"Do you honestly think she'll stick to that?"

"Well, we never know what she's got cooking with Mike. We can hope. What about Dan?"

Raine told him about the store incident with Kym, Tricia, and Tricia's mother. When she had finished, he looked thoughtful.

"Does he call you often?"

"Hardly ever, and when he does, he says little. He did say he's giving me time to get over the shock of his return from the dead."

Jordan raised his eyebrows. "It's hard to know what Dan has in mind. He's the most devious guy I've ever known."

"That goes double for me. I told him after I talked with you last night that I'm going to file for divorce."

"How'd he take it?"

"He didn't say much. I started to call you, but I felt you had enough trouble with Rita."

"Look, love," Jordan said urgently, "Dan and Rita are both our problem. They're the ones standing between us and the life we've got a right to with Kym. We deserve better, and for that matter they deserve someone who wants them."

"You're right, of course. Oh, Jordy."

"I can't stay long," Jordan said. "Sweetheart, I'm going to have to go to Malaga, Spain, sometime within the next month or so."

"Oh," Raine said, "that's where Dan said the people in the mountains found him and kept him from dying. Somewhere in the general area of Torremolinos, Malaga."

"Bright woman! When Matt Hinson, who's one of my best accounts, asked me to set up security for him at a plant he owns there, I jumped at the chance."

Raine's heart fell a little. She hated having him go away so soon.

"Once I get things set up," he said, "could you take a day off, or maybe two, and join me? I'll be going over in early December. Tack a Friday and a Tuesday onto the weekend, and we've got a great mini-vacation."

"Oh, Jordy, yes! Could we take a side trip to Madrid and visit the Prado?"

Jordan hesitated the briefest moment. "There may not be time, although the security setup won't take me long. I've—we've got other fish to fry. We're going to visit those mountains, Ray. See what we come up with."

Raine looked at him and closed her eyes. "I have a feeling, my love," she said, "that you've developed into a man I want to be with always."

"I'd hoped you'd feel that way."

A group of parents came up to congratulate Raine on the festival. One was an older community woman who had a painting entry. She kissed Raine's cheek.

"Well, I'm no Lois Mailou Jones," she said, speaking of a highly revered Washington artist, "but I do my best, and oh, how I enjoy painting."

Raine introduced them to Jordan and the group walked down to the woman's painting of sunflowers. It was simple, arresting.

"You did yourself proud," Raine told her, "but then you've done so many remarkable paintings."

Walking on, the group admired other paintings until they came to Jimmy Coles's sweeping portrait. The blended blues and grays and hints of black blended with undetectable red: a magnificent scene of nature at her angriest—a storm at sea. It was a magnificent rendering, much advanced for a boy of his fourteen years.

Jimmy came up quietly. They all congratulated him, and his response was somber. "I feel like I've got God guiding my hand when I paint," he said simply. "Having folks like my parents and Mrs. Gibson like my painting means a lot to me."

Raine, Jordan, and Jimmy moved away from the others.

"Jimmy, this is the friend I said I'd ask about a job for you." She introduced him.

"We've got a world of need for someone like you," Jordan told him. "I've got security schemes you could work on for me at home. Make copies, that kind of thing. We have a good, old copy machine you could use. We need an artist."

Jimmy's face lit up like a sun. "Oh, gee, sir, this is going to be wonderful."

"Will you be able to get into D.C. some Saturdays?"

"Every Saturday if you say so. We've got neighbors who can see after my mom."

"Then you're on."

The man and the boy shook hands. Looking at them, as much as she loved Kym, Raine hoped with all her heart she'd be fortunate enough to have a son with Jordan. Still, if it never happened, her precious little girl would be enough.

Lunch was served at twelve thirty: a smorgasbord of piping hot chili, baked hams and turkeys, fried chicken, corn pudding, macaroni and cheese, big baked and buttered yams, and collard greens. Salads in big bowls spread their cheerful color palette, and desserts of early-season fruitcake and devil's food cake complemented angel food and bundt cake.

Both Raine and Jordan ate lightly of the delicious food that the community women had prepared. When Raine painted most, she found she ate little food, but drank beverages copiously.

Mrs. Quarles came up to be introduced to Jordan; the two liked each other immediately.

STILL IN LOVE 95

Kym nearly burst with wanting to tell everyone that Jordan was her dad, but her mom had cautioned her not to talk about it for now. She still had trouble with her pride at having a dad conflict with wanting her mother all to herself.

Raine found the chili delicious and chose hot red-clover herb tea, one of her favorites. Sipping the smooth tea, she couldn't help but be happy—in spite of Dan, in spite of everything. But she couldn't help but wonder what Jordy hoped to find in the mountains of Spain.

Looking across the auditorium, Raine's heart sank nearly to her shoes as Dan came in sight, followed by two photographers and a woman with a yellow writing pad. A reporter? They usually came a bit later when the crowd had grown even bigger. And there was an electricity in the air that hadn't been there for the show last year. The four reached them.

"Are you surprised to have your husband back alive, Mrs. Gibson?" This began the rapid-fire questioning.

"I'll bet you were happy to see him. Tell us about it."

The brashest of the two photographers was snapping away like a small-time paparazzi. "Che-e-e-esecake," he called as if he were a room away from her.

"What paper are you from?" Raine asked when the reporter moved in for the kill.

"Oh, we're the *Minden Sentinel*. We're new, so we didn't cover you last year. But oh my, this year. Everyone loves a good human interest story."

Raine found she didn't hate it so much for herself as for Kym. Poor kid. She was catching hell: a newly discovered daddy she couldn't talk about, Dan trying to dance attendance on her to curry favor.

Kym came to her, and Jordan fought to keep from catching her hand, but his loving eyes said it all. "Hang in there, tiger!"

Coolly Raine turned to the newsgroup.

The brash guy said, "You might as well give us the story because we're going to haunt you until you do."

"Oh, yes, I know," Raine said.

Jordan shepherded her with his eyes.

"Who're you?" the reporter asked Jordan.

"I'm Jordan Clymer, a friend," he said. The press group reminded him of when the kid had been shot in his father's possession as deputy sheriff. They were too young to know about that, so Dan must have told them.

"Jordan's my cousin," Dan said heartily. "He and I go way back.

"Don't bother the lady," Dan said. "She's got her hands full with this show. I told you it'd be a better idea to cover us at her home."

"No, this is better for human interest," the reporter said, laughing. "Oh, man, this could help make my reputation as a reporter."

Mrs. Quarles swept up, every inch the queenly principal she was.

"I'd like to offer you a room where you can talk and take some photos," she said. "That way you can get your story right."

They followed her to one of the smaller conference rooms, and she stood at the door, arms akimbo, as the reporter questioned first Dan, then Raine and Jordan, whose face was pinched with anger.

When they turned to Kym, Raine quickly protested. "I'd rather you didn't question her."

"Why not? Everything in the name of human interest."

"Not where my daughter's concerned," Raine snapped.

Mrs. Quarles stepped up. "Come with me, darling," she said to Kym. "There're some things I want you to help me check on." Together the two left the room.

The next hour dragged for Raine. Mrs. Quarles kept Kym busy, and Jordan left for the appointment he had mentioned earlier. In the same small conference room where they had chosen to talk with the reporter and the photographers, Jordan's lips barely grazed Raine's cheeks when the newspaper group left.

"I hate having to leave you to deal with this," he said.

"The worst is over. Thank God you were here."

As they stepped out into the auditorium, they found Scott and Caroline standing there. Caroline hugged her quickly.

"Miss Vi told me what happened," Caroline said. "What a rotten thing for Dan to do."

"I'm just glad Jordy was here," Raine said.

"You don't know how relieved I am I was able to be here," Jordan said, then to Scott, "Why don't you stay until the close of business? That way we can guard against more of Dan's shenanigans."

"I think he'll leave soon," Raine said. "He's proved his point. It's almost as if he and Rita are working in tandem."

"What a horrible thought," Jordan said.

Jordan left, and Raine began to circulate through the small throng of people again. Parents praised the exhibit and congratulated her as a teacher and an artist.

Jimmy's mother came in a wheelchair. As he brought her up, having returned home to get her, Raine bent and kissed the surprisingly young woman's cheek.

"You've got quite a son here," she said.

"And he's got quite a teacher. You've been so good for my boy."

"Just wait until he gets to the Ellington School of the Arts," Raine said.

Mrs. Coles shook her head. "I know they're good over there," she said, "but you'll pardon me for thinking you're as good a teacher as he could have."

Raine blushed.

"It's no flattery," Mrs. Coles said. "On the way over here, he told me your friend's going to give him a job. Thank you from the bottom of my heart."

"You're so welcome. Jimmy is such a good kid."

"That's my son, all right."

Scott walked around, meeting people, checking out the paintings, and Caroline came back to Raine just as Jimmy and his mother moved away.

"How're you holding up?" Caroline asked.

"Quite well. I guess by now I'm numb with shock."

"I can surely see why."

"How are you and Scott getting along?"

Caroline thought a few minutes. "You know, he's actually gotten a bit softer, and he holds me only at elbow length instead of his full arm. It helped a lot, your telling me about his ex-wife's savaging him. I can see where that would leave you raw. Well, whatever comes, I can take it."

"But you do like him."

"Oh, yes, but I'm not letting myself dream too much. Where's Rita, the other part of your square?"

Raine shrugged. "Jordan said she's gone back to Montreal for a few days, then back to New York for he doesn't know how long."

"Thank the Lord for small favors."

"Jordan's going to Spain—Torremolinos, Malaga—in early December. He wants me to join him later."

"Go, girlfriend! Don't even consider not going."

Raine smiled broadly. "With much of what's gone on today, I need that trip to save my sanity."

Mrs. Quarles came up with Kym. "Now I don't want you to worry about what Dan Gibson pulled this afternoon," she said. "I overheard him talking with the reporter. He set this up, and I think it smells to high heaven. We're living in a day and age when I think people can see through this. You thought he was dead. You had a right to go on with your life."

Raine hugged the older woman, who smiled, saying, "I remember Dan in high school. We never knew what was coming next with him."

STILL IN LOVE 99

The three women and Kym moved to the outside to get some fresh air. Raine stood admiring the cloudless bright blue sky when she saw Uncle Prince sitting on a small bench along the front wall.

Going over to him, she sat down beside him. "Tired out from just watching your wife move around?" she asked, chuckling.

Uncle Prince smiled. "My wife is a human fireball," he said. "But I wouldn't have her no other way."

He drew in a harsh breath and bent over a moment.

"Uncle Prince, what's wrong?" Raine asked.

He straightened slowly. "A mite of indigestion, I'd guess," he said. "She's been after me about all that rich food I eat. Doctor's been after me, too. Guess I'll have to cut back, but I love to eat. You know that. And I married a woman who loves to cook."

"You two are still so much in love," Raine said softly.

"I know I am," the old man said, "and I'm pretty sure she is. She's been the best wife a man could have."

Raine hugged him. "I could leave early so you can get home. I think that's a good idea."

"No. I'll stay. Her heart's set on seeing the prizes awarded. Don't tell her how bad I've felt. It'll pass."

Raine thought quickly, setting up a plan.

"Now I'll tell you what. I don't feel too well, either. Too much rich food for me, too. How about my leaving early and you coming along to keep me company? Caroline will bring Miss Vi and Kym."

"Why is Caroline going to have to bring Miss Vi?" Miss Vi asked, coming up. "I wondered where you two had absconded to," she continued, then suddenly with a note of alarm, "Lord, Prince, I don't think I like the looks of you, honey."

"Why'd you marry me then," he grumbled in jest, pretending to feel better."

"The problem is I've eaten too much of that chili and

it's upset my stomach," Raine said. "Mrs. Quarles will be perfectly satisfied to finish this up. It's two thirty already, and we close at four. I'm going to have to go home, Miss Vi, and I'd like Uncle Prince to go along so I can have a grown-up for company. Caroline can bring you and Kym home."

"Well, sure," Miss Vi said slowly. She turned to Raine. "There's something I need to say to you that men oughtn't to hear." She winked at her husband, whose face creased with smiles.

The two women walked out of Uncle Prince's hearing, and Miss Vi wrung her hands. "It's him, isn't it? You want to take him home and bless you for that. He's looking poorly again. There's nothing wrong with you."

"Well, my stomach's a tiny bit upset after that debacle with Dan."

"Well, I told you earlier how I feel about that. Dan Gibson's no good to try to hurt you." She paused. "But about Prince now—he's looked puny to me several times lately. He just loves good food. But at least he'll get his rest, and he still works hard, so that's exercise."

Raine smiled. Miss Vi subscribed to health magazines and newsletters and stayed on top of the health picture. She ate everything, but sparingly.

Miss Vi went on. "I'm goin' t'see he goes to the doctor tomorrow. Thank you, missy, for helping me to look after my husband."

Twenty minutes later Raine and Uncle Prince pulled from in front of the school on their way home. She would see to it that he lay down once he got there.

At a filling station in Minden, Raine was unpleasantly surprised to see Dan Gibson and Wayne McClure, his cousin, whom he'd hung out with when both were boys.

When she got out of the car to draw gas, Dan walked over to her.

"Pretty interesting set-to we had with the newspaper people, wasn't it?"

"Dan," Raine asked tightly, "how could you?"

Dan raised his eyebrows. "That newspaper filly asked me about the story."

"No. You set it up."

"All right, I did. I want you back, Raine. You put my insurance money into that farm and I want it back by getting you back."

"The insurance company is asking for the money back," Raine said. "Fortunately Jordy can let me have it. It's no go with us, Dan. Surely you know that."

Dan looked abashed. "I just said that to throw you off balance. It's you I want back, Raine. You always did belong to me."

"I belong," Raine said, pulling herself up to her full height, "to myself, and to my child and Jordy."

Dan's fists clenched at his sides. His face was a study in malevolence. "You better reconsider, wife. The law says you're mine, and I intend to live within the law."

"Dan," Raine said as calmly as she could, "it was over for us when you joined the Army. I didn't care about a divorce because there was no one for me. But it was over then. I'm begging you to please let go. I'm going to file for divorce."

"And I'm fighting it," he said quickly. "Now my month here is nearly up, and I go back to Fort Riley, so you won't be seeing me around. I thought I was getting out of the Army, but I decided not to just now. Things are rough all over out here. I can support you and Kym on my Army pay."

"I don't want your support. Kym doesn't need it."

"Yeah, I'd guess. Jordy seems to be doing very well. Well, I was doing all right as a coach, if you remember. I made captain in the Army. Seeing you since I've come back excites me. I'd nearly forgotten what a good-looking woman you are."

With an ugly laugh and a broad wink, he walked back to Wayne McClure's car and got in. They rode away. Wayne, Raine thought, was a worse heller than Dan. McClure was the son of the man who had sworn Jordy's father had shot the boy in his custody. Some townspeople thought otherwise, but there were those who believed it. Delman McClure, the father, had been there and common gossip said he had done the shooting. He had accused Jordan's father and had stuck by his lie.

"Your hands are shaking," Uncle Prince said when Raine got back in the car. "I hate that this is happening with Dan. Want me to drive?"

"No. I'm okay." She added softly, "Loving Jordan gives me strength, Uncle Prince, even more strength than I have loving the rest of you."

As Miss Vi rushed home to check on her husband, a happy Kym and Caroline told her that Jimmy had taken the expected first prize.

That night Kym's earnest being was all nurture. She fretted over Raine as Raine fretted over and comforted her in her rare illnesses. She made tea from echinacea herbs and dried red clover.

"Now you drink this," she said, propping herself up on pillows as Raine lay resting. "I put in a soup spoon of honey and a big slice of lemon, so I'm sure it's good. I'll get you well."

Raine smiled, but sighed a bit, too. It would have been a gloriously perfect day if Dan had not been in the picture.

NINE

Torremolinos, Malaga, Spain, is beautiful the year around, but it seemed especially beautiful this December to Raine: a city of waterfront hotels and villas and sun-washed beaches. The weather was a pleasant mid-sixties. Or did it seem so beautiful because she and Jordy had followed through on their plans? She had arrived that afternoon and taken a brief nap because she had slept on the plane. They stood on the balcony of their villa, watching a brilliant sunset. Jordy turned to her, his face pensive.

"We've got to straighten out this Dan business, cupcake," he said. "I've got some gut hunches, and I'm going to play them."

"We're going to go into the mountains to see if we can find someone who knew Dan?" Raine asked.

"Yeah. I've gotten the cooperation of U.S. Secret Service personnel here who've been able to narrow it down. We know where he most likely lived."

"But what if he was lying? What if he wasn't in Spain then at all? He wasn't writing home."

"He was here. We've tracked him from Army records. My Secret Service buddies have been invaluable."

Jordan smiled, then his lips were caressing her face, his hands gently massaging her entire back.

"Relax," he said.

"How can I?"

"You can and I'll see that you do. How did Kym take your going away?"

"Well, she wasn't too happy until she found I was coming to be with you. Then, of course, it was okay. I think you're slowly winning that kid's heart, Jordy."

"And she's taken me over."

"She'd better not have."

"Except for you, of course."

His lips found the hollows of her throat and traced kisses up to her forehead, then back to her mouth where he found the honey he sought. Her body was supple and yielding, her skin soft and tenderer than anyone else's he'd found.

"Do you want to lie down? Rest a bit. We have a driver coming for us around twelve. The trip over here must have left you tired."

"No. No, really. I don't even have jet lag. Herbs took care of that. Remember, I'm the one who suggested we get started our very first day and get it over with. I'm anxious. Aren't you?"

Jordan nodded. He pulled her into his arms again, began to kiss her, then gently let her go.

"I want us to get to Nevada Mountain," he said. "Stay here and we're going on a ride for thrills that won't be stopping anytime soon."

"We're allowed one kiss of passion."

"Well, my nerve endings are closer to the surface than yours where making love to you is concerned. It takes only a caring look from your beautiful eyes to start my engine roaring."

Raine laughed softly. "I'm not that far behind you in timing. Oh, Jordy."

He watched a flicker of pain cross her face. "What are you thinking?" he asked.

"About when I lived in New Orleans."

"You and Dan." It hurt him in ways he couldn't imagine. Here in his arms, she was remembering Dan. Why? But the

STILL IN LOVE

look had been one of pain. She hadn't wanted to talk very much about her life with Dan, and he wouldn't press her. All in good time.

"Whatever it was he did to hurt you, I'm sorry," he said. "I'd take every second of pain that bastard caused you into my own heart and suffer it for you if I could. You know that."

She brushed his face with her fingers. "Yes, Jordy, I do know that. It's why I love you so."

They took a picnic hamper prepared by the villa staff and ate part of the delicious sandwiches, cheeses, fruit, and nuts as they rode, sharing the lunch with the driver.

"Senor and senora," the driver teased them, then "I will help you find the man you seek. I will make this a honeymoon you will not forget."

Jordan squeezed Raine's hand. "Thank you," he said, then said in a low voice, "It should be our honeymoon."

They rode on the backseat of the spacious black Volvo, cushioned in soft black leather. Now Jordan whispered to her as he nuzzled her ear. "I'm pretending we're married. Be with me. I'll never try to force you to carry anything through you don't want to."

Raine laughed throatily. "What could you want me to do that I don't want to do?"

He kissed her deeply then, as the driver rode through the city with its throngs of tourists and gentle breezes that caressed the lovers who sought it out.

They reached a small settlement in the lowest part of the mountain, which was called a *sierra*, in little more than an hour. They had been referred to a patriarch who had lived a lifetime in these mountains and knew the lives of everyone there. The driver got out, then helped them out. The weather was colder in the mountains, with a crisp snap to it.

"Some of the people speak English," he said. "I am an excellent interpreter for the others. How do you find my English?"

"I couldn't be more pleased," Jordan said.

"It's wonderful that the hotel sent us someone like you," Raine added.

"We want you to come back," the driver said, "so we give you our best."

As they parked to finish lunch, the driver, whose name was Roberto, pointed out benches along the road. They got out, stretched, and finished a leisurely lunch, topped by a bottle of delicious claret with the lunch and a scintillating, fruity white wine with the dessert of strawberry tarts.

On the lower mountainside, there were clusters of houses, with some a distance from any neighbors. Jordan began with a cluster where the Secret Service men had said he'd find Senor Rodriguez. He had photos of Dan both with and without a beard—head shots, full-length photos, and profiles—and turned them over on the seat between Raine and himself.

As they parked in front of a country store, a grizzled old man—a *viejo*—ambled up to the car, smiling his greeting.

"Buenos dias, senors, senora!"

The old man spoke little English, but Roberto interpreted well. Then the man held up his hand for Roberto's silence, said a few words, and went back to the front of the store.

"Does this mean he won't answer our questions?" Raine asked.

Roberto shook his head. "No, no. He goes to get himself a chair. He is very old, he said, but it is a good thing you come to him because he sees and hears of everything that happens here at one time or another. If he cannot help you, he will tell you who can."

STILL IN LOVE 107

Jordan breathed a sigh of relief. Roberto walked over to carry the chair for the man, and a gaggle of children and one woman came over to inspect the car—and its occupants. Jordan got out and helped Raine out. The oldest of the children stroked the car, murmuring, *"Bello,"* while the smaller came to stand at Raine's side. They were beautiful children.

"Bello," Raine said of the children, and the mother of some of them smiled shyly. "You are *bella.*"

The mother was absolutely lovely except for her half-rotted teeth.

Roberto interpreted something the woman said to Raine.

"She would like you to come with her so you can be with the women of the family."

Yes, Raine thought, these were the mountains and the genders were often separate socially. She could learn from them, and she went willingly. She took a few photos with her. Their happiness was infectious.

At his request, the old man sat in the backseat of the car with Jordan, and Roberto turned around in the front seat, interpreting.

Dan held up a photo. "Senor Rodriguez, have you seen this man before?" Jordan asked him.

Senor Rodriguez studied the bearded photos carefully and looked through the stack before he spoke.

"Caramba, I would never forget this hombre!"

Jordan and Roberto looked at each other, and Jordan felt excitement climb in his breast.

"What did this man call himself?" Jordan asked.

"Aaron Gibbs," Roberto translated.

Jordan nodded. It was a close approximation of Dan's last name which was what people often did when they hid. And Aaron was Dan's middle name.

Roberto kept translating as the old man talked. "He grew a mighty beard and moustache, and we began calling him the bearded one: *barbudo.* It was plain to me that he hid from something." The old man shrugged. "In these mountains we are very poor. Life is cruel to us, and we have long ago learned not to question too much. We do for each other what we can. There are many Gypsies here, and we are not foolish enough to look down our noses at them as so many Spaniards do. We have in this settlement and higher up in the sierra—which is our word for mountain—a large family that comes from an American brown baby, the offspring of a man from your country. Mestizos."

Excitement raced along Jordan's veins as the old man continued talking, drifting a bit.

"Did this man Gibbs, this American, take a wife or live with a woman?"

"Sí! He took the daughter of the mestizo family for a wife—a lovely girl, with black eyes like ripe olives and such a fine figure of a woman." His gnarled hands described a Coke bottle, and his face lit up.

"I want the senora to hear the rest of this," Jordan said. "Would you send for her?"

The old man called a nearby child and instructed her to get Raine from the house where she sat in front of a fireplace in a group with the women, eating a small dish of paella and drinking homemade wine from the grapes in the long arbor outside the house.

When the small girl stumbled in her haste to get Raine, her mother scolded her a bit. The child finally got to say that the *viejo* was summoning Raine. The woman gasped. "Why didn't you say so quickly, mia?" Turning to Raine, the woman said, "Then you must go. Since Papa became old, he has little patience now. Go in peace, and God bless you for you are a lovely woman."

Raine returned the compliment as this woman and the three other women hugged her and kissed her cheeks. She had waited too long to show the women the photos, so she couldn't ask if they knew Dan.

STILL IN LOVE
109

Going down the hill, the little girl clutched her hand and looked up at her with clear blue eyes in an olive face.

At the car the men piled out to stretch their legs and told her what had happened. Roberto spoke swiftly to Senor Rodriguez and relayed his message.

"The woman you seek is Serafina Jiminez. She lives with her family in a settlement similar to this one higher up the mountain. She has a small child born a little over two years ago. The woman and her child are brown works of art. She was so happy to find a man like her American grandfather."

"Are we going to see her?" Raine asked.

Roberto relayed her question as Jordan said, "I think we'd be best served to come back tomorrow, and earlier."

"You are wise," Senior Rodriguez complimented Jordan. "Tomorrow would be better. There is little reason to hasten because Serafina has gone—"

"Gone?" Jordan queried. "You mean she left with Dan?" Neither he nor Raine could contain their displeasure at this news.

"No," the old man said slowly. "Like the *sin vergüenza*—scoundrel—he proved to be, he abandoned her. She went to America to look for him. He had no memory when he came to us here. He had been beaten and robbed of everything. Then a month or two ago he regained his memory, went to the American authorities here, and they gave him money to return home. I think he said he was from a place called New Orleans."

"He lived there," Jordan said, his eyes narrowing as he restrained the desire to grab Raine and kiss her in jubilation at what they were finding.

"This woman was a cousin to me," Senor Rodriguez added. "We take family seriously. I hope for his sake that he doesn't seek to return. We would draw and quarter him. And the child . . . poor little bambino. The image of his father."

Sleep almost overtook Senor Rodriguez as he sat in the

car. He yawned widely. "I am old and must nap often. Come back tomorrow, and I will go up farther up the mountains, and you can talk with the family this rascal married into."

Jordan and Raine thanked him profusely and said they'd be back.

"What would make you happy for us to bring you?" Jordan asked.

Senor Rodriguez's eyes crinkled shut with mirth. "God has granted me ninety-three years of life. My mind is clear. My heart is merry. What could you, what could anyone give me that matters?"

Jordan bowed to the man. "It is clear that you are a sage, and forgive me for asking what I could bring you."

Senor Rodriguez reached out and patted Jordan's arm. "Yours is a good heart, and you are a fine couple. If you brought me a gift of a fine cheese, I would not refuse it. It should be enough for the small army of my family."

"You shall have the finest," Jordan told him, "and thank you from the bottom of my heart."

"Vaya con Dios!" the old man said heartily as if in benediction.

Raine and Jordan made it an early evening to see Torremolinos.

"A city of night owls," Jordan said as they walked along with many others.

Dressed in a filmy navy lace miniskirt with navy satin pumps and a navy lightweight coat, Raine felt she looked well.

"Bella," a male passerby murmured, looking at Raine.

"Am I going to have to cover you in harem clothes, put you in purdah?" Jordan said, laughing.

"I'm happy here with just you," Raine said. "But to tell the truth . . ."

"Yes?"

STILL IN LOVE 111

Raine shrugged. "I'll let it go for now. It had to do with Dan."

"Talk to me. I'm a willing listener. It helps to talk about pain."

"And humiliation."

"Dan?"

"Yes. The art show vendetta. After saying he'd do nothing to antagonize me, he pulls a stunt like that."

"As you said, it's vintage Dan. At least he's back in camp for several weeks."

A pretty young flower seller offered them red roses, and Jordan bought a dozen for Raine.

"Profligate man!" she exclaimed. "They'll be wilted by the time we get back to the villa."

"No, senora," the flower seller said helpfully. "I can wet them from my water can and wrap them in cellophane."

"Muchas gracias," Jordan responded.

"Roses are like kisses," the girl said, laughing. "One can never receive too many." She watered and wrapped the flowers.

They passed blocks of Chinese restaurants, some tiny and crowded, others elegant and spacious.

"This is the last place I'd have expected Chinese food," she said.

"The world has changed," Jordan answered. "We are truly beginning to be a global village."

A full-bearded dark Spaniard passed them, focused on them for a moment, and Raine's face clouded.

"You are bothered. He reminds you of Dan."

"Yes."

"Suddenly you seem sad. We can take a taxi back to the villa and come out tomorrow evening. Or we can stay in indefinitely."

He stopped and took her in his arms as passersby smiled. He kissed her with softly tender kisses, and her heart leapt with desire, the pain greatly lessening.

"No," she said. "I'm hungry. Let's go in."

The small Spanish restaurant he had chosen was elegant with its snowy damask, crystal, and silver. The maitre d' led them to a table close to the water and seated them.

They chose white wine and ate the tiny finger rolls on the table while waiting.

"What are you hungry for?" Jordan asked, teasing her.

To his delight, Raine laughed. "Not food especially," she answered, her eyes alight. She flirted with him outrageously, and he loved it.

"Woman," he said, "be careful! You wouldn't want me to carry you out of here in my arms."

"Wouldn't I?"

"You're a wonderful woman, Ray. I hate the years I've been without you."

"I keep praying we can make up for lost time."

"We seem to get a better chance for that every day."

"I only hope the old man is right and that it is Dan who married Serafina Jiminez. That's certainly grounds for divorce if he doesn't go to prison, unless he's telling the truth about having amnesia.

"I won't file charges if he's lying. I just want him out of my life."

Jordan nodded. "Rita hasn't called lately. She's been seeing Mike again. He's stringing her along, but I think he loves her. It doesn't matter. She'll tire of giving you and me trouble. Rita is her own worst enemy—"

He broke off as the waiter returned. "What would you like, love?" He asked Raine.

"By all means the shrimp in garlic sauce. And a large varied lettuce salad. I can taste it before it gets here."

Jordan gave the order.

"And I know right now," Raine said, "I want flan for dessert."

"I'm not sure we'll make it through dessert," Jordan said, his eyes flashing wickedly as Raine leaned forward, smiling at him.

Excellent music of several guitarists added gaiety to the already joyful atmosphere in the restaurant. It seemed almost completely a preserve for lovers this night. The colorful costumes of the guitar players made Raine want to paint them—she asked Jordan about it.

"I'm sure it can be arranged, but why don't you let me bring you back to Torremolinos. You always say you need time to plan what you paint."

Raine nodded. "I'd like that."

They talked more of Dan and of Rita, and violins replaced the guitars. Jordan got up and went around to her side of the table. "Ah, senora, may I have this dance?" Jordan asked.

Raine rose gracefully, walked the short distance to the dance floor and into Jordan's arms. The orchestra played an old Spanish love song. With her lissome, warm body close to him, Jordan felt excited by every tender curve.

"Any minute now we're going to become as one," Raine murmured.

"Good. The sooner the better."

The world seemed far away to Raine just then. They had their own private world and it was wonderful—but threatened. Jordan's tongue found the corners of her warmly luscious lips and kissed them. She opened her mouth a bit to all that tenderness, and his tongue found hers for brief moments.

"We need to be alone," Jordan said.

"In a short while, tiger. Patience."

"A much overrated virtue much of the time."

The waiter brought their food, and they went back to their table. With the dishes uncovered, they served themselves and the food was delicious. The shrimp in garlic sauce came with bread and olives, and the mixed green salad was as colorful as a painting.

They ate slowly, enjoying every bite. Raine slipped her foot from her shoe and placed it on Jordan's chair edge, between his legs. He laughed aloud.

"You're asking for real trouble, Ray. Keep it up and I'll see that you get it!"

"Promises," Raine said somberly. "As delicious as this food is, we should have stayed in."

"The food is good, but we could skip the flan."

"No. Flan is one of my favorite desserts."

"The flan can't compete with what I've got for you when we get home."

"Don't brag. I believe you."

They ate in warm silence, flirting with each other, in prelude to a lifetime of seeking from and giving to each other. After a while, they moved their chairs closer together and fed each other tidbits of the delicious dinner.

A shadow of sadness passed over Raine's face.

"What is it, my darling?" Jordan asked.

Raine's hand paused in midair. She sighed. "Jordy, I keep thinking we have to take it slow. We don't know yet that it was Dan who married the girl in the mountains. We hope so. And how do you handle Rita's clinging to you in spite of the divorce? Lord, when I remember how close we were . . ."

"How close we are."

"Yes. And that's all the more reason. We don't want to hurt each other."

"You're saying we ought not to make love."

"Yes, that's what I'm saying. Or rather I'm thinking it's not too wise. Right now we're racing toward . . ." Raine paused, unable to express just what she felt and aching for the man beside her so much she thought her heart would break. She repeated, "We're racing toward . . ."

"Toward heaven," Jordan said evenly. "Look, I'm not

going to plead you into bed. I know you want me as much as I want you, but if it's any help, I'm scared, too. I don't want to be hurt again, either. But do you agree we've got to do something? Perhaps I should have chosen another place to relocate."

"Oh, Jordy, no. If you hadn't been there when Dan came back, I don't think I could have stood it. I've loved your being back."

"Yeah, the same way I've loved being back, but we add complications to each other's lives. Yet it doesn't matter because as long as we're alive, I'm going to fight to be free for you."

"And if the old man in the mountains is right, I'll be free, too."

Jordan summoned the waiter and ordered champagne. In a short while they lifted their glasses in a toast.

"To freedom and to love," Jordan offered.

"Hear! Hear!" Raine answered immediately, feeling the champagne and her and Jordy's love in her bloodstream, lifting her.

The flan proved worth waiting for. Served with a very long stemmed red rose, the delicate pale yellow custard with its sweet, browned crust was delicious and a fitting end to a delicious dinner.

Back at their villa before midnight, Jordan kissed Raine good night at her door, as she held the dozen roses over his shoulder, together with the long rose from the restaurant.

"I love you, sweetheart," he whispered. "Whatever you want for us is what we'll have."

They lingered outside her door, unable to break away before Raine suddenly left his arms and fished through her bag and found her keys.

"Jordy, come in for a moment anyway," she said, her voice trembling with passion.

For a moment Jordan looked puzzled, then his face was wreathed in smiles.

Raine put the roses in the small refrigerator and started to her dressing room which lay between her room and Jordan's. She felt she floated on a lovely cloud of loving and lightness and being loved. Jordan reached for her and took her into his arms. His lips crushed hers until they hurt. Pressed in to him, she could feel the hardness of his body and the special hardness that told her how he wanted her.

"I'm going to undress," she said. "Jordy, I don't want to wait any longer. If this comes back to haunt us, then it's just a chance we'll have to take."

With a groan of passion, Jordan's hands began to roam her body. Slowly he unzipped the back zipper of the filmy lace dress. Garment and lining slid from her body, and she pulled away from him and stepped out of the circle the dress made on the floor. He unhooked her heavy satin and lace bra, and his caressing hands slid the bikini panties down her hips until they fell to the floor and she stepped out of them.

Looking at her, he began to hug her again, but she had begun to remove his clothes, and she was not so gentle as he had been.

When they were both naked, he pulled her to him, reveling in the feel of her silken skin, inhaling the jasmine fragrance of her, the flesh that felt warm and cool at once. He wondered somewhere inside himself if he wanted to just devour her, and realized he wanted to save her much more.

So it would be both saving and devouring as they held each other close. She raised her slender legs to ride his hips, pressed into him, and she could not believe the length of time he held her there. She was, after all, she thought, not a thin woman. But his well-exercised strength held fast.

He took her to their king-sized bed and gently laid her

down, marveling at his own ease when he wanted to quickly go inside her, deeply inside her and remain there for a long time.

His hands covered the sides of her face, and she felt blocked off from all else save him. "Jordy, Jordy," she moaned.

Jordan wanted so badly to spend time in extensive foreplay, wanting to pleasure her to her maximum, but the shaft of his manhood was demanding its due and would not be denied.

With his shaft inside her body throbbing with love and wonder, Raine felt the height of glory she knew now and had known with Jordan in the past. It had been love like this that had created Kym.

At first he planted wild kisses on her breasts, then took the nipples and sucked them gently, then harder as she moved rhythmically beneath him. Pushing him back, she let her tongue glide over his flat nipples, knowing from the past how it excited him.

"Oh, Lord, you remember," he exulted.

"I have never," she whispered, "forgotten anything about you, lover."

"And I certainly remember every move you so lovingly made."

To slow himself, Jordan withdrew and held Raine close to him, stroking her and sweeping feather kisses over her body. He made himself think of cool streams and the mountains they had recently visited.

This time he entered easily and stroked with deep strokes as Raine wept lightly with passion. He kissed the tears from her face. "Sweetheart," he said. "I want to make you happy. Tell me what you want and I'll do it for you."

"I'll tell you," she said. "Be with me all the days of my life. That's all I ask and nothing else will do."

She brought her legs up and over his back before he rolled her over so that she sat astride him, the wings of her dark hair framing her face. He felt bathed in nectar as her warmth surrounded him inside her body, and he gasped with sheer joy as he moved into a deeper area and felt her clutch him. Oh, glory night!

And Raine felt happy, appreciating his efforts to be with her as long as he could.

This time her hands cupped his face and her tongue went into his mouth, probing, discovering honey and loving his masculine fragrance as she savored their kisses.

She raised above him, then slid down easily onto him and he felt the splendid quake of his loins as he rushed into her like the tide roaring onto the shore. The waters were calm outside their open balcony—it was early morning. But his loins preceded the tide that would sweep in later.

Raine felt the quickening of him as he crushed her down onto him, and her very soul gave way to ecstasy as she matched his tender passion with her own. No, surely it had not been over nine years, but only yesterday when they had lain together the way they did now.

The lovely middle-aged woman, Mrs. Duenas, who had rented them the villa, had left fresh flowers and champagne and had stocked the refrigerator with Jordan's and Raine's choice of foods.

Getting up, feeling relaxed and livelier than she had in months, Raine rummaged in the refrigerator and found the makings of piña coladas. She took the drinks back and got into bed with Jordan.

"I keep wanting to cook something for you," she said. "Do you like sourdough pancakes—for breakfast?"

"There're things I want to do for you, too," he said, "but it isn't cooking, although as you know I'm a good cook. Yes, I like sourdough pancakes. Very much. But I adore you."

"I get there first adoring you," she answered him.

They sipped the drinks slowly. "Jordy," she said, "I went through so much pain when you left. Sometimes I thought I'd go mad, what with my father's long illness and his death and your leaving. I thought you'd abandoned me, and I wanted to die."

Jordan set his piña colada on the night table, then took Raine's from her hand and set it on the table, and took her in his arms. His mouth claimed hers with fervent kisses that quickened her breath. Then he murmured against her throat, "Still feel abandoned?"

He expected her to smile, but she didn't. Something had her in a rough hold.

"What is it, Ray?"

She reached for her drink and with a few gulps swallowed it.

"Hey, hold it. That was, too—"

Tears misted her eyes. "I think I can tell you now what happened, Jordy, what happened between Dan and me."

He stroked her back, her arms, her breasts, her face, not talking, listening for whatever she had to tell him.

"I was pregnant a year after I married Dan."

Still he listened carefully. Finally she said, "Dan kept pressuring me to have a baby, then he lied and said that since I didn't want his child, he'd had a vasectomy. Like a fool, I believed him . . ."

"How could you know? Don't beat on yourself, Ray."

"All right. When I was five months pregnant and teaching, painting, Dan came home roaring drunk. He told me then how he'd tricked me into getting pregnant, and I told him what a monster I thought he was. He said he'd saved me after you left me, and he got no thanks. We were on the back porch, and he struck me. One of the rotten banisters gave way, and I fell . . ."

The memory was worse than she'd thought it would be after all this time, and the waves of old fury and terror washed over her. She had wanted the baby once it was inside her, even if it was Dan's.

"He screamed at me that I was no good, that I lusted

after you even as I lay in bed with him, and said I knew what that made . . .

"What could I say, Jordy? I did lust after you."

"You love me, the way I love you, so of course you wanted me."

"Yes, well, I've always had these incredible dreams about you. You're almost there with me even when you're not."

"Don't you know, my darling, I have the same kind of dreams about you? I don't kid you when I say we're fated to love each other. Raine, I'm so sorry. If only things had been different."

Suddenly Jordan was silent. They had drifted away from her pain.

Very gently he asked, "And the fetus, Ray? What happened to the baby you carried?"

His compassion melted her, and all the unshed tears of the past few years broke a dam inside her, and she cried with terrible, broken sobs.

"You lost your child," he said gently again as he gathered her in his arms.

"My darling," he said, stroking her, cradling her head on his chest." I am so sorry. And I could kill Dan for hurting you like this."

"That isn't all," she finally said.

"Okay, I'm listening."

"His hitting me and my fall off the porch through the broken banister damaged my womb so that I can no longer carry a child."

Would it matter that much to Jordan? Raine wanted to lift her head and look at him to see if she could tell how he felt about what she'd just told him. His voice was tender and full of compassion when he spoke.

"We've got Kym, Ray. I don't know about you, but I'd like other children if you and I could have them. But if we can't, I can live very happily with just the three of us."

"Most men want a son."

"I'm not most men. Don't you know that by now?"

"The doctor I had then said that in time perhaps an operation would make it possible for me to have another child, perhaps not. Oh, Lord, I wanted to tell you ever since I first saw you again, but so much has happened."

Jordan covered her hands with his. He looked deep into her eyes as he told her, "I love you, Raine, and nothing is ever going to stop that love. When I'm around you, when I talk with you, make love to you, I'm home. And I don't want to be anywhere else."

"Thank you," she told him, relief like nirvana in her bones.

She lay on her back with him above her. Putting her arms around his neck, she brought his mouth down to hers. As if on cue, passion like wildfire swept through her veins.

"I love you, Jordan Clymer," she said fiercely. "If I could have nothing else but you, ever, I'd be happy—and satisfied."

He ran the pad of his thumb over her lips, then pressed one small kiss against them. "Darling, you'd be cruel not to love me. Cruel and oh, so foolish. I'm your gold at the end of the rainbow. There's nothing I wouldn't do for you. Nothing."

He untied the sash and slid the robe from her body first, then his own and laid her gently back. Her ripe, firm flesh was his for the taking, as he was hers for the taking. Relaxed now and at ease the way they hadn't been before, they had the time and the psychic energy to search out the sweet, secret parts of each other.

Jordan nibbled at her ears, swept kisses over her face, and she responded with sweeping kisses of her own. She felt for the moment free of pain and longing. If these moments lasted only the night, they would belong to her forever.

Her breasts tautened under his onslaught of passion, and she felt her loins tauten with wanting him. He kissed each part of her body, slowly, carefully, maddeningly, his tongue relishing the sweet, sweet taste of her flesh. Crying out his name, she arched upward and he entered her smoothly and slowly, with love driving him to make this moment all that it could be for both of them.

Raine felt a heavenly sense of limpid warmth course along her veins. These now were new sensations, sensations bathed in trust and yearning. Dan and Dan's world were outside her world. What she had here, he could never understand, and for the first time she felt sorry for him.

What had the old man said Dan was? *Sin vergüenza*—a scoundrel without shame.

Jordan saw her suddenly become pensive and correctly guessed that thinking of Dan had pulled her down again. "Let go of it for now," he said. "I need you, Ray. I need everything you've got to offer just now."

She listened to him and found she could let go. They were the concentric circle of life that mattered, that never hurt except when it could not be helped: the ying and yang of living, female and male, best friends, lovers.

Oh, God, Raine thought as the glory of simply being with Jordan moved her so that she was drifting on a sea of loving grace. And Jordan reflected in his haze of passion that not since he had known her as a young woman had his feelings been so deep, so intoxicating. And this time he could indulge in all the prelude she needed to gain full measure of their love. He thrilled, knowing that this time he could make it last until they had the fulfillment they both needed and wanted. The woman he took in love and passion graced his life the way nothing else had ever done.

TEN

Nevada Mountain was mistily beautiful that next morning, with sunlight striking through. Raine and Jordan had slept late. Roberto picked them up for the drive to the settlement higher up on the mountain, and riding up the mountainside Raine thought that the weather mirrored her mood, relaxed and warmly happy. She squeezed Jordan's hand as Roberto sang them a love song in his clear tenor.

"Something tells me we're getting close to the truth about Dan," Jordan said, stroking her hand. They had been so close to heaven the night before, and he felt he would do anything to keep that closeness.

"You're awfully quiet," he said.

"I feel good right to the center of myself," Raine replied.

"So do I. Ray?"

"Yes."

There were many things he had been about to say, but he found himself intent on saying just one thing: "I love you."

"I'm glad because I love you."

Roberto had finished his song, and they thanked him. He made them welcome to his talent because he liked this couple who were so much in love, but who seemed bothered, too. They sought a man, an American. He wished he could help them.

At the lower mountainside settlement, they picked up Senor Rodriguez, who sat on the front seat with Roberto.

When the old man was settled, Jordan told him about the hoop of excellent cheddar cheese in the trunk of the car, and the man's face lighted up.

"Cheddar is one of my favorites," he said. "It will keep my big family happy for a few weeks. *Muchas gracias,* my son!"

Inside the fairly large log cabin, Raine, Jordan, Roberto, and Senor Rodriguez sat in the front room with Rosita, the mother of Serafina, the woman Dan had married, Rosita's mother, and an aunt. Children played merrily outside. The mother's skin was the cinnamon brown of Raine's skin. Her sparkling brown eyes were merry but held sadness, too.

"You are welcome," the mother said. *Bienvenidos.* Through Roberto she continued, saying how sorry she was that her daughter and Dan had left.

Then very shyly, talking to Roberto, the woman made conversation.

"She wants you to know that she is mestizo, of African and Spanish blood, the child of this lady and a black American soldier. Her daughter has lived in America."

The middle-aged grandmother beamed, and Roberto translated her words. "My husband was a fine man. He did not desert us. He went home and while he was planning to send for me, he died. After all these years my heart is still heavy sometimes."

Getting up, she went away and came back with a large framed photograph. There were four photos, one each of the mother and the black American soldier, of the mother, and the daughter. The fourth photo was of a bearded Dan.

"Barbudo," the woman said, laughing—the bearded one.

Roberto was kept busy with questions and answers between all three women, Raine, and Jordan.

In answer to a question from Raine, the mother said, "My daughter has not been gone more than two weeks. She was heartbroken not to hear from Dan after he left. He has no memory, and we were afraid something happened to him.

STILL IN LOVE

"She will go to a place in America called New Orleans and another place called Minden. She will put a picture in the paper at each place. My daughter has not always lived in the mountains. She has a bit of education and knows how to do these things."

Dropping her glance, the woman also said, "I had so hoped that her life would be happy. Now it seems there is a curse on us where American men are concerned."

Jordan and Raine looked at each other.

"I hope she doesn't go to Minden while we're away," Raine said.

The mother asked Roberto what Raine had said, and he told her.

"No. She plans to spend two weeks in each place. New Orleans first. You are Dan's sister?"

Sadly Raine answered, "I am his wife."

The announcement was electrifying. "I see," the mother said. "He is a man with no memory—"

"He has regained his memory," Jordan said.

"Ah, then he will have to choose between my daughter and you," she said to Raine.

Raine shook her head. "I will divorce him, and he can be with your daughter."

As Roberto spoke, the woman's face lit up. "You are in love with this man. Your eyes adore him." She pointed to Jordan. "And he loves you."

Roberto's rich tenor rang out in laughter. "They are, indeed, in love, senora," he assured her. "You are a wise woman."

The woman served them delicious mixed berry wine and small vanilla cakes.

A little more relaxed now, Raine looked around her. The floors were spotless, scrubbed nearly white. Afghans were thrown about, and a large religious picture hung over the mantel, glowing with spirituality. Poor and proud, Serafina had come from no mean background. She deserved better than Dan, Raine thought.

With the lingering taste of wine on their lips, Jordan said they must leave. They had to prepare to go back to America. He thanked the women for their help. The mother turned to Roberto. After listening a few minutes, Roberto turned back to Jordan and Raine.

"She is sorry you cannot stay longer," he said. "She says you are good people, and she would like to know you better. She asks that you say *vaya con Dios* to her daughter and say as she said to her that she will always have this home. She says it is as if she is reliving her own husband's going away."

Impulsively Raine hugged the woman, who cried.

Roberto's next translation was more sobering. "She says that Dan was a good man in the beginning, but he changed."

Senor Rodriguez nodded and again used the word he had used the day before in describing Dan's character—*sin vergüenza.*—sleazy, without shame. From what she remembered of Dan in his last days with her, the words might well have been created to describe Dan. It saddened Raine to think of the suffering he had caused the people in his life.

All three women hugged Raine as they walked out into the brilliant sunlight.

The great-grandmother spoke for the first time, repeating her daughter's words *"Vaya con Dios."*

Raine kissed her feathery soft, lined cheek and gravely returned the wishes the woman had tendered.

Dan, Raine thought, how could you do what you did to these women and to me?

"When will we be together for good?" Raine asked.

"It will happen," Jordan said. "Every hour of the day we know that we can and we will make it happen. We need to

STILL IN LOVE 127

give Kym more time to get used to me and to wait until you are no longer afraid."

"Speaking of Kym," Raine said. She set up her cell phone and dialed a number.

Kym answered. "Mom?"

"Yes, sweetheart, how are you doing?"

"Mom, I don't want to worry you or anything, and we're all fine, but I wonder when you're coming back."

"We're on schedule, and I'll be there tomorrow afternoon. You know that. Why do you ask? Lonely?"

"Yes. I miss you and—can I call him Dad yet, Mom?"

"Darling, I think it's better if you just let it ride for the time being. Just call him Mr. Clymer. You and I know he's your dad. He knows it. Can you live with that?"

"Oh, sure. I'm getting to be kinda glad he's my dad."

"And he couldn't love you more."

"Mom, Mr. Gibson, my other dad, is back. Miss Vi asked me to call, and I was going to do it later. She wants to talk with you."

Raine's heart jumped, and she hated the confusion this was causing in her child's life.

"Put Miss Vi on, sweetie, and I love you very, very much."

"I thought you'd want to know that Dan is back," Miss Vi said, clearing her throat. "He hasn't come by, but he's called. We didn't tell him where you were, just that you're out of town for a few days."

"What kind of mood was he in?"

Miss Vi thought a moment. "Well, Dan always did affect me like rough fingernails scraping my skin. But I really couldn't read his mood. He asked me to tell you to call. You know where he's staying."

"Yes, at Wayne McClure's house."

"When I think about the hell Wayne's daddy put Jordy's father through—lying in his teeth—with Jordy's daddy going to his grave without his name being cleared of shooting that boy. Neil Clymer was a fine man. He didn't deserve what he got." She sighed. "I guess I've rattled on enough."

"Say hello to Uncle Prince, will you?" Raine said.

"You know I will. He's gone into town. And Raine, just one other thing. Someone called you yesterday. Said she was Mrs. Clymer."

"Yes, I imagine that would be Rita, Jordan's ex-wife. Thank you, Miss Vi. I'll deal with her when I get back, as best I can."

"Well, I'll talk with Jordy, and you have a good time now. I've heard Spain is a lovely country."

"Yes, it is. Oh, Lord, Miss Vi, I'm forgetting to ask how Uncle Prince is going. How is he?"

Miss Vi chuckled. "As ornery, as sweet as ever—I sure wish he'd go on a diet like the doctor keeps telling him, but he won't. And because he's not fat, he keeps saying everything is all right. His pressure's up. I tell you, I'm holding my breath for him."

"Just keep trying to get him to follow doctor's orders, will you? We need more men in the world like him."

"Amen to that."

Raine handed Jordan the phone and lay back to look at his fine physique, the tautness of his muscles and the warmth of his expression. Pure love welled in her breast when she reflected on what they meant to each other.

So both Rita and Dan had called, she thought—both sides of an evil coin.

"Do you know what I wish?" she asked him.

"What do you wish, love?"

"That we could bring the people we love here to Torremolinos and leave Dan and Rita a million miles away."

Jordan looked at her sharply. "But you know how you love Challenger Farm."

"Bring it along, too, since we're in wishville."

Jordan's thumb traced her jawline.

"Stop worrying and trust me," he said. "Ray, we're going to make it."

Get 4 FREE Arabesque Contemporary Romances Delivered to Your Doorstep and Join the Only Book Club That Delivers These Bestselling African American Romances Directly to You Each Month!

4 FREE BOOKS

LOOK INSIDE FOR DETAILS ON HOW TO GET YOUR FREE GIFT.....
(worth almost $20.00!)

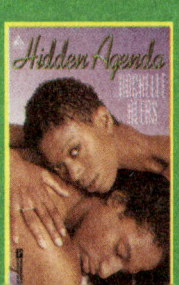

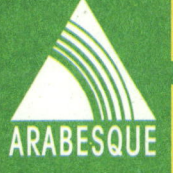

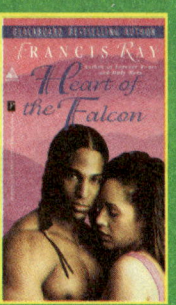

ARABESQUE

WE INVITE YOU TO JOIN THE ONLY BOOK CLUB THAT DELIVERS HEARTFELT ROMANCE FEATURING AFRICAN AMERICAN HEROES AND HEROINES IN STORIES THAT ARE RICH IN PASSION AND CULTURAL SPICE...

And Your First 4 Books Are FREE!

Arabesque is an exciting contemporary romance line offered by BET Books, a division of BET Publications. Arabesque has been so successful that our readers have asked us about direct home delivery. Now you can start receiving four bestselling Arabesque novels a month delivered right to your door. Subscribe now and you'll get:

- 4 FREE Arabesque romances as our introductory gift—a value of almost $20! (pay only $1.50 to help cover postage & handling)
- 4 BRAND-NEW Arabesque romances delivered to your doorstep each month thereafter (usually arriving before they're available in bookstores!)
- 20% off each title—a savings of almost $4.00 each month
- A FREE monthly newsletter, *Arabesque Romance News* that features author profiles, book previews and more
- No risks or obligations...in other words, you can cancel whenever you wish with no questions asked

So subscribe to Arabesque today and see why these books are winning awards and readers' hearts.

After you've enjoyed our FREE gift of 4 Arabesque Romances, you'll begin to receive monthly shipments of the newest Arabesque titles. Each shipment will be yours to examine for 10 days. If you decide to keep the books, you'll pay the preferred subscriber's price of just $4.00 per title. That's $16 for all 4 books with a nominal charge of $1.50 for shipping and handling. And if you want us to stop sending books, just say the word.

See why reviewers are raving about ARABESQUE and order your FREE books today!

WE HAVE 4 FREE BOOKS FOR YOU!

ARABESQUE

(If the certificate is missing below, write to:
Zebra Home Subscription Service, Inc.,
120 Brighton Road, P.O. Box 5214, Clifton, New Jersey 07015-5214)

FREE BOOK CERTIFICATE

Yes! Please send me 4 *Arabesque* Contemporary Romances without cost or obligation, billing me just $1.50 to help cover postage and handling. I understand that each month, I will be able to preview 4 brand-new *Arabesque* Contemporary Romances FREE for 10 days. Then, if I decide to keep them, I will pay the money-saving preferred subscriber's price of just $16.00 for all 4...that's a savings of almost $4 off the publisher's price + $1.50 for shipping and handling. I may return any shipment within 10 days and owe nothing, and I may cancel this subscription at any time. My 4 FREE books will be mine to keep in any case.

Name _____

Address _____ Apt. _____

City _____ State _____ Zip _____

Telephone ( ) _____

Signature _____ AR0399
(If under 18, parent or guardian must sign.)

Terms and prices subject to change. Orders subject to acceptance by Zebra Home Subscription Service, Inc. . Zebra Home Subscription Service, Inc. reserves the right to reject or cancel any subscription.

ARABESQUE

4 FREE ARABESQUE Contemporary Romances are reserved for you!

(worth almost $20.00)

see details inside...

GET 4 FREE ARABESQUE ROMANCES TODAY!

ZEBRA HOME SUBSCRIPTION SERVICE, INC.
120 BRIGHTON ROAD
P.O. BOX 5214
CLIFTON, NEW JERSEY 07015-5214

AFFIX STAMP HERE

ELEVEN

On his third morning back in D.C., Jordan found his former father-in-law, Max Wilson, waiting for him in his office.

Deep in thought, the older man stood with his hands behind his back, facing the floor-to-ceiling windows. He didn't hear Jordan come in, he was so deep in thought. Realizing this, Jordan crossed the room.

"Good morning, Max. What brings you here?"

Max sighed and turned to face Jordan. "More than I can say in a few words. How are you, Jordan?"

"I've seen better days and worse ones."

"Coming back from a trip, are you?"

"Yes."

"May I ask where?"

Jordan cleared his throat. "It's a very private matter, Max. I'd rather you didn't ask."

Max chuckled dryly. "I know, of course. In a business like mine, we have to have the finest in security, a position your firm once held."

"I still won't talk with you about my trip."

Max Wilson looked suddenly aggrieved. "We were close once, Jordy. You were the son I wanted and never had. I thought I'd be a grandfather several times over by now by the grace of you and Rita."

"Did you ever talk with Rita about your plans for being a grandpa?"

"Briefly. She said you weren't interested. I'd hoped you just wanted to settle down first."

Jordan's mouth opened with astonishment. He wanted no part of putting Rita down to her father, but this was a lie that he didn't intend to have against him.

"Rita always told me she preferred to wait, that we'd have children eventually. Those were her words. Had it been left up to me, we'd have had a kid the first year."

Max's black eyes squinted in his pecan-brown face. He was a tall man, bald, a little shorter than Jordan, and imposing.

"You mean that, Jordan . . . ?" he began, broke off to peer at Jordan, then continued. "Of course, you mean it. I could hate your guts, and I'd still have to give you credit for being honest. You've never lied to me, but Rita is all I have now."

"I'm sorry, Max," Jordan said patiently. "As you know, Rita walked out on me. She had Mike Allen to keep her company. If I'd been a different man, I could have raised hell about it, but I didn't. I was busy building my security firm."

"Now you're in love with someone else."

"Yes." Jordan's answer was straight from the shoulder. "I told Rita about Raine—how much I loved her, how disappointed I was when she married my cousin."

Max whistled low. "It looks like you had your work cut out for you, and I'm sorry." He glanced sideways at Jordan. "You're not going to reconcile with my girl, are you? No matter what I say."

"No, Max. I'd be living a lie if I did."

Max put his hands behind his back and began to pace again. After a few minutes Jordan excused himself and went to the small kitchen nook and poured himself a cup of coffee. He leaned outside the doorway, asking, "Can I get you a cup of coffee? Tea? Cocoa?"

"Yes, just pour me out black coffee, and I'll come and get it. You still take cream and no sugar?"

"Yes."

"I miss having you for a friend, Jordy. If I could have just made that girl of mine walk the track she should, you'd have had a no-nonsense wife and I'd be a happy man."

Jordan chuckled, but his heart hurt a bit. He and Max Wilson had been really close. Max was like the father he'd lost as a teenager.

"You spoiled her," Jordan told him. "She expects the world to give her what you've given her—everything."

Max nodded. "Yes, I know, and I'm sorry. It's just that she looks so much like her mother. I love my daughter, and I loved my wife. If Rita's mother had lived . . . She was a beautiful, level-headed woman. I wish my daughter had one third of her mother's common sense."

"What brings you here, Max?" Jordan said abruptly, for the second time.

Jordan sat down in one of two deep chairs beside his desk, and Max sat in the other, sipping his coffee slowly.

"Rita's in trouble, Jordy. I don't think even she knows the trouble she's in."

"What kind of trouble?"

Max expelled a harsh breath. "You don't have to tell me she's in love with this playboy, Max Allen. The boy's always had too much money to play with, and too little guidance. Oh, I know his family well."

He seemed to be having a hard time getting to the point, and Jordan waited patiently. Finally Max breathed a deep sigh. "Rita's taking up motorcycle riding, a Harley-Davidson. I know lots of people ride nowadays, even people my age. But unless they're damned fools, they don't drink and ride."

"How long has this been going on?"

"She didn't say anything to you about it?"

Jordan shook his head.

"It's not like you had time to listen with a sizzling love affair."

Jordan felt his temper rising. "Look Max, I won't be called to account where Raine is concerned. She's always come first with me, and I told Rita what she meant to me many times. I have passionate feelings for this woman, and I won't apologize for those feelings."

"Didn't she marry someone else before you could get ready for her?" Max scoffed. "Listen, I'm sorry I said that. Sometimes you fall in love with one woman or one man, and there just is nobody else for you. Since my wife died, I've never loved anyone enough to bond with and marry."

"What do you want me to do?"

"Talk with Rita. Let her know you care, even if she's not your wife anymore—or at least your first responsibility. Rita settled a lot after she married you. If she was still wild, she hid it from me, at least until now.

"She's drinking too much, Jordy. A cop pulled her over and told me she was riding drunk. She and several of her other friends are on a joy ride. I hope to God no drugs are involved."

For a moment Max looked utterly defeated as Jordan listened carefully. When he spoke again, his voice was choked.

"Mike Allen rides his big, expensive, glorious hog. If you don't know the parlance, that's a Harley-Davidson motorcycle. He's become a man from hell: smart, capable, good looking. And he's throwing it all in the river—no, going to hell in a handbasket. And my girl's following him straight down.

"Jordy, I know you're making big money now, but you're still not in my class. Be friends with her for a time until she can get herself together. I'd make it worth your while."

Jordan shook his head. "You still don't really know me, do you, Max?" Jordan said slowly. "There's not enough money in the world to make me hurt Raine by being too close to Rita. But yes, I'll let her know I still care about her, and Raine wouldn't mind that. She's a compassionate woman."

Max smiled widely. "I've met the lady. She's what the young folk call a fox."

"You met Raine? Where?"

"Well, you know Miss Caroline Lindsay owns Lindsay's Art Gallery. I've picked up paintings there from time to time. I'm trying to get her to sell me one now that your lady doesn't want to part with. It's a little-bitty world, my boy, and was I surprised to find out this artist was the lady who was breaking my little girl's heart."

"No," Jordan said firmly. "Raine isn't breaking Rita's heart. Like I said, Max, Rita's spoiled. We all have to take our knocks. Did Raine sell you the painting? Which one was it?"

Max seemed to glide past the question at first. "By the way, I didn't give her my last name. She wouldn't know from looking at my girl because she looks like her mother, not me." He paused a long moment before he said, "No, she wouldn't sell me that painting. She called it A Prince. I begged her. Offered her all kinds of money. That's a damned good painting."

"I know the man who modeled for that painting. And yes, he is a prince. I'm not surprised she wouldn't sell. That man and his wife manage her small farm."

"Well, hell. But back to Rita, will you promise to help me with her? At least get her off that damned motorcycle."

"Max, I'm going to say something you're not going to like. Again and again in this conversation and in others, you've called Rita your girl, your little girl. Rita and I are both thirty years old—time enough for a fair share of maturity. She still sees the world as a place where Daddy can buy anything or anyone.

"Now she's in love with Mike, and you can't buy him for her because Mike is the same spoiled brat she is, and his daddy's bought him out of scrape after scrape with women. I think he cares as much for Rita as he can care for anyone, but he'll never try to be faithful to her the way I was."

"Yeah, I believe you were, son. I believe you kept yourself zippered for Rita until she began acting up."

"And even after she began acting up."

Max ran a thoughtful thumb over his chin. "I know Rita complained that you had another woman after you two were having trouble. I never believed it. I've never known anybody to work like you."

"I love my work."

"And you love this other woman."

"Yes."

"But you'll stay friends with Rita . . ."

"I'll be friendly. I'll try not to let her make me fly off the handle. But one day, Max, Rita is going to have to wake up. She's still a Sleeping Beauty waiting for Mike to kiss her awake. She waited the same way for me."

Jordan slapped the desk with the palm of his hand. "One day she's going to have to stand on her own feet, and the sooner the better. The world comes closer to kicking you instead of kissing you when you demand what it isn't about to give."

Max laughed without mirth. "I guess I call you and others 'boy' a whole lot, too. But make no mistake about it, Jordan, I respect you as a man."

"Thank you. It's the way I respect you."

"You'll talk with Rita?"

"Yes, and you'll stop treating her like a child?"

Max Wilson looked suddenly sad. As a child Rita was the sole link between him and the dead wife he still adored. Take that away, and Rita was a woman like her mother who died, leaving him alone.

"I know myself," Max said huskily, "and I'll slip again and again, but I promise you I'll make the effort. You'll call her soon?"

"Yes, but it's never going to be what she's looking for. Rita wants what she can't have. When I was hers, she didn't want me. Maybe she doesn't want Mike when she can have him. I don't know. I do know I can't be so close to her that it damages my relationship with Raine. I'll do what I can. And Max, I'm sorry."

Max nodded. "Thanks, Jordy. I've tried to get her to go into therapy. There's a good place on the Maryland Shore. There's the Betty Ford Clinic, Hazelden—lots of good places."

"But Mike drinks," Jordan said thoughtfully. "Mike races motorcycles. He's in with a group that drinks and rides, and Rita is in with Mike from what you tell me. You can't find a better way to be close to a man than to be interested in what he's interested in."

Max stood up. "Thanks, Jordy. I've got a few people to see while I'm here. I wish you could have been my son-in-law for keeps. But I'll appreciate any help you can give Rita—and when help comes to my gir—, my daughter, it comes to me."

Jordan didn't fail to notice the glimmer of tears behind Max Wilson's eyelids.

The following Saturday Raine stood at her kitchen counter with old newspapers spread out, repotting a bronze chrysanthemum. Crumbling the moist dark loam brought on a sense of awe at the feel of the earth sifting through her fingers. She found it like nothing else, this bonding with the earth itself.

She breathed deeply as she finished and checked her work. First the larger clay pot, then the rocks on the bottom, a layer of charcoal, the richly mixed loam, packed just so around the plant, then watered with a weak solution of plant food.

Ah, she thought, in a month or so, this one was going to be even more beautiful.

Admiring the plant once more, Raine pushed it to the back of the counter, washed her hands, and walked out to her easel which she had set up on the sunny back porch. Lifting it, she took it into the kitchen.

She had begun painting Jordan's portrait. At first it had proved surprisingly difficult. She wanted the essence of the man—the lover, the fighter, the husband, and father within. She studied the angular planes of Jordan's likeness. What wasn't she capturing? Her portrait of Uncle Prince had turned out to be one of the best she'd ever done. A New York buyer had offered a princely sum for it, but she'd decided against selling the portrait. It would be her Christmas present to Uncle Prince and Miss Vi.

She'd gotten the walnut hue of Jordan's skin perfectly, the lines of his face were excellent, and his unique expression, the mixture of joy and sadness and an unusual compassion. . . . Raine sighed. She'd work on it tomorrow and make some time that afternoon.

She glanced at her watch: noon. Kym and Miss Vi were away shopping in a mall near D.C. They'd be gone at least another hour. Uncle Prince was over at Caroline's art gallery helping with the unexpectedly large group who were dropping in to study Raine's new show.

Raine leaned back in her chair and studied the palette, not really seeing it. Looking at Jordan's unfinished portrait brought back all the glory of their recent trip to Spain. She could still feel Jordan's kisses on her face and body. She felt his fingers go through her hair and massage her scalp, felt his tongue in fervent kisses.

She brought herself up abruptly. No sense in reliving the past so ardently when their future would be even better. Better? She wondered about that. If they truly had found Dan's other wife, or at least the fact that she existed, then she was free.

STILL IN LOVE 137

But what about Jordan?

Getting up slowly, Raine went into her bedroom, showered, letting the warm water course over her body, scrubbing with a long-handled loofah sponge. She was to meet Jordan at Caroline's gallery. As she dried off and dressed in her pale-yellow shift, slipping on her tan leather pumps, she wished for the beginning of the week when she and Jordan had lain in each other's arms.

The intensity of her longing heightened when she looked at the green orchid in the refrigerator. Jordan was such a love. First, there had come a purple orchid, then on the second day, peonies, then red roses, pale yellow roses, a green orchid. What would today and tomorrow bring?

Glancing out the window, she saw the florist's delivery truck, and answered the door, laughing.

An older man stood beaming as he handed her a dozen white and red striped carnations.

"I'd say somebody's in love, ma'am," he said. "Don't let him get away."

Raine laughed again. "I'm going to take your advice." The scent of the carnations was sweetly spicy. She got money from her purse to tip the man, but he said as he'd said the days before.

"Oh, no, ma'am. The gentleman came into the shop and asked me to deliver them every day. That's why I'm always the one who delivers these. And he tipped me handsomely."

The older man placed his cap back on and touched it. "Good day, ma'am. Enjoy your blessings. From where I stand, you've sure got hold of a lot of them."

Smiles simply pulled at Raine's face as she got a ruby crystal vase that beautifully displayed the flowers.

"Jordan," she breathed. "Who else but you?"

Each day there had been the card: Ray, I adore you. Jordan.

Even though this was the sixth day of the flowers and the cards, Raine felt a lump in her throat, and her eyes misted over with tears. She took a green orchid from the refrigerator and pinned it on the wide lapel of her pale yellow dress.

"Oh Jordy," Raine murmured. "I love you."

Lindsay's Art Gallery was located in a bay-windows-fronted town house on Capitol Hill. There were twenty to thirty people milling about.

Max Wilson stood with Caroline and two other people. He had been in a month ago and expressed an interest in Uncle Prince's portrait.

Jordan was there, but his back was to her at first as he talked with one of his clients. He excused himself and came over to Raine.

"You're really something," she said, kissing his cheek.

"Inundated with flowers?" he asked.

Raine touched his face. "Never inundated, but you'll be going broke. Darling, the carnations are really lovely."

He touched the orchid on her lapel. "And my little green friend is lovely, too. I don't want to overwhelm you. The flowers stop tomorrow."

"No deliveries on Sunday, or have you bribed them to stay open?"

Jordan shook his head. "I'm the deliveryman tomorrow. Happy birthday tomorrow ahead of time."

"Thank you."

"I'm taking you to a little inn down Virginia way. They're pulling out all the stops."

"You've already pulled out all the stops."

"You've got to admire a man who goes all the way to prove his love."

"Yes. And you've got to admire a woman who has so much love, she couldn't prove it in a lifetime."

"Raine, I got carried away." Jordan frowned. "Rita's father is headed over here."

"Rita's—" She broke off in midsentence. "That's Max.

It's all the name he ever gives. He's been in here a time or two. I never connected the Max you occasionally spoke of and this man."

By then the man named Max had reached them.

At the introduction Max bowed. "A very pretty, classy lady, I must say, Jordy."

"I'm glad to meet you," Raine said.

"I'm Rita's father," Max said, "but I suppose you know."

"As a matter of fact, I didn't," Raine answered. "I guess there're some connections we're slow in making."

"Ma'am," Max said, "I'm sure my being here complicates things, and I'm not fond of unnecessary complications. But you've got a painting you know I much admire. Today I met the subject of that painting: Mr. Prince Thomas, a mighty fine gentleman."

"I agree with you wholeheartedly," Raine said.

"I'd be mighty pleased if you'd sell me that painting, and you can name your price. I always say, What good is money if it can't buy you what you want?"

Jordan looked obliquely from one to the other of the two people with him.

Raine smiled broadly and shook her head. "I'm delighted that you like my painting, Max. More delighted than I can say, but it's not for sale. But yes, it is one of my best."

"And don't I deserve your best?" Max asked.

"Of course you do, but there are other paintings."

"And all of them good. Sycamores in Fall, with that one lonely, winsome little girl standing among the trees, is excellent, and that would be my second choice. But I crave the Prince painting. Won't you reconsider? That man's a dead ringer for my own pa."

Raine drew a deep breath and shook her head again.

"This is a very personal painting."

"Then I'm very sorry you won't sell, because watching this painting and having met the man tells me that you're an artist of great talent."

He paused a moment as Raine thanked him. Jordan was silent and smiling.

"Would you consider painting my portrait?" Max asked.

Both Raine and Jordan looked surprised. Raine thought about it a moment and found herself stammering.

"I-I don't know. I'm terribly busy just now." She frankly appraised him. "You would make a challenging subject, Mr. Wilson."

"Understatement of the year," Jordan drawled.

"Keep on calling me Max. Will you consider it, please ma'am?" Max said. "Like I said, price is no object. You name it, and I'll pay it."

"I'll do that," Raine said gently.

Max raised his shoulders, shook her hand, and bowed again. "Well, I guess I'll quit this great little gallery—a disappointed man. But I'll dream. I didn't get where I am taking no for an answer."

"Better get used to it, Max," Jordan said. "She can be stubborn."

Max left then, and they watched him walk to the door. More people were coming in and staying longer.

Raine turned to Jordan. "What a civilized and ridiculous situation. Rita would like to fry me alive. Her father wants me to paint his portrait."

"Max is a lonely man these days," he said. "I think Rita's trying to break away from him—growing up, maybe."

There was something in his voice that made Raine's heart hurt a little. Was he protecting the woman who had been his wife and left him? The thought chilled her.

Jordan continued. "Max is worried sick. Mike's become a motorcycle rider, and Rita's taken it up, too. I'd guess she does it to be close to Mike. Cycling can be damned dangerous."

"You sound bothered."

"I hate to see people turn in on themselves—hate to see her become self-destructive."

Raine thought from what Jordan had told her, Rita had been self-destructive from the beginning, throwing away a man who loved her and pursuing someone who cared much less.

Jordan sighed. "I guess I'm to blame a little anyway. I felt I had to be honest. I told Rita how much I'd loved you. But I was prepared to make the absolute best of it if you'd stayed married to Dan."

He broke off, then continued. "God, the mess we make of our lives. Ray, we've got Dan pretty much off our backs, legally, even if he doesn't yet know it. But the trouble with Rita is getting deeper, I'm afraid."

Very gently Raine asked him, "Do you think that being too close will help Rita?" She held her breath for his answer.

Jordan shook his head. "No, because that wouldn't work. I'm with you now. She wanted the divorce. I've told you and myself that again and again. If I got too close to her, we'd just be destroying three lives. Or am I being presumptuous to think I'd ruin your life if I went back to being close to Rita?"

Raine drew a quick breath and was surprised to feel the rise of anger. "I'm not going to back away from an answer to that, Jordy."

Jordan bent and kissed the corner of her mouth.

"Settle down, tiger," he whispered. "I'm not going anywhere."

Scott and Caroline strolled up, arm in arm.

"You've made quite a conquest," Caroline said to Raine. "Mr. Richbucks Max is smitten with your work."

"And perhaps with the artist herself," Jordan said dryly.

Raine blushed. She had felt that Max Wilson was more gallant than necessary.

"He's about worried me crazy, begging me to lean on you for Uncle Prince's portrait."

"He can't have it. You know I've stayed largely with flowers and water. This is one of a few portraits I've done."

"You're really good, sweetheart," Jordan said fondly, "and to think you're mine."

Raine murmured, "yes, I'm yours completely."

Scott pulled Caroline to him, and they stood side by side.

"She's growing on me like ivy up a solid brick wall," he said to Jordan and Raine.

"Be glad, old sworn-never-to-marry again," Jordan told his friend. "You've gotten lucky, man. Count your blessings."

Caroline smiled shyly. "Maybe I'm the one who should be counting my blessings. I find Scotty a wonderful man."

Jordan crossed his arms and stroked his jaw. "Now when have I heard this walrus called Scotty," he said. "Caroline, my friend, something tells me you're in love."

Caroline blushed.

"Don't leave me out of that caring circle," Scott said.

Caroline had spoken of love, Scott of caring. Raine didn't want Caroline hurt the way she had been hurt before in a close relationship.

She thought to herself that she felt Jordan loved her. He was the one who'd spoken from the beginning of being fated to love her. Silently she prayed that neither she nor Caroline would be hurt the way they'd both been hurt before.

TWELVE

On her birthday, a blustery wind whistled around Raine's corner room, and she'd dug in for a short nap before getting up.

"Good morning, birthday girl!"

Raine came fully awake to the buzzing of her bedside phone. Groggily she picked it up. Jordan had spoken before she could say anything.

"Good morning, sweetheart. Since I didn't get a chance to answer, you could be wishing the wrong person happy birthday."

"I recognize your breathing by now."

Raine laughed. "You're hopeless, you know."

"Ready for a round of fast courting?"

"Courting at any speed feels wonderful."

Raine stretched and relaxed. Jordan's voice was soothing, tender.

"Why don't you come out for breakfast?" she asked him.

"I think I could arrange that—spend a leisurely day with you and Kym. Talk some more with Uncle Prince about his World War Two days. Then tonight's the night we tie on a bit of heaven at that Virginia inn."

"You're such a profligate with me."

"I just don't want you ever to doubt my love again."

Raine thought a moment before she said, "I don't want to doubt your love for me, Jordy, but given our situation, it's difficult to feel constantly assured."

"Yeah, I know. When we're past this, we can look back and smile."

"And I, for one, hope that's soon."

"Well, I'll see your shortly. Chin up, birthday girl. You sound a bit down."

"I'm pretty happy. Even happier hearing your voice. See you soon."

Very gently, Raine replaced the ivory phone in its cradle. Jordan had gone back to D.C. early the day before for a meeting with a client. She mused a moment about Max Wilson, Rita's father. Stretching again, she thought how charming he was. His only child was in trouble. She wondered about Rita and the headstrong and reckless Mike.

But she wondered most of all about Jordan. Max had done a lot for Jordan, and he was grateful, but he said he had no illusions that Max had put him on top. He was his own man, and he said he was hers.

Kym knocked and came into the bedroom.

Hi, Mom, how's it going?"

"Not bad. How's it going with you?"

"Fine. Happy Birthday!"

As Kym had come into the room, she held both hands behind her. Now she thrust a small, well-wrapped package in front of her, holding it out to Raine.

"Did you wrap this? Great job."

"Miss Vi helped me. Open it! Did you think I was going to forget your birthday?"

"It would have been all right if you had. I know you'd remember it at some point."

Kym shook her head vehemently. "No, I'd never forget. You never forget mine. Gee, Mom, I think it's neat the way Mr. Clymer's sent you all those beautiful flowers."

"There's one more to come. I wonder what that will be."

"I hope I marry someone like him. I love it now that he's my dad."

Raine's heart beat faster. So Jordan had won Kym over.

"I love it, too, honey."

Yes, she thought as Kym hugged and kissed her. I want the world to know he's your dad.

"Open the package, Mom, won't you?"

"Impatience, thy name is Kym."

"Kym Clymer." The girl tested the sound of the word, her face wreathed in smiles. She hardly ever mentioned Dan anymore.

Slowly Raine undid the ribbons, laying aside the big yellow bow cluster to save. Inside the white, waxy paper lay an object wrapped in fine yellow tissue, yielding a gold-framed, artfully arranged selection of colorful wildflowers.

"Oh, darling, it's beautiful!"

"I made it, Mom. My teacher showed me how to do it."

Raine hugged Kym again and held her close. "There just isn't anything in the world you could have gotten me that I'll enjoy more."

"Well, it isn't as great as flowers for seven days."

"Don't compare what you give and do with what others give and do," Raine said gently. "It's such a waste. I value you and love you as much as I ever have or ever could love anyone."

Again, Kym threw her arms around her mother. "You're sweet, Mom. You're just swe-e-e-t, that's all."

"Well, you're a little jar of honey yourself, toots."

Kym laughed delightedly at the name and jumped off the bed.

"Listen, Mom, I'll get dressed and you get dressed and we're having sourdough pancakes." She puffed her chest out. "And I'm making them."

In less than an hour Jordan was there. Raine's seventh flower proved to be a bird of paradise.

"Oh, Jordan, really. How exquisite!"

Both Miss Vi and Uncle Prince admired the plant, but Kym stood studying it with awe.

"I've never seen anything like this in my life!" she exclaimed.

"You haven't been around for that long, cookie," Raine told her, "but yes, it is beautiful."

Jordan suggested that he be allowed to serve as Kym's helper with the sourdough pancakes and blueberry syrup.

"I warn you. She's a bossy little missy," Miss Vi volunteered.

Kym smiled. "I'm like you, Miss Vi. Mom always says so."

Uncle Prince whooped with laughter. "Wife, she's got your number."

"Oh, never mind," Miss Vi admitted. "I'll own up to my failings anytime."

"Pay it no mind," Raine said to Miss Vi. "You're a sweetie-boss. I can live with that easily."

The two women exchanged glances of camaraderie and got busy setting the table.

Uncle Prince licked his lips. "Already I can smell the sausage frying, taste the buttered pancakes under a blanket of blueberry syrup. Heaven don't come no better."

Miss Vi shook her head. "You're gonna see heaven soon enough, unless you stop eating so much rich food, honey," she told her husband.

Uncle Prince drew himself up in a mock huff. "Some things just ain't worth living without," he said.

Miss Vi put her hands on her hips. "Well, I thought you felt I was the only thing you couldn't live without."

"Oh, wife, you know that goes without saying." He got up, ambled over, and planted a smacking kiss on Miss Vi's forehead.

With her birthday breakfast done, the bird of paradise serving as a breakfast table centerpiece, Jordan turned to Raine. "Walk with me down by the pond."

Raine nodded, got a tan woolen coat from the hall closet, and they set out. It was a lovely morning, a bit overcast and misty: invigorating, cold.

"What's on your mind?" she asked.

He got right to the point. "You're upset about Max asking for my help with Rita, aren't you?"

She didn't dodge the question. "Yes, I suppose I am, Jordy. Marriage is a hellishly strong institution. Don't forget I've been there. Sometimes people stay in marriages because they don't see anywhere else to go even when they want to, or don't see their way clear.

"You've slept with this woman, known her, lived with her at times from minute to minute. I believe you love me, and God knows I love you. But there are others in the picture, although as far as I'm concerned Dan isn't a player anymore. Then there's you and Max. You two go back a ways. He helped you to be the prosperous man you are."

"I'd choose you, Ray, over anybody else on earth."

He took her gloved hand in his.

"I believe that. It's just that I'm saying I'm free, and I don't want you psychically ensnared. Rita needs help. She didn't need you when she first took up with Mike. And he wanted her the way he doesn't seem to now. She seems to be on the edge."

Jordan cleared his throat. "I'm being brutally honest about this, Ray. I'm not sure I can help Rita, and I won't sacrifice our relationship. I think a treatment center is her only hope."

"And Max thinks you may be her only hope?"

Jordan sighed. "Let's take this up a little later. I have something for you."

"I don't need anything but you, love."

"Maybe it's why I want to give you everything I possibly can. Ray, in my whole life you're the only one who makes me feel on top of the world. Now there's Kym, too. You're my wife in spirit, even if we don't have it straightened out yet. You're the wife of my heart, and I'm crazy about you—crazy for you. That trip to Spain has spoiled the hell out of me.

"We haven't changed. We still turn each other on, Ray—on to life itself. I don't think that kind of love comes along too often."

From his inner jacket pocket, he took a small blue velvet ring box and gave it to her.

She snapped it open and gasped. A beautiful white diamond, oval shaped and flanked by other diamonds set in gold, winked up at her.

A second plain gold wedding band lay just behind the other ring.

Raine gasped with delight. "Thank you for the rings, my darling," she said as he slipped the engagement ring on her third finger, left hand.

Impulsively going close to him, she threw her arms around his neck and hugged him fiercely, closing her eyes as they kissed, the cold wind failing to dampen their ardor.

The sound of clapping hands interrupted them. Raine opened her eyes expecting to see Uncle Prince or Miss Vi, although that was not their style, she thought.

Instead she froze as she saw Dan and Wayne McClure standing a few yards from them. Too bad a neighbor had borrowed the hounds, Ripley and Lilac, for the day for hunting.

"How dare you!" Raine sputtered.

As Dan and Wayne walked closer, Raine and Jordan could see that the two men had been drinking heavily.

"Making love to my wife right out in the open now, are you?" Dan growled. "A man could get killed for less."

"Too bad you left the shotgun back in the truck," Wayne said, leering wickedly.

With a quick glance at Raine, Jordan moved in front of her. He was remembering what Raine had told him about

STILL IN LOVE 149

Dan pushing her through the broken porch banister. He nearly choked with fury.

"Now, cousin," Dan grated. "Don't go playing knight on a white horse. I'm never going to let go of Raine."

"Be quiet, Dan, and listen to me," Jordan said through clenched teeth. "We know about your Spanish wife, Dan."

Plainly all the air went out of Dan. Suddenly he looked very frightened. He began to stammer. "You know I had amnesia," he began. "You can't hold me responsible for that."

"Maybe you did have amnesia," Raine lashed out at him. "And maybe you didn't, Dan Gibson. We're going to lay our cards on the table with lawyers, and you'd better be able to prove your amnesia."

Dan began to sputter. "I've got witnesses back there in the mountains. They'll swear for me."

Jordan shook his head. "You didn't leave many friends back there, Dan. People don't feel too kindly where you're concerned. Serafina's family doesn't much care for you, and Senor Rodriguez thinks you're a scoundrel from hell."

Dan looked crestfallen. "You talked with Serafina's family? You saw Serafina?"

He seemed to be trying to cut Raine out of the conversation, talking directly to Jordan. Raine reflected that Dan was like that. To him women had a place, and he did his part to keep them in it.

"We saw Serafina," Raine said glibly. The lie slipped easily off her tongue because she felt the more he thought they knew about him, the less he was prone to attack.

"Well," Wayne said. "My man here said you'd be snooping around trying to dig up what dirt you could cover your own sins. A man can't help having amnesia. You ain't got a damned thing that'll wash in court. This woman is Dan's wife."

Some of his drunkenness seemed to return as Dan lurched toward Raine. "And maybe I'll just claim some of that wifely love, beginning today. Come on baby, there's room in the pickup for you."

He moved toward her, and Jordan sprang into action.

"I'm warning you, Dan. Don't touch her! She's not going anywhere with you."

"I'm certainly not," Raine said angrily.

Dan moved several feet closer and Raine backed away, her eyes flashing fire.

"Don't press your luck, Dan. You hurt me once, bad. I'll never let you do it again."

The anger on her face—and his guilt—roiled in Dan's breast so powerfully that for a moment he couldn't breathe.

Uncle Prince came running down the cobblestoned pathway.

"What's going on here?" he demanded.

"A whole lot that ought not to be happening," Jordan said.

"You need my help, you got it," Uncle Prince said, his big, rough hands clenched.

Dan threw back his head, and his laughter was coarse, ugly, as he turned and spat.

"Old man, don't you know your time is past? Better go back to Miss Vi's apron strings."

"Why, you no-good young punk," Uncle Prince thundered. "Even if I didn't think much of you, I treated you with respect."

"Damn you and your respect, old man. You've always been in Jordan's pocket, the same way you were in his papa's pocket. And to hell with the McClures."

Uncle Prince looked tense with rage. "Well, I'd say the McClures got what they asked for. Your pappy drove a good man to an early grave with his lies."

With a roar McClure lurched toward Uncle Prince and stumbled. Jordan stepped between the two men.

"I'd advise you to leave," Jordan told them, "unless you want to spend the rest of the day in jail."

Miss Vi came running down the path. "What on earth is going on here?" she asked, panting as she went to her husband's side.

"No fool like an old fool," Dan sneered. "Got your whole crowd around you, eh, Jordy? Well, it won't work because I'll never give Raine up."

The cords stood out in his neck as he went in on his favorite line of fury. "I raised your kid even when it nearly killed me. And she can't say I ever took it out on her."

"No, but you took it out on me," Raine told him.

"Damn you, woman," Dan thundered. "There are names I could call you."

"I wouldn't if I were you," Jordan said evenly, his muscles knotting with anger. "I'm not spoiling for a fight, Dan, but I won't back away from one."

Suddenly Uncle Prince clutched his throat as he turned to Miss Vi. "Honey," he choked, "I can't breathe!"

Her arms flailing, Miss Vi railed at the two drunken men.

"Get away from here, or I'll kill the both of you. You two brought this on."

His mouth quivering, Dan backed away. Wayne tried to stand his ground until Raine glared at him, hell's own anger in her eyes, and he backed down. The two lumbered off to their waiting pickup truck parked on the road that ran past Raine's house.

"I'll call an ambulance," Raine said as she shed her coat so that Uncle Prince would have something to lie on. Jordy pulled off his coat and spread it over him.

Raine was up to the house and on the phone in record time calling for help.

"What's wrong, Mom?" Kym asked. "I was watching a Sunday special for kids."

"It's Uncle Prince, honey. He may be having a heart attack."

She was lucky. The 911 call was answered within a couple

of seconds. The dispatcher told her not to move the patient and gave her other instructions.

Still, it seemed ages to Raine before the ambulance came, and the ambulance crew hurried down to the sick man. It had taken only ten minutes. Raine looked up the road to where Wayne McClure's blue pickup had been parked, and she cursed the place their truck had sat in.

"Darling, stay here," she said to Kym, "and answer the phone for the moment. Then we'll all go to the hospital with Uncle Prince."

Kym's eyes were wide with fright, mirroring the way Raine felt in her heart.

At Minden's small, excellent hospital, Miss Vi, Raine, Jordan, and Kym sat in the waiting room. Miss Vi wrung her hands constantly, full of anguish.

"Why didn't he listen to me?" Miss Vi said.

"You mean about eating too much rich food?" Raine asked.

Miss Vi nodded.

"Well, I think this could have been wholly brought on by the things Dan said to him. Dan can be real mean. I ought to know."

"I pride myself on being a peaceful man," Jordan said, "but I came within a hair's breadth of losing it today. If he had touched you, cupcake . . . And that had to be the way Uncle Prince felt."

Miss Vi chuckled mirthlessly. "My Prince has a place for women in his heart nearly as big as the world itself." She closed her eyes and said a little prayer: "Please, God, don't take him now. I know I ought to pray your will be done, but I can't. I love him too much."

Raine's eyes filled with tears, listening. It was a prayer that she repeated silently.

STILL IN LOVE

Jordan and Kym walked down to the cafeteria to get coffee and milk. "I'd better stay with Miss Vi," Raine told him.

"I want to say go ahead," Miss Vi told her, "but I can't. Everybody says I'm so strong, so good at tending others. But if that man goes to his Maker, I don't see myself wanting to stay here without him."

Raine took her in her arms and let the woman cry on her breast. She cradled her for a few moments, and Miss Vi sat up, drying her eyes on the sleeve of her sweater.

"I keep remembering how we love each other," Miss Vi said. "As old as we are, I guess maybe others would consider it foolish, but I still love the feel of his skin. You see how smooth he still is—and he still tells me I'm a good-looking woman, that these young birdies can't hold a candle to me. Oh, he's far from the truth, but I love it. It just fills my heart right up to brimming."

"I want you to remember to tell yourself what you told me when Papa died," Raine said. "That we cannot ever lose the ones we love when they pass on because in so many ways we are them. So we simply wait for eternity."

"I remember telling you that," Miss Vi said. "It was what my mama told me when my own papa died. We've been close a long time, Raine, even if you are just a baby chick."

Raine chuckled. "No, I've got to be a young hen—not even a pullet. I've got my own baby chick now."

"Yes, indeed, love, and I don't know what I'd do without the two of you. Now Jordy's come back, and I've prayed every night that things can work out for you."

Raine mused, sitting there, that was Miss Vi—thinking about someone else when her own problems were overwhelming.

They had been there three hours when the doctor came to the door.

"How is my husband, doctor?" Miss Vi asked.

The doctor's face was somber.

"The prognosis is a whole lot better than I thought it was

at first," the doctor said. "Come with me and I'll talk about it with you on the way to his room."

Miss Vi got up, the relief on her face palpable, and went with the doctor.

Jordan and Kym came back with a cup of coffee for Raine.

"I just thought you might need one," he said.

"I do and thank you."

Kym wandered about the room as Jordan sat down and looked closely at Raine.

"Any word yet on how Uncle Prince is doing? And where's Miss Vi?"

"The doctor came out and got her. Apparently he's better than they thought he'd be."

"That's certainly good news." He paused a moment before he said, "Birthday sweetheart, we'll just have to delay our plans. I canceled while Kym and I were in the cafeteria."

Raine nodded. "That's good. I want to wait until Uncle Prince is a lot better. Besides, you've already given me a birthday fit for a queen."

"The dinner and dancing will be just lagniappe." He laughed. "A little something extra. I'd have a good excuse to hold you close to me and love you while the music's playing."

"And even when it's not." She smiled, then turned serious. "Jordy, we haven't had a chance to discuss what brought on Uncle Prince's attack."

"Because I haven't wanted to bring on my own heart attack—that bastard of a cousin of mine."

"Dan can be really nasty when he's drunk."

"Yeah, I owe him one for pushing you through that porch rail."

Jordan's fists were clenching and unclenching. He bore the look of a man deep in his anger as he drew Raine to him.

"Darling, I'll be making up what Dan did to you for the rest of our life."

Kym moved around the room restlessly. Finally she came to where they sat holding hands.

"Is Uncle Prince going to be all right?" she asked. Apparently she hadn't heard what Raine had told Jordan.

"Not quite all right just yet," Raine said, "but it's not as bad as we'd thought."

The doctor came back out with Miss Vi. As she sat down, he sat in one of the easy chairs in front of the couch, facing the three.

"I'm talking to your husband in no uncertain terms," the doctor said to Miss Vi. "His heart is surprisingly strong. He was having some fibrillation, which is perfectly normal even in a much younger man given the circumstances you tell me about.

"But we did find his arteries clogging a bit. We can handle that, but he's going to go on a lower-fat diet."

"Like I haven't been trying to get him to do that for ages, ever since you doctors have been talking about low-fat diets, and even before. Put my husband's head beside a stone when it comes to eating, and the stone is softer."

The doctor smiled. "I think he's hearing you say low fat, and I happen to think that lowered fat is good enough. What most people don't realize is that food can be truly good with less fat and less sugar.

"Your husband tells me you're a great cook, Mrs. Thomas."

"I reckon I am above average in cooking," Miss Vi said. "Not to brag about it."

"Then go to work turning out good recipes and less fat. Keep working on him. His face really lights up when you're around. You've got something valuable in your love, and you're doing this will help you to help him."

The doctor shook Miss Vi's hand. "Just hang in there, Mrs. Thomas. You're there for your husband. And with friends like these to help you, I wager Mr. Thompson is one lucky man. I predict that with a little cooperation he's got many years ahead of him."

The doctor left.

"They're keeping him the night and probably for a few days," Miss Vi said. "The doctor said it's a good thing he got upset, because if he'd gone on the way he was headed, there was going to be trouble with his arteries soon."

Jordan expelled a harsh breath. "So even from Dan," he said, "something good can come."

Once they were home and in the house, Raine turned to Miss Vi.

"Your house is locked up. Stay the night with us. You sleep with me or Kym, or in the guest room. I don't like the thought of your being alone."

Miss Vi smiled sadly. "Now whoever said I'd be alone? If ever I was to lose Prince, he'd still be right there with me. That man and I have built some powerful memories."

Raine and Jordan looked at each other.

"I hope we'll be able, Raine and I, to do the same," Jordan said softly.

Jordan and Raine walked Miss Vi to her door and waited until she was in and settled. Walking back past the pond in the moonlight, Jordan took her hand.

They watched as the light in Kym's room went out.

"The little lady's had a busy day," Jordan said.

"We all have. Kym's amazingly strong and resilient. She has to get so much of that from you."

"Don't sell yourself short."

"No. I don't sell myself short. The rings are so beautiful, Jordy," she said.

"Damn Dan and his games. We'll get this straightened out soon. I'm tired of being starved for love the way I was before I found you again."

His voice was urgent, full of pain and longing.

Jordan drew her to him and held her close through her

heavy gray woolen coat. "Birthday sweetheart," he said. "You've got a raincheck on that dinner and dancing."

He kissed her long and deep and, with her blood like honey flowing from his touch, she relaxed completely. She was all his in love and hope, and he groaned with desire.

"Ray," he whispered. "Don't do this to me."

After Jordan left, Raine lay in bed, going over that day's events. She felt lonely without Jordan, and she wanted him with her. She felt the peace of hope where Uncle Prince was concerned, but Max Wilson's presence and his plea for help with Rita from Jordan saddened her. So Rita was in trouble with her motorcycle and her life-style, based on Mike's life-style.

Welcome to the real world, Rita, she thought, where we pay for our parents having spoiled us rotten.

No way, she thought, could she know how Jordan truly felt about Rita. Did even he know? She sought reassurance from the beautiful rings he had given her, the week of gorgeous flowers, the plans for dinner and dancing. But she didn't find it there. It came with his kisses that went to the depths of her soul and with his touch that gave truth to their relationship.

And lying there, an unwanted image forced itself into her mind. She hadn't wanted to worry Jordan or Miss Vi, so she hadn't mentioned it, but hadn't she seen a blue pickup truck half hidden by bushes as they passed a fork in the road on the way home? That was Wayne McClure's pickup truck that had brought evil into a perfectly delightful day. She trusted a sixth sense that made her certain it was him.

THIRTEEN

Uncle Prince mended rapidly. By the end of the week, he was out of the hospital, his arteries that had been partially clogged now clean. Raine found it a joy to have him listen to Miss Vi's blandishments about his diet.

One morning when Raine was home getting over a touch of flu and Miss Vi had already walked part of the way with Kym to the child's school that was eight blocks from her home, Uncle Prince, Miss Vi, and Raine sat at breakfast in the older couple's kitchen.

"I reckon I have to admit," Uncle Prince said, "that I like being able to stay alive around you, wife, enough to give up some of my puddings and cakes."

"You're a sweetie pie," Miss Vi said.

He turned to Raine. "And you, missy, I'm the reason for you and Jordy missing your birthday bash."

"I'd say you're worth any trouble you caused," Raine said. "Jordy's hit a rosy streak now with new clients. We'll set up another dinner and dancing date as soon as things simmer down with him."

"Where's he off to now?" Miss Vi asked.

"Chicago and Madison, Wisconsin. I'm beginning to worry about him pushing himself too hard."

"You can slow him down," Uncle Prince said. "I notice he listens to you. I'm real sorry about him being messed around with by his ex-wife."

Uncle Prince got up.

"I reckon I'll ease on into the living room and watch my morning talk show. Leave you two ladies to catch up on the gossip."

Miss Vi watched him as he left the room.

"I guess I owe that scoundrel Dan a debt of gratitude. It's like Prince's doctor said. If something evil hadn't made him lose his temper, it may well have been too late when he passed out the next time."

"I'm so happy he's going to be all right," Raine said, drinking the last of her coffee and chicory.

Miss Vi's eyes twinkled, but she also looked serious.

"I guess you've wondered why I still percolate my coffee on the stove, in spite of the fact I've got drip pots and all the newfangled stuff."

"I've wondered a little."

Miss Vi drank the rest of her coffee and turned the coffee cup on a slant toward Raine. She sounded anxious in her concern.

"Missy," she said, "learn to read tea leaves and stove-percolated coffee dregs. You've got the gift same as I have. Oh, maybe not so deep and maybe you don't want it to be so deep, but it's useful. It can be a help in living, saving yourself and those you love."

"You're talking about being psychic, having second sight?"

"Yes. My mother, who was dead long before you were born, had the gift of second sight." She threw back her head and laughed. "I think you smart folks call it extrasensory perception."

"Miss Vi," Raine protested, "there aren't many people much smarter than you are."

"Well, thank you. I guess I've got my good points," Miss Vi conceded. "Mama also said I wasn't to pay too much attention to what was on my outside, that it was what was inside my head that mattered."

"You're a pretty snazzy lady from the outside, too," Raine complimented her.

"I'm plain. God knows I am. But I try to fix myself up nice for Prince. I don't see getting old is the same as getting dowdy, especially if you've got a man who loves to notice good-looking ladies of all ages."

"He's a doll, your man is," Raine commented.

"He thinks a lot of you, too. Always has. I don't mean to meddle in your life, honey, but I want you to just pay attention to what your senses tell you. God gave you the gift of second sight. Use it."

Raine leaned forward. "What makes you bring this up now?"

Miss Vi thought a long moment. "Because I keep having the feeling that something is going to happen. Prince is out of danger. I had a feeling before he took sick, but it wasn't so strong.

"I'm having dreams where I'm wringing my hands and crying, and I'm trying to warn someone and they're not listening."

"Is it me you're trying to warn?"

Miss Vi sighed. "If it is you, you're in a mist. I just can never see the face."

Raine noticed that Miss Vi was wringing her hands as she spoke. She reached out and took both the older woman's hands in hers.

"Don't you worry about my not listening to you ever. Before Papa had cancer, you took me aside and said you saw troublesome days ahead for me and just to be careful."

"I hope I didn't scare you to death."

"No. You soft-pedaled it—said you weren't sure."

"And that's right, too. We can't ever be sure we're right. Only God can do that."

Raine nodded. "So much has happened to Jordan and me lately. I find myself wondering if something isn't going to get worse where Rita is concerned."

"I surely wish I knew. I'm praying about this and asking for His guidance. But I'm telling you because a person can best know their own destiny."

Raine got up and hugged the older woman. "I'll be asking you to tell me some of what you know," she said.

"It's not like somebody else can really teach you," Miss Vi said, "and I think you know that. But you've told me about feelings you've had you didn't understand. Before Jordy came back, you said you felt you were waiting for something good to happen. Remember?"

"Yes, very well. For a while the morning Uncle Prince got sick, I felt a sense of worry. Something wasn't right. But I thought it had to do with Dan. You see, I may listen better than you think I do."

Miss Vi squeezed Raine's hand and shook it a little.

"You love the land the same way I do, Missy. I'll bet the stars make you real happy just watching them, not to mention the moon and the sun. People like us, Raine, we wouldn't care if they took all the store-bought trappings and gave them to somebody else. Except it is dangerous now not to have a fair living—a door to lock against outsiders."

Raine stood up. "Miss Vi, I love you, and I could stay here all day listening to you talk, but I've got to go. Did Kym seem all right when you left her? She complained of a headache this morning."

"Oh, yes, she seemed real happy. She told me about the headache. Said you'd given her a children's aspirin. I guess that child is about as happy as she can be since she found out Jordy's her papa."

Raine laughed. "No matter how happy she is, she's only half as happy as I am to have him back."

"How's Rita acting these days?"

"I haven't heard anything else from her. I guess she's concentrating on Mike for the moment."

Miss Vi shook her head, chuckling. "You young folks got

some strange ways of running your life these days, but then I guess we wasn't always on the straight and narrow when I was a girl. It seems to me you young'uns don't let yourself be mired in misery the way we felt we had to be."

Pulling her glasses down her nose, Raine ventured, "Wouldn't you say that's a better way to be, not standing still with misery?"

Miss Vi sighed. "I don't reckon it matters what I think. One thing I know for sure. You and Jordy have a right to each other. I never saw two people so well matched."

"Jordy's always said we're fated to love each other."

"And he may be right at that."

As Raine walked up the path from the pond to the house, she noted it was warming up. She saw someone look around the corner of her house and hurried, walking around the house to the front.

"Buenos dias. Good morning," the woman said eagerly as Raine reached her. "I am Serafina Gibson, and you are Raine Gibson?"

Raine took in the small ginger-colored woman who held a small boy's hand. That child bore a remarkable resemblance to Dan, with his curly hair and olive skin.

"Buenos dias," Raine said and continued, "Since you speak English, I have to tell you that I speak very little Spanish. Are you comfortable speaking English?"

"Yes," the woman said in a voice little above a whisper. She looked frightened. "I have lived in this country before."

"Oh? May I ask where?"

"In New Orleans." She threw her head back laughing, all fearfulness momentarily forgotten. "You should have seen the look on my husband's face when we found him after a bad accident, and I spoke English to him. But I forget

STILL IN LOVE 163

my manners. This is my son, our son, Dan. Say hello, my love."

"Buenos dias," the little boy said and clutching at his mother's hand, hugged her legs.

"This is all strange to him," she said, "and he is nearly three and does not want me out of his sight."

Thinking of strangers and the fact that she didn't know this woman, and many negative incidents had begun to happen even in a town the size of Minden, Raine asked her to sit on the porch in the swing, although it was really too cold to sit there.

The woman caught on quickly. "You do not know me. You are kind, but I do not expect to come into your home. In the mountains of Malaga we always say, 'Trust your heart with strangers!' You will seldom be fooled."

Raine reflected that Serafina and her family had been fooled by Dan.

Looking at the small woman's tranquil round face that was so much like a female Buddha, Raine smiled.

"I will trust my heart and invite you in," she said.

The child looked hungry as they went through the house into the kitchen, pausing to help the two to take off their coats and hang them in the hall closet. Raine asked if they would like something to eat.

"I cannot impose on you. We have eaten."

But she looked wistfully at the Danish pastry Raine opened.

"It wouldn't be an imposition. I'm going to fix something for myself. You would do me a favor if you kept me from eating alone."

As Raine prepared ham and eggs and hominy, the two women chatted as the child played with plastic bowls and stainless steel pans Raine gave him.

"What is your name?" Raine asked him.

"Yan," the child said.

"Dan?" Raine asked.

The child looked absolutely delighted and banged on one of the pans with another pan.

"You're a little angel," Raine told him. The child looked at her shyly at first, then held out his arms. She picked him up.

"Breakfast in a very few minutes," she said, waiting for the Danish to heat through.

When the ham and eggs and cereal were ready, she heaped their plates full, fixing coffee for Serafina and chocolate milk for Dan.

"You are divorced from my husband, then?" Serafina said.

Raine shook her head. "No. I suspect he forgot his marriage when he lost his memory."

"No. His memory was gone for only a year or so. There was great happiness in my heart when it returned. You look puzzled."

"It doesn't matter," Raine said. "I'm going to divorce him very soon. Are you telling me that Dan has had his memory back several years?"

Serafina nodded, then clapped a hand to her head. "Dan has told me not to speak of this to anyone. And here I have betrayed him. I am sorry."

"No. He betrayed you by marrying you while he was still married to me. But it will be all right."

"He also told me his real name is Gibson. The others think he is called Gibbs."

Serafina looked frightened again. "I am a stranger to the laws in your country. Since you are the first wife, I will be the one to lose. But you spoke of a divorce."

"Yes."

"Then he will still be my husband. I love him more than I have ever loved anyone, even my sainted mother or my father, who died when I was a small child, or, God forgive me, even my own child."

"Dan is all yours," Raine assured her.

Raine noticed how the little boy wolfed his food. Although his mother ate slowly, there was an eagerness about the way she handled the food, as if she were afraid someone might snatch it away.

Only after she'd finished eating and sipped her coffee did she turn to Raine.

"I talked with my mother on the phone," she said, "and she told me there were people who came to the mountain asking about Dan. A man and his wife."

"I suspect she was talking about me," Raine told her. "A very dear friend went with me."

"You love this man you speak of."

It was a statement of hope, and Raine nodded. "Once Dan and I are divorced, Jordy and I will be married."

"And Dan will be free. I am sorry for the trouble to us all."

"So am I," Raine said, wondering about her own statement that once she and Dan were divorced, she and Jordy would be married. That equation left out Rita, who toyed with Jordan.

"Have you found Dan here in Minden?" Raine asked.

Serafina nodded and looked perplexed. "He is confused. He did not want me to come to see you, but he is away in Philadelphia for a day. So I came."

So this small, attractive woman, Raine reflected, was in many ways her own woman.

Raine enjoyed listening to the lilt of the woman's voice. She spoke with a slight accent, but it was evident that Dan had taught her to speak English well.

"Did Wayne go with Dan?" Raine asked.

Serafina nodded. "They both went to Philadelphia. They will not return until tomorrow. Or he said perhaps they will be away for several days.

"Please. You will not tell him I came, or that I told you—only you—that he has his lost memory back for a long time? Or that I came to see you?"

Raine leaned close to her, patted her hand. "I will say nothing about what you've told me. You can trust me."

There were tears in Serafina's eyes as she stood up.

"Thank you. My mother said you seemed kind. I must go now. I have much to think about."

"Did Dan tell you that he was in the Army?"

Serafina nodded. "He hates the Army. It is one of the reasons he was untruthful about his memory. He would have had to go back."

"But he finally did go back."

Serafina nodded. "It seems he changed his mind. Perhaps it is because he found his heart wanted you again."

Her voice was so low, Raine had to ask her to repeat her statement.

"I doubt that," Raine scoffed. "I've told you that we quarreled bitterly even when we were still together. I don't know why Dan left you and went back into the Army. He has a strange mind, and perhaps he simply wanted to hurt you as he hurt me."

Serafina shook her head. "It does not matter when you love a man, that he hurts you."

Under her breath, Raine said as she looked compassionately at Serafina, and thought about her own wounded womb, oh yes, it matters.

Breakfast finished, the woman and the child stayed in the kitchen.

"You will divorce him, then, and he and I can be married again."

"Yes, I am talking to a lawyer now."

"I am happy, but sorry for your trouble."

The woman glanced at her watch and rose.

"We must go. I said I wanted to go into town for some things for Dan. Mrs. McClure does not know we are here."

She seemed very agitated.

"Is something wrong?" Raine asked.

"Yes. I married a man who it seems is not my husband.

I do not know, as you say, where my child and I stand. Please help me."

Raine touched the woman's shoulder.

"I will do whatever I can," she said.

Raine had intended to paint for a while when she left Miss Vi and Uncle Prince's that morning and before Serafina came. Now she found herself agitated. Going back to the kitchen, she put the breakfast dishes in the dishwasher and uncovered the portrait of Jordan she was working on.

Studying the painting from many angles, she found it pleased her immensely. Like every portrait she painted, she sought to understand and portray the soul of the person. With Jordan, she had been successful beyond her wildest dreams. She smiled as she thought of the pleasure she would bring him in unveiling this painting.

There were art magazines she had intended to peruse, lesson plans to work on, and she needed to call Mrs. Quarles, her principal. In a few hours Kym would be home. Her thoughts were interrupted by the telephone ringing.

"Just wanted to know, missy, if you want me to pick up Kym from school. You seem to be feeling much better."

"I was," Raine said. She proceeded to tell Miss Vi about her visitor.

"Well, I never!" Miss Vi declared. "That Dan's got a lot to answer for. You said you thought he might be lying about having long-term amnesia. Looks like you were right."

"I came to know Dan so well. He's nothing if not devious."

"What do you reckon he's doing in Philadelphia?"

"I have no idea. Being Dan, we can be sure it's no kindhearted deed."

Miss Vi chuckled. "Well, honey, he met his match in you.

That little lady you just told me about is getting her heart smashed. And I feel so sorry for that child."

For a moment Raine saw in her mind's eye the affection mirrored in the little boy's face as he had held up his arms to her this morning.

"Please pick up Kym for me," Raine told Miss Vi. "I was feeling a lot better when I left your house. You know, if there's anything to paying attention to your psychic side, I'm feeling really strange, in ways I've never felt before."

The door chimes sounded, and Raine opened the door to a happy Jimmy Coles, one of her students. Raine invited him in, exclaiming on how happy he looked.

"What's going on in your world?" Raine asked him.

He handed her a big manila envelope. "Mrs. Quarles sent over these forms you asked for, and I've got a few drawings I want you to look at."

"Would you like a cup of tea?" she asked.

"Make it chocolate and you've got a taker."

"You need a coat on," she chided him.

He grinned. "These are Navy-issue flannels. And I've got on long johns. I'm doing fine."

Later, in the living room sipping coffee and with Jimmy sipping chocolate, she and Jimmy talked about the fact that it was his last year with her as his teacher.

"I've liked the year we've spent with you better than all my school years," he told her. "You've taught me so much."

Hearing him, she felt humble. "I'm glad. You've really developed wonderfully well. I think you're going to be an important artist. Oh, yes, I know, all artists are important, to themselves if to nobody else, but you know what I mean."

Jimmy blushed. "Well, gee, Mrs. Gibson, I mostly got that line of reasoning from you—respect—how important that is."

"Next door to love," Raine said cheerfully.

"For sure."

He munched on a slice of the Danish she had shared with Serafina and her son, and accepted a second piece which finished the pastry.

Raine dozed on her queen-sized bed, nebulous dreams of pain and betrayal floating around her. Jordan was there, but she couldn't reach him. He walked away with Rita as they both laughed happily. In the next dream Rita called to say that she and Jordan were going to Torremolinos to renew their marriage vows. Then Jordan called to tell her how happy he and Rita were.

Still in the dream, she pleaded with him not to leave her, but he hung up, laughing.

She came abruptly awake to the actual ringing of the telephone. No dream.

Rita's voice, flute clear, delicate, mocking.

"Hello, Raine. Remember me?"

"I'm afraid I do."

"I want to know if you'll have lunch with me."

Raine thought a long moment. "I'm home ill today, at the end of a light siege of flu. When do you have in mind? Tomorrow?"

"I was thinking about today, but the secretary of your school said you were home ill. I guess I'll have to settle for tomorrow."

Plainly she had been drinking. Her words were slightly slurred.

"No, wait," Raine said. "I'll still be at home tomorrow. Why don't you come here?"

"You're inviting me to your home?"

"I'm inviting you to my home. Can you make it?"

It was Rita's turn to pause. "Sure I can. I'll burn the roads up." Then abruptly she was weeping. "Raine, can I come today? Now?"

"Rita, what's wrong?"

"Do you know where Jordy is? Scott won't tell me, and I've got to know."

She sounded frantic, and Raine suspected that she was drinking as she talked.

"Doesn't your father know where Jordan is?" Raine asked.

Rita laughed nastily. "Since you came into the picture, Jordy's not so close to Dad. You've ruined everything for me, you little bitch."

"Rita," Raine said abruptly, taken aback. "I won't tolerate that kind of name-calling. I'm hanging up and no, I can't tell you where Jordan is. Good-bye."

Raine hung up to loud cries of protest from Rita.

When the phone rang a moment later, it was Raine's impulse not to answer it, but she did. It might be Kym or Jordy.

"Oh, my God, Raine, I'm sorry," Rita said, sounding as if she'd momentarily sloughed off all the liquor.

"I accept your apology, but I'm not feeling well, and I really don't want to talk with you."

"Please, I've got to talk with Jordy."

"Rita, I'm not going to tell you again that I can't give you his number."

"Raine," Rita said as humbly as a child.

"Yes."

Sobbing, Rita sounded heartbroken. "Oh, God, I think I'm going mad."

"What's wrong, Rita?"

Through strangled crying, Rita got out, "It's Mike." Then she was caught up in a new storm of weeping.

"What about Mike? Has something happened to him?" Raine coaxed, as the hysterical sobbing continued.

It was a long time before Rita spoke, and when she did, her voice was drained, lifeless. "Mike married someone else today!"

"Oh, good Lord," Raine soothed her. "Rita, I'm terribly

sorry. But do you know this for certain? Perhaps he's teasing you to bring you around."

"No. He's really married. The bastard. It was on the Internet. He had it put on one of the places we watch. He knew I watch that group no matter what. He's cruel. Why would he want to hurt me like this?"

Raine couldn't get over the irony of all this. Here she was comforting Rita when Rita had brought her nothing but pain.

"Have you talked with your father?"

"He's incommunicado right now," Rita said. "Probably buying up another company or selling one. By the time he calls, I could be dead. Remind me next time around to get a real father."

"Rita, pull yourself together!" Raine said sharply. "Think about the good times you and Mike had."

Rita began to sob again. "I took up that damned motorcycle only to please him. But never mind. I can fix that."

"Listen," Raine said urgently. "I want you to call a hospital emergency room and tell them what's happened—or a grief hot line. They'll help you. And I'll get in touch with Jordy and have him call you."

By then Rita had hung up. She didn't answer when Raine called her back.

This spoiled child of privilege was having a hellish time, Raine thought, as she paged Jordan.

To save herself, still a little weak with flu, she couldn't think of how best to help Rita. She didn't think Rita would take her advice and go to a hospital emergency room or call a hot line.

And what had Rita meant when talking about taking up motorcycle riding to please Mike? "I can fix that," she had said.

Later that afternoon Raine sat on the back porch, bundled up, and painting. It was a beautiful, crisp day, and she felt nature's beauty keenly in the crisp, sunny day. Jordan's beloved image looked back at her, made her happy.

What were they going to do about Rita? She had gotten in touch with Jordan and asked him to call.

He had sounded weary as he said, "You'll forgive me if I don't take this too seriously. It's like the case of the shepherd boy crying wolf once too often. I know it's got to hurt her like hell that Mike's married and didn't even bother to tell her, but she probably did something to him."

Raine had listened, saying at the end, "For what it's worth to you, I think Rita's very hurt and very upset this time. I know temper when I hear it, and this was much more. This was hurt, Jordy, deep hurt. Please do call her. She said she hadn't been able to get in touch with her father."

"No. She wouldn't be able to. He's somewhere in Central America, possibly having trouble with communications. Rita's pitched a few fits in her day, until she gets her way, then you'll never see a quicker or sunnier smile.

"Listen, I'm worried about you. What about your flu? Are you taking care of yourself?"

"I am. I'm a whole lot better, and I want you to do the same."

"Ray, I don't want you to think I'm being heartless where Rita's concerned. It's just that I've been through the mill, trying to get along with that woman, and my nose is sttill pretty bloody from getting a reasonable divorce. So don't expect me to be too sympathetic."

"I know, darling," Raine said. "I'm pretty angry with her myself."

She told him about Serafina's visit, and he expressed pleased surprise.

"Speaking of divorces," she continued, "I'd think we're clear enough on Dan. Even if he had amnesia, by his own admission, he doesn't anymore. But he does have another wife, and he apparently didn't intend for anyone to know that."

"Well, the cat's out of the bag now. Honey, I'm running late for yet another meeting. I love you, and I'll call again tonight when I have more time to talk."

"I love you," Raine said, "so very, very much."

Just as she gently placed the phone in its cradle, she heard Miss Vi in the kitchen. Joining her, she was surprised to see the older woman frowning deeply.

"What's wrong?" she asked.

"I'm just getting back from walking down to Vera McClure's house. She called, wanting some help—said she keeps having feelings that something's going to happen."

Miss Vi chuckled. "I thought, but I didn't say, With a man like your son living with you and now someone like Dan, there's no way something's not going to happen. Wasting my time like that.

"I guess she could see the look on my face because she apologized for bringing me out. Got real sweet, telling me how sorry she was about Uncle Prince, when not one of those three devils in that house came or called to see if they could do anything."

Raine walked over to the older woman as she stood by the window and hugged her.

"You're letting yourself get into a state. Listen, Miss Vera's none too sociable. I think Wayne gets his ways from her and his daddy. Now, with Dan there, they make an unholy three. Don't let it get you down. I'm not. And I've got more to worry about than you have."

"Well, my nerves are down, what with that scare with Prince. Vera wanted me to tell her some of what I knew about herbs. She said her nerves were shot, and she can't figure it out. She's just depressed, I think, and Wayne's no help what with him drinking like a fish, and now having a drinking buddy in Dan."

"But she's had little to do with you, hasn't she?"

"Well, yes and no. When we were in high school together,

whenever she had problems, she'd run to me. But when I had problems, it was a different kettle of fish."

Miss Vi stood with her arms akimbo. "I just wonder what her need is now. I'll bet that it's only that son of hers that's dragging her down."

Raine told her about Rita's call, and Miss Vi sympathized.

"Things sure are gettin' all mixed up with you and Jordy, the last two people on earth who deserve it. Lord, if only I could shake this really strange feelin' I'm having."

Raine looked at her carefully. Miss Vi was really bothered, she saw.

"It's funny," Raine said, "how you cautioned me to use whatever sighting sense I own. I'm beginning to feel in the marrow of my bones that something bad is going to happen, and soon."

It was the sense that something was going to happen that led Raine to call Rita's number at Jordan's apartment. Rita sounded sleepy, but fairly calm.

"Are you all right?" Raine asked cautiously.

"It depends on what you mean by all right," Rita said slowly.

"Have you been able to get in touch with your father?"

"Not yet, but he'll call." She sounded sly as she said "Jordy called."

"He said he would. I'm glad you're better."

"I doubt you're glad, but I am better. You're probably thinking I'll hurt myself because Mike got married, aren't you? Maybe even kill myself . . ."

"Rita, please."

"No. I'm serious. You see, Raine, this is why I don't have to need Jordan. Because I can trust him the way I never could trust Mike."

With some bitterness, Raine thought: Let no good deed

STILL IN LOVE   175

go unpunished. "But you're punishing him and yourself by continuing to cling to him."

"You think he doesn't love me? At least some?"

"I have no way of knowing that," Raine said sharply, surprised at the stab of pain she felt. At least they were divorced. "Well, I'll say good-bye since you're okay."

"I wouldn't say I'm okay, but thank you. A doctor friend of Jordy's gave me tranquilizers. A new prescription drug: Zyprexa. Have you ever heard of it?"

And before Raine could answer, Rita said, "But no, you'd never need a tranquilizer, would you, Raine? You're so strong. I'll bet you'd never need to cling to a man."

"Good-bye, Rita, I hope you feel even better," Raine said, hanging up. At that moment, she reflected that Rita was wrong—if Jordy were here, she'd hold onto him for dear life and never let him go.

Quite late that same night, with Kym tucked in bed, Raine was well on the way to being caught up with some of her reading. Her dreams were now so full of turmoil, she hated to go to sleep. She paid a good deal of attention to her dreams, studied them, felt they helped guide her.

Rita was really a puzzle to her, a puzzle that was presently helping to blight her life. Somehow she felt that Dan would no longer be a problem. He might hate the Army, but he'd gone back, and they wouldn't take it lightly if he tried to hold onto two marriages. She had locked her fingers over her head and yawned deeply when the telephone rang. It was Jordy.

"Raine," he said, "I've got some bad news."

"Yes, sweetheart. What is it?"

"Rita's been hurt in a motorcycle accident out in the Virginia hills, down near Richmond."

"Oh, good Lord! What happened?"

"After I talked with you, I called her. She seemed upset,

but not out of it. In fact, she seemed fairly calm. I tried to soothe her, even so.

"She asked if we could have lunch together, and I invited her to have lunch with me here. I told you she was hurt, Jordy. She said she'd come and even sounded appreciative at first."

She told Jordy about Rita calling her an ugly name.

"I'm sorry about that," he said. "Rita can be a real sewer-mouth at times. That's very mild for her."

"How badly is she hurt?"

"Pretty badly. She has a crushed collarbone and spinal injury. She'll be in the hospital a while. The doctor said it's way too soon to tell for certain, but there's a chance that she won't walk again."

"Oh, my God! Are you going down to Richmond?"

"Yes. I'll be flying out in the morning—early. Raine, this in no way interferes with my love for you. You know that, don't you?"

"Yes, Jordy, I know. But it certainly changes things. You have to be decent to her, show some compassion."

"She's healthy, and the injuries won't last forever. Keep in mind what I've always told you, Ray: We're fated to love each other. We'll be together."

"Yes, my darling, I certainly hope so," Raine murmured. They talked a long while, reassuring each other and expressing sorrow for Rita's pain. And when they finally said good-bye, Raine found herself thinking about their being fated.

She sat, mulling it over. Kym now said she loved Jordan. Her marriage to Dan would soon be over. And Jordan was divorced and free, but with Rita still making demands.

They would be together, she felt. But when?

FOURTEEN

By the beginning of April, the feeling of impending doom hung over Raine like a storm cloud. Jordan had no more trips planned until June. Rita still couldn't walk, but her doctor had told Jordan it could well be psychosomatic. Otherwise, she had mended well. Was it another way, Raine wondered, to cling to Jordan now that Mike was no longer in the picture?

Raine was early at school with no outside duties. She pulled out her desk drawer and looked at a recently taken photo of Jordy and Kym, feeling a small thrill of satisfaction.

Dan had been no more trouble. He still called, but after his drunken visit, along with Wayne McClure, he seemed to have simmered down. Then, too, his Spanish wife, Serafina, had come into town. Miss Vi told Raine that Dan had arranged for Serafina and her son to stay with a relative of the McClures. Dan was rumored to have said he wanted nothing to stand in the way of his getting back together with Raine, a statement that puzzled Raine and Jordan. Did he intend to use his apparent amnesia of the past to legally and personally excuse his bigamy?

Raine pushed her shoulders back and forth to ease her tension. She had no outside duties this entire week. Too bad, she thought, because she would have welcomed the activity to ease her stress. She felt she would snap in two at any minute. What on earth was wrong with her? Her psychic side was telling her nothing. Or was it?

* * *

Dan Gibson warned himself not to drive too fast. This caper had to work. Getting Kym in the car with him hadn't been too easy, but he'd managed to pull it off. He tweaked his bushy false black moustache and smoothed his black Afro-style cap wig. The fake moustache and wig changed his appearance quite a bit.

"You okay, kid?" he asked now.

Shortly after 8 A.M. they were out on the highway from Minden heading toward the Baltimore-Washington International Airport. He had a head start. By the time Raine found out, he and Kym would be in New Orleans with the tickets he'd purchased as Rudy Hoover.

"No, I'm not okay," Kym said crossly. "Why didn't you tell me the truth? You spanked me once for lying to you."

Trouble was the kid was nine going on forty.

Dan chuckled.

"I had to say your mom and Jordan were waiting for you at Miss Elly's shop, that the four of us would talk. I'm still hoping that will happen, sweetie. The thing is, I've got to go the long way around to make it happen."

"Where are you taking me?"

"Where do you want to go?"

"Home."

"I'm taking you to a new home for a little while." Yeah, he reflected, and after that to Mexico or Central America. He had outlaw ex-Army friends in New Orleans, and they had helpful friends in El Salvador. He'd given Raine every chance. He knew she'd go to hell to get Kym, and in Central America, the law would be on his and his friends' side. He would kidnap Raine, and Jordan couldn't do a damned thing about it. She would be his for good.

Now he really was in hot water. Serafina didn't know how to deal in lies. She was such an open soul, and it was going to cost her her spurious marriage to him.

STILL IN LOVE

If Serafina hadn't come, he could have toughed it out, maybe persuaded Raine to go back to him. His shoulders hunched with fury, thinking that Jordan had always been the winner. His own parents had spoiled him up until their death and had left him well off. But Jordan was the lucky one. Always smarter than Dan, better liked, more successful, Jordan had gotten the one woman he, Dan, wanted. Once Dan had married her, it hadn't taken him long to know that he couldn't take Jordan's place in Raine's heart no matter how he tried. Now Jordan was fast becoming far more successful than he'd ever be.

He never thought about the women he'd pursued during the short times he'd courted Raine and the years they were married. It was the nature of a man to roam, he felt. Being faithful was for women.

The kid was too quiet. He was going to have to watch her.

"How do you feel about going to a new home with me?" he asked Kym.

Kym shook her head. "I don't want to go anywhere with you, Mr. Gibson," she said—polite, contained. He admired her.

"Oh, please, honey, you called me Dad for years. Let's not change a good thing."

"You're not my dad."

Dan felt an unreasoning sense of anger. His head began to throb. He'd married Raine so this kid could have his name. Raine had been so hurt, so frightened when Jordy had left. Remembering, his jaws clenched. Raine owed him big-time. Now he was afraid. Something was coming apart in him, and he needed someone he could trust. Raine. And the kid everybody thought was his was going to make her see the light. He wanted to stay married to Raine. Damn Jordan.

Forcing himself to breathe slowly, he told Kym, "I was all the Dad you knew for a lot of years, up to this fall when Jordan came back."

"I'm glad he came back. He's nice."

"And I'm not?"

Kym got rattled. Plainly Mr. Gibson was mad, and she was afraid of him, the way she used to be when she was little, just before he went into the Army.

"I never said you weren't nice."

"Do you think I'm nice?"

Some sixth sense warned Kym.

"Yes, you're okay."

"But Jordan's nicer."

"Mr. Clymer's okay, too."

She wondered that Mr. Gibson seemed mollified at the fact that she didn't choose between them, and she noted that.

"Where are we going?" she asked.

"You're a spunky kid. I'm glad you're not scared. Are you scared?"

"Not really," Kym said. But she was scared. She just didn't feel it would be good for him to know that.

He patted her skinny knee. "Then that's good because you've got nothing to be scared of. I love you like you're my own kid. I'll bet nobody ever told you that I love you like that."

Uncomfortable, Kym said, "Mom used to say you loved us." She didn't add that Raine had said that Dan had loved them a long time ago.

"I'm not going to harm you, Kym, and I want you to know that. You're as safe with me as you would be with Raine or Jordan. Hell, you're safer than you'd be with Jordan. He left you and your mom, and he didn't give a damn if you lived or died."

The vehemence of his words made Kym catch her breath.

"I know you took care of Mom and me," she said, "when we lived in New Orleans."

"Yeah. Great place, New Orleans. Would you like to go back there?"

STILL IN LOVE 181

Kym shrugged. "I don't know. I like Minden."

"You and me and your mom had a great time in New Orleans. I coached at one of the local high schools, had award-winning teams every year. I was Mr. Gibson in spades, Kym. You were too little to know much about it when I left."

"I remember."

"I'll bet you do. You're a great girl, Kym. Relax. You've got nothing to be afraid of."

But the older black Chevy was taking her away from the security of Raine's love and her newly found love of Jordan, her real dad. The child's heart ached with fear, and nothing this man said could do other than frighten her even more.

Dan gauged his plans and bit his dry lips often. He'd gotten an old model black Chevy in Philadelphia and some temporary license plates with a bogus name. He'd had a new name in Spain: Aaron Gibbs. Now he was Rudy Hoover. Twitching uncomfortably, he wondered how many more aliases it was going to take. He liked his own name.

They'd be in New Orleans late this afternoon where he had a cousin he got along with well. Yeah, Bennie, the cousin, was both relative and buddy. There wasn't a better combination. This was another McClure cousin that he could trust. Dan worried about trust and never wondered that he himself could hardly be trusted.

They were nearing the Baltimore-Washington International Airport parkway, and he had to fight nervousness.

"I've got to talk to you, Kym. Now, please listen."

"Yes, sir."

Dan cleared his throat. "If anybody asks, you're my little girl, my young lady. Your name is Kitty. Kitty Hoover."

"Why? That's not my name."

"Knock it off, Kym. Your middle name is Katherine, and so your nickname could be Kitty. Hoover is a name I have to take to get something done.

"Now I know Raine has raised you to be your own little person, and I'm willing to let you be just that up to a point.

But this is serious business. I need your help, and this is the only way I could get it."

He paused a moment, his head threatening to split wide open.

"Look," he said. "I'm sorry, but this is the way it has to be." He glanced at the brown curly Afro wig that he'd made her put on. It looked so natural. Wayne's mama was something. That was her idea.

By noon when her nervousness had grown worse and she could find no immediate cause for it, Raine decided it was somehow connected to her menstrual period that went haywire sometimes and decided she'd take her materials and do her planning period at home.

In the office she called Mrs. Marshall, Kym's teacher, only to be told that Mrs. Marshall was home that day. She gave the message to the secretary that she would pick up Kym early. Raine noticed with dismay that she twisted her hands in anguish. She felt her psychic powers were telling her that something was wrong, that something bad was going on. With Kym? With Jordan? Or was there trouble with Caroline, Miss Vi, or Uncle Prince?

She stood up, thinking that if something were wrong with Kym, the secretary would have told her. She didn't want to alarm Jordan unnecessarily, so she decided to get a grip on herself. In a little while she would call Jordan. She went outside for fresh air to steady herself.

As she stood talking with two other teachers, the school secretary came up, plainly agitated.

"Mrs. Gibson," she said. "The school secretary at your daughter's school wants you to get in touch with her right away."

It was Kym. It had to be. Was she suddenly ill with the seizure of a nervous stomach she sometimes had? Or the occasional sudden bouts with allergies?

STILL IN LOVE

Her feet refused to move fast enough. When she picked up the phone and answered, one of the school secretaries at Kym's school said with alarm, "Mrs. Gibson, Kym isn't in school today. We haven't had the manpower or we'd have called you at school and at your home to find out about her."

Quickly hanging up, Raine dialed Miss Vi.

"Is Kym with you?"

"Why no, she left for school a little late, but she went. You know she begged you to let her walk. She said the little Kramer girl would join her."

"Did she say anything about not feeling well?"

"No, not at all. Raine, where is she?"

"Oh, my God! I don't know! She never made it to school, and that's been around four hours. I'm going to call Jordy, and I know I don't have to tell you to please call me if you hear anything."

"Oh, Lord in heaven, let her be safe," Miss Vi cried.

Raine stopped for a moment to steady herself as her co-workers rallied around. Most of them had children in school.

She managed to steady herself enough to dial Jordan's number. He picked up his phone on the first ring, and she told him quickly that Kym was missing, steeling herself not to cry.

"Where could she be?" she asked him.

"I don't know, but I'll move heaven and earth to find out. Listen, Raine, you sit tight, except for one thing. Just on a hunch, call the McClures' house and speak with Dan if you can. See if you can intuit his having anything to do with this."

"Dan?"

"Yes. I've been getting a feeling that Dan isn't hitting on all eight cylinders. There's something wrong here, and I can't figure out his game plan. Okay, honey, let's get moving. I have several calls to make, and I'm coming to pick you up. You're in no condition to drive."

Dully she hung up the phone, hating the thought of calling the McClure home. Put a broom and a pointed black hat on Vera McClure, and you had a made-to-order witch. She dialed the number.

"Hallo," Vera's gruff voice answered.

"May I speak with Dan, please?"

"Well, he ain't—he stepped out for a while."

"Do you know where he went?"

"This Raine?"

"Yes."

"Well, honey, you oughta know. He's your husband. Your man."

Raine was about to retort that he wasn't her husband, but she thought better of it.

"You never even let him keep the girl he raised for so long."

"Mrs. McClure, I don't want to get involved in an argument with you, but Dan never asked to keep Kym."

"Would you have let him?"

"No." She wasn't going to lie.

"You see. Well, I'll tell him you called."

"Have you any idea when he'll be back?"

"Soon, I think. He said he'd be back soon. I'll tell him you called. You want him to call you?"

"Yes, please. And thank you."

Vera McClure slammed down the phone.

Raine hung up, her hands shaking. Talking with Vera had been like playing cat and mouse. There had been something full of gloating and malice in Vera's voice when she talked about Kym. And why did she bring Kym into this? Had Dan taken her somewhere? Legally he was her father. But he'd never asked to have her visit since he'd been back. He'd simply come to Raine's house, and he'd paid little attention to Kym. What was going on?

STILL IN LOVE 185

At the thought of Dan's toying with Kym, her heart constricted with fury. Kym had been trained not to speak with or get into a car with strangers. But Dan was her adoptive father, having adopted her when she was a baby. He had a right to pick her up. And if he had, he must have picked her up on the way to school.

Raine sat in the school office surrounded by friends when Jordan arrived in record time. He took her hand.

"Is there anyone who can bring your car home?" he asked.

She nodded. "I've already called Caroline. She'll take the bus over here."

"Then let's go. We've got a world of planning to do. I want to stop by your police department and report a missing child."

Taking Raine home, Jordan felt a sense of fury he had seldom felt. Since the beginning of their lives, he and Dan had been adversaries. His father was the brother of Dan's mother. His aunt had constantly and bitterly complained that his grandparents favored Jordan's father. Others hadn't seen it that way. To them the aunt had simply had a harsh, unforgiving personality. She had grown up mean-spirited, haunted with spite. She had been full of resentment, guile, and malice. His father had been a taciturn, settled man who lived and let live.

Fueled by his mother, Dan had taken up the cudgel against his cousin and had never let go. Quite simply, he hated Jordan and would go to any lengths to indulge that hatred.

As they rode along in his dark blue Mercedes, after leaving the police station, Jordan kept as careful an eye on Raine as on the road.

"How're you doing, sweetheart?" he asked her.

"I'm as okay as I can be," she answered. "Don't worry

about me breaking down on you. I know I have to be strong."

"I'm glad to hear you say that, but I'll surely understand if you break. At certain moments I feel close to breaking."

Raine nodded. "We both know we have to keep on. Jordy?"

"Yes."

"I'm so glad the police decided to get involved right away."

"So am I. We'll go right to the McClure home, and the police will meet us there."

Riding now, with his knuckles blanching on the steering wheel, Jordan couldn't remember a time when he'd felt more helpless. But he felt imbued with a peculiar strength and power, too, that came from knowing in his heart that there was nothing he wouldn't do to bring his newly gained daughter safely home again.

After talking to the sergeant on duty at the police station, Raine and Jordan were advised to go to Wayne McClure's house. Police were on their way there.

Raine was happy to see that Paul Sanders, a police sergeant, and a young blond rookie were already at the McClure house on the front porch.

Sergeant Sanders, a beefy chocolate man with an engaging smile, greeted Raine and Jordan, as Vera McClure glared at them.

"You two have brought me nothin' but trouble lately," Vera grumbled to the policemen.

"Mrs. McClure, please," Sergeant Sanders said. "We're here on a serious matter. A little girl is missing."

"Well, you can look under every bed and into every closet we got, and you won't find her," Vera McClure said.

"I've asked if you've seen the child lately."

Vera harrumphed. "I haven't seen that girl twenty times

STILL IN LOVE

in her life. We ain't good enough for the likes of the Challengers, Raine's people, or Jordy's. We're just common folk. But Dan now has always thought well of us."

Sergeant Sanders nodded impatiently.

"Then I can say that you haven't seen Kym Gibson today or yesterday?"

"I'll swear on my Bible. I ain't got a thing to hide."

"Have you seen Mr. Gibson—Dan?"

"He stays with us. Nosey as you policemen are, I'm sure you know that."

The policeman nodded. "And has he been here all day?"

"I been a little sick lately, and I been in bed. I haven't seen Dan since yesterday. He said something about going back to Philadelphia. In fact, he may be moving there. That help your search any?"

"Maybe," the sergeant answered. "I'd just be real pleased if you'll give us what information you can."

"I'm doing my best."

"Is your son around?"

A bloated Wayne came around the corner. "I been listening, Sergeant, to your questions. I'm around, all right. Far as I know, Dan headed back to Philly late last night. I haven't seen him since."

His shifty, flat look said he was lying.

"And he hasn't called you?" the sergeant asked.

"I'd tell you if he had."

"Mrs. McClure," Raine pleaded, "if you hear anything at all, please call us or the police."

Wayne looked obliquely at Raine, laughing up his sleeve. It wasn't likely with the moonshine liquor he handled he'd be calling the sergeant about anything. And with the hostility he felt toward Raine and Jordan, it wasn't likely that he'd be calling them, either.

But Wayne nodded pleasantly even as he saw his mother clamp her jaws shut.

"Listen," Wayne said, "I'm telling all three of you Dan

ain't had a fair deal. He married this woman when this man had dumped her. There's a lot of shady dealing going on here, and my buddy's getting shafted."

Sergeant Sanders said evenly, "I've heard rumors about a woman from Spain showing up here lately claiming to be Mr. Gibson's wife. And this lady is his wife."

Mrs. McClure shifted a wad of snuff in her mouth and spat into a spittoon.

"Dan's had amnesia, in case you didn't know," she said, "Bad car accident over there. If he married two women, there's a good reason. You want to question the Spanish woman, she's living with my cousin."

The four visitors on the porch rose. Mrs. McClure remained seated. Wayne leaned against the porch rail.

"Thank you," Sergeant Sanders said. "I guess your cousin is a good person to visit. And we need to talk to the Spanish lady. Ma'am, thank you and thank you, Mr. McClure, for your help."

Mrs. McClure stared at the floor, and Wayne didn't invite them to return.

Out on the street, the sergeant and the rookie were parked just beyond Raine and Jordan. They stopped to talk.

"Ma'am and sir," the sergeant said. "I want you to know we're doing everything in our power to help. We've first got to get a bead on where Mr. Gibson would take your daughter, if he's the one."

"I can't think who else it would be," Raine said tightly. "Of course it could be a random kidnapping, but Dan's just disappeared, too."

"The lady said he may have gone to Philadelphia. They aren't sure—"

"Yes, I know," Jordan cut in, "but they know more than they're saying."

Sergeant Sanders nodded. "I get that impression, too. Still, we have to tread lightly, what with complaints and lawsuits and all. We've got bulletins out from coast to coast.

We're checking airports, bus and train stations, and notifying state highway patrols. Even if someone decides to hole up in a rural area, lawpeople there, well, they're plenty savvy, too."

"I can't help feeling Dan has taken Kym," Raine said quietly.

"Any special reason, ma'am?"

"Just a hunch. He's been too quiet after a time of threatening me."

"Threatening you how, ma'am?"

"I can't say exactly. He kept saying he wanted me back. He didn't actually say he'd hurt me or Kym, but I got odd feelings whenever he was around."

She told him at length about Dan's recent visits.

The sergeant's glance shifted to Jordan.

"Mr. Clymer, I wonder if you and Mrs. Gibson would invite me in and give me a clear picture of what's gone on between you three. You're a security expert, and it'd sure help me do my job if I knew more about the background here. But first, I think we need to pay the Spanish lady a visit."

They found Serafina home. Raine thought she looked frightened as the two cars pulled up and the sergeant and his aide, then Jordan and Raine, came up the steps onto the porch and knocked on the door.

"Won't you come in?" Serafina said barely above a whisper.

They sat in the musty, dark living room where little Dan played on the floor with blocks and toys.

"How are you, Serafina?" Raine asked quietly.

"I am well," Serafina answered. "It is Dan you are seeking, isn't it?"

"Yes. How did you know?"

"I know when things are not right," she answered. "I

love Dan as much as a woman can love a man, but I will not help him to do evil to you and this man."

Raine's heart leapt at the thought that Serafina might be able to aid them in some way.

"Can you tell us where Dan went?" Jordan asked her.

She shook her head. "I do not know. We quarreled and he struck me." She pulled back her hair to show a long, angry bruise near her left ear. "I wanted to go to you, to phone and tell you. I knew in my heart what he had planned. He spoke of going to Mexico or El Salvador, saying he had a difficult time deciding. The one thing he was sure of, he said, was that he'd take Raine with him. He hurt me so."

She paused, and her voice was strangled and half hysterical. "I thought he meant to kidnap Raine. He was so obsessed with her. I never dreamed it was the little girl he would take."

She looked imploringly at Jordan. "Forgive me. I was angry and jealous of Raine. I thought to myself, very well, let him take her to some other country. She is strong. She will know how to get away from him. And I brooded that he would want her when she didn't care, and not want me when I would die for him."

Raine got up, went and sat beside Serafina, and took her in her arms. "I am so sorry," she said.

"No. I am the one who is sorry," Serafina told her. "Ask me and I will tell you anything I know about Dan. And you can trust me. I want to save him from this madness inside him."

"Did you talk with him last night?" the sergeant asked.

Serafina shifted and sighed.

"He came by. I fixed dinner for him, and he slept all afternoon. While he slept, I looked in some bags he had brought, and I saw a medium brown wig and a dress or a blouse. There was a black cloak in one of the bags. He caught me before I could look at the garments and yelled at me horribly.

"I accused him of wanting Raine and not me, and he said I was right about that. He said he'd hurt me if I didn't stop meddling, and he took the bag and put it under his pillow and went back to sleep."

The woman's voice was a wail as she continued. "I wanted to call you, warn you, but I couldn't. I was sick with jealousy, and I am afraid of Dan."

Serafina buried her face in her hands, sobbing, as her little son went to her with a sad face saying again and again, "Don't cry, Mamacita. Don't cry."

Raine picked the boy up and stroked his back. "Mama will stop crying in a little while, Dan." She kissed the soft tan velvet cheek.

"I'm sorry, Mrs. Gibson," Sergeant Sanders said, "to have to question you when you're so upset, but you understand, don't you?"

"Oh, yes, I want to help in any way I can. If only I had called you last night," she said to Raine.

"We just can't know the best thing to do all the time," Raine replied. "I want you to know how grateful we are that you're cooperating now."

Jordan shifted slightly, looking directly at Raine first, saying silently: We're in this together, my love. Have faith.

"Do you remember what color the garment you saw in the bag, was, Serafina?" Jordan asked.

Serafina thought a moment. "Sky blue, with small white flowers. As I told you, he snatched the bag before I could hold the garment up. It could have been a woman's blouse or a child's dress. And there was another garment that looked like pants. Dark blue pants. I have no way of knowing what size they were."

"That info can be helpful," Jordan said. "Have you any idea what direction he's headed, if he's the one who took Kym?"

Serafina hunched her shoulders as Dan climbed onto her lap. She was silent, thinking.

"Philadelphia?" Jordan prompted. "He was in Philadelphia a short while back. You said he might be moving there."

"If you will trust my feminine intuition," Serafina said slowly, "I believe I can really help you here. When he and Wayne are here, they have talked of little but New Orleans for the past several days. I knew they had something bad in mind. They were like two devils, plotting evil. I told you what he said about taking Raine to Mexico or El Salvador."

Jordan felt the bile rise in his throat even as Raine felt the fear rise in hers.

"What part of New Orleans did you live in?" Raine asked abruptly, pursuing a line of thought.

"A great question," Sergeant Sanders put in. "Ma'am, it would be most helpful if you could tell us that. And if you and your husband talked recently about where you lived there."

"We lived in a place across the river—Algiers," Serafina said quickly. "We went back and forth to New Orleans by ferry. I remember the address: 32 Sunfield Street."

"Serafina, you were single then. I think Dan will head for places he's lived in down there," Jordan said.

"Then you'll need to know where I lived with Dan as well," Raine offered, giving the address. "It's out past Elysian Field on Gentilly Boulevard."

"I'll send additional bulletins down that way as well as to Philadelphia," the sergeant said. "Thank you, Mrs. Gibson," he said to Serafina.

Jordan and Raine thanked her, too. Her information could be crucial.

"We're flying down to New Orleans," Jordan said to Raine. "Scott can take care of things for me here. You'll need to notify your principal, and we'll have to throw together a few things and get moving."

Sergeant Sanders cleared his throat. "I know you're the best in security, Mr. Clymer, and I really respect that, but you're so close to this."

"She's my kid. It doesn't come any closer," Jordan said.

The sergeant looked surprised.

Jordan laughed shortly. "I won't keep you waiting, Sergeant, for the info you need. Please, if you two will come with Raine and me to her house, we'll fill you in on the details."

Serafina came to Raine and hugged her. *"Vaya con Dios,"* she said. "May God go with you."

By the time they got to Raine's house, Caroline, Uncle Prince, and Miss Vi were gathered in the living room. Miss Vi's face was wet with tears.

"Poor baby," Miss Vi said. "Who else would have taken her but Dan?"

"We're pretty sure it's Dan because he's missing, too," Jordan said slowly.

"Damn that rascal. Has he taken her to Philadelphia?" Uncle Prince asked. "That's where he seems to have been going lately."

"We think Philly might be a cover," Jordan said. "Serafina said they've talked about New Orleans almost exclusively. There's been nothing to stop them going to Philadelphia as well as flying to New Orleans. They were gone both times long enough to accomplish that."

Miss Vi pressed Jordan's shoulder, then kissed Raine. "Uncle Prince and I will take care of everything here. You don't have to worry about a thing here. Just concentrate on getting Kym back."

Raine got up to answer the door. Caroline stood there. Hugging Raine, she told her sadly, "I can't tell you and Jordy how I feel. Kym's like my own child."

Raine's eyes were dry and aching. Jordan and Caroline

and Miss Vi went into the bedroom to help her get some things together. Was she a strong woman or not? Raine chided herself. And she decided tears could sometimes be the greatest strength. Jordan looked terrible, drained. Turning to her, he said, "We'll find her, Ray. You know we will!"

The tears she hadn't shed came then as she stood there. He held her tightly as she cried bitter tears, his own tears mingling with hers.

So this was the evil she had recently felt in her bones, Raine thought now. Her psychic side had worked well. She didn't think she would ever come to have the second sight of Miss Vi, but she prayed for guidance and for her love for Kym and Jordan and her friends to see her through. And she prayed for strength to believe in her inner sight and to trust it to help show them the way.

Dan was elated that he had been able to spirit Kym through the Baltimore-Washington International Airport and on to New Orleans where his cousin and Army buddy, Bennie Durham, had met them. Dan chortled to himself: Lord, he and Bennie had raised some hell in the Army. A light-skinned man with several prominent gold teeth, Bennie spoke with a whine and had a shrill laugh.

"Nice kid," he told Dan. "I don't blame you for claiming her."

"It's her mother I'm after," Dan said shortly. "I'm just using the girl to bring the mother to heel."

"Yeah, I remember you talking a lot about your wife."

"The girl's not mine. I married her mother because I loved her and to give the girl a name. She was fathered by my cousin. Now after all this time I've taken care of her, he wants to claim her as his."

"The hell you say."

"Yeah. Where're we going, Bennie?"

"To a friend's place, a wild little island in the Gulf of Mexico, not too far from New Orleans. We got a place over there, even the law don't like to set foot on."

"Will the girl be safe there?"

"As long as she's with you and you're with me, as safe as in her mother's arms."

"Bennie?"

"Yeah, honey."

"You know I'm going to rope Raine—that's my wife's name—in, and the three of us are headed for El Salvador."

Bennie looked at him sharply. "Decided on El Salvador, huh? Thought you was leaning toward Mexico."

Dan thought a moment. "Right now, I'm leaning toward El Salvador. I've got closer friends there, helpful the way you're helping me. If I can get Raine away from so-called civilization entirely for a year or so, I think I can bring her around to loving me again."

Bennie whistled. "Some plan, Dan. I wish you luck, and you can count on me to do my part. I remember from her photo this Raine was one peach of a woman."

"She's more than that. She's smart, too. Trouble is, she's too smart. It's never been good when a woman is too smart."

"You got my agreement on that."

Listening to them as she sat on the back seat, Kym felt like crying out with fear. Her hands were clammy, and her eyes hurt with unshed tears. She understood peripherally what the men talked about. But even without understanding completely, she knew she was in danger and that her mom would be in danger, too, if they could draw her here.

Bennie brought out a bottle of Scotch. "Toast ya," he said, "without the glasses to toast with. The bottle will have t'do."

Dan shook his head. "I never drink when I have to use my brain. You see, I can tell you Jordan Clymer will be hot on my tail—along with Raine."

"Is that the dude's name, Clymer?"

"Yes. The same. Jordan Clymer."

"You told me a long time ago, this dude was your cousin, but I forgot his name. Hers, too. But I remember how torn up you was, Dan. You really love that woman."

"Well, if it's not love, it's the next best thing. You bet I love her. I'm going to have her or go down trying."

"Hey, man! Hold on. It's too early in the game to talk about going down."

Bennie looked at Dan narrowly. His friend had changed. The Dan he had known in the Army was slick, sophisticated. Whoever he might have loved, he loved himself a whole lot more. Now this Dan had become driven, his line of conversation off the wall.

"I borrowed my friend's car," he said. "We leave it and take a boat to my place—my island. We've got a reputation. The devil himself wouldn't come there if he could help it."

Lifting the bottle high, Bennie chortled, "To Raine. May she be your love forever!"

FIFTEEN

By the time they'd reached New Orleans and rented a car at the airport, Raine felt numb with fear and grief. It was very warm for April. At police headquarters Jordan went to meet with an old Secret Service buddy, who after retiring had become a missing persons detective lieutenant with the city. Martin Davis was a handsome, sympathetic man.

Seated in his office, they quickly got down to business.

"We're going to pull out all the stops to help you to find your daughter, ma'am. I promise to give it my very best shot."

His café-au-lait face was furrowed with concern.

"I've missed being around this guy, Mrs. Gibson," he said of Jordan. "I hope you know he's the best."

"Yes, I do know."

"Now what makes you think the child was brought to New Orleans?" He centered his questions to both of them.

Jordan told him about the tangled background of this case. Lieutenant Davis's face showed no emotion except empathic listening.

When Jordan had finished his brief spiel, Lieutenant Davis sighed. "Our work is getting dirtier and dirtier. And the dirtiest of all the cases is where kidnapping is done by a parent or stepparent. Who do you know in New Orleans?"

"No one," Jordan said, "except you."

"I exchange Christmas cards with a woman who lives out on Gentilly Boulevard," Raine said, "just after you turn off

Elysian Field. We're no longer that close, but we keep in touch."

"Name, please."

"Mrs. Rena Clark."

"You knew her when you lived here. And by the way, what was your address when you and Mr. Gibson lived here?"

"Across the street and several houses up from Mrs. Clark. Her husband was alive then. They were very helpful to me and to Kym. They were wonderful people. I don't know how I could have gotten through what I went through with Dan if it hadn't been for them."

"Did your husband abuse you?"

Jordan took a sharp breath when Lieutenant Davis asked the question, and the detective took note of this.

Miserably Raine wondered if she would ever get over the jagged edges of pain that cut her spirit when her miscarriage was brought to mind. But it was better with Jordan's love.

"Yes. He was abusive."

"Verbally? Physically?"

"Both. And emotionally."

"Did he abuse your little girl?"

"I would have hurt or killed him first. No. But I guess I'm a little wrong here. He yelled at her toward the end."

"By the end, you mean before he went into the Army?"

"Yes. He was changing, drinking more. Women were openly calling the house and asking for him."

"Did you ever discuss marriage counseling?"

Raine nodded. "I guess one of the biggest quarrels we had was when I mentioned marriage counseling. He accused me of saying he was crazy."

"Do you think he might be psychotic?"

"If she doesn't, I do," Jordan replied.

Lieutenant Davis smiled grimly. "And you, Mrs. Gibson, what do you think?"

Raine thought a long moment. "I'm sure it's possible. But the Army took him. Doesn't that mean something?"

"Not necessarily," Lieutenant Davis replied. "Psychotic people sometimes operate in spells of emotional clarity. I'm sure you know how many generals, heads of state, and the like are finally proved psychotic. It covers well, sometimes for a very long time. Some hold that we're all a little bit off. Was Mr. Gibson ever in an accident that you know of? You said he was a coach."

"Yes, he was badly injured when breaking up a fight between two rival gangs at the school."

"When was that?"

Raine shrugged. "A couple of years before he got so mean and vindictive."

"Did he see a doctor?"

"Yes, but the doctor wanted him to come in for treatment and he refused. Lieutenant Davis, Dan is the epitome of the macho man. He saw any illness as a sign of masculine weakness. Women were sick, he often said—not men."

"That's about the way Dan has always felt," Jordan came in. "His dad, my uncle, was like that, too. My aunt, my father's sister, was never well. Remember, honey?"

"Yes, very well," Raine said. "Yet she outlived her husband by a few years."

"It often happens." Lieutenant Davis leaned back in his chair, then sharply forward again. "You do plan to go out to Mrs. Clark's house. I think that would be a good beginning."

"Yes," Raine said. "Dan might be visiting whoever lives in our—that old house."

"And we know about criminals visiting the sites of their past," Jordan said. "What are your thoughts about where Dan has taken my daughter, Marty?"

"I think it's a good gamble that it's right here. Dan has years of living here in New Orleans. From what you tell me, he's hardly had time to get much set up in Philadelphia.

What do you think, Jordy, that he's savvy enough about police work to realize that we'd be looking for him in a place he knows well?"

Jordan thought a moment, his thumb worrying his face. "It's never smart, Marty, to underrate the opposition, but having known Dan all my life, he is an action man, as Raine told you, a macho man—all coach. No, I don't think he'll be giving much thought to what law enforcement is thinking about. I'd say Dan goes for what he's pulling across at any given moment."

"Mrs. Gibson?"

Her own last name, her name that marked her as married to Dan Gibson, was rubbing Raine raw. She thought almost hysterically that she didn't want the name of the beast who had her child.

"Lieutenant Davis," she said, swallowing hard, "please call me Raine."

"Good idea," Jordan said immediately.

Lieutenant Davis looked at them both intently. He liked the affection and loving interaction between these two, and he tensed with wanting to do his best work here.

"Look," he said, "by nightfall there'll be posters over the city and across the river: HAVE YOU SEEN THIS CHILD? You did bring photos with you?"

"Oh, yes," Jordy said. Raine reached into her handbag and brought out a pack of sharp, clear photographs of Kym. Looking at them, she blinked back tears, and Jordan reached over and took her hand.

"We'll get these on TV and radio," Lieutenant Davis said. "And another thing, I'm going to follow you out Elysian Field to Gentilly Boulevard to Mrs. Clark's house. If she's not there, I'll go back. Now, do you have a place to stay?"

"We made reservations at a bed-and-breakfast out Gentilly way," Jordan said.

"Well, you're more than welcome to stay with me and my family," the lieutenant said.

"We might be taking you up on that later," Jordy said. "You know we're grateful."

"Is Mrs. Clark the only person you know down here now?"

"Yes," Raine said. "I'm sorry to say I didn't keep up with people once I left, except for Rena Clark. New Orleans was all mixed up with Dan in my mind. He was the one who wanted to move here, and I wanted to forget."

"I understand," Lieutenant Davis said. His eyes on his friends were gentle, kind. He was thinking that if Dan Gibson was here in New Orleans with Jordan Clymer's kid, he damned well was going to wish he'd gone somewhere else.

Rena Clark hadn't changed in the few years since Raine had seen her. The dark coffee skin was still like smooth silk, her eyes clear and sparkling brown, and her figure ample. At sixty, she didn't look a day over forty-five.

"Ma chere," she exulted when she answered her doorbell. She hugged Raine tightly.

"Christmas cards were never enough for us," she told Raine, "but I always knew that you were trying to forget, and I was a part of what you had to forget. Oh, honey, how is the little one? Although she's a big girl now."

For a moment Raine felt her breath would stop with grief. She looked at Jordan. "Please tell her," she said. "I can't, and tell her what you told Lieutenant Davis."

They stood on the porch, waiting, as the detective pulled his blue Pontiac into a parking space near the corner. Jordan briefed Rena Clark on who he was and what he was to Raine, then what had happened. When he had finished, Rena's face blanched.

"Oh, my God," she said, and felt suddenly dizzy.

Raine looked across and up the street, reliving for a brief moment Dan's pushing her: the rotten banister, and blood that snuffed out a new life. But there was no time to think about that now. Kym's life might hang in the balance. They had to stop Dan.

Inside Rena's cool beige living room, Rena thought of something.

"Being a policeman, you know Remy St. Cyr?" she asked Lieutenant Davis.

"Ace rogue cop? Blackmailer? Extortionist? I guess I do, since I was one of the ones he tried to hurt."

"Are you aware he lives up a few houses across the street? The same house Raine and Dan lived in?"

"I hadn't given it a thought," the detective said. "I wasn't sure where, but I just knew he lived out this way."

Her eyes a bit glazed, Raine told Jordan, "The white house three houses up and across the street with the black shutters and the side porch. That's where Dan and I lived, Jordy."

Jordan froze for a moment. He wanted to see that house again, to obliterate the terrible memories for her.

"Why do you happen to mention Remy St. Cyr?" the detective asked Mrs. Clark.

"Well, I guess I was thinking that whatever goes on that's bad in this city, he knows something about it, if he's not in on it."

Detective Davis looked as if lightbulbs had gone on in his head.

"Thank you, Mrs. Clark. I'll get right on this."

Rena Clark grew thoughtful. "Another reason I mention it is that I'm a neighborhood watch team all by myself as well as with the others. There's been a lot of movement, cars going and cars coming out of that driveway the past day or so. There were people going in, and I door-popped."

She explained to Jordan, "Door-popping's a term we use in this city for being nosey."

Jordan nodded and she continued. "Last night, there was even more movement, and I saw two men and either a child or a little-bitty woman go into that house onto the side porch. Remy hardly ever uses the side entrance. The child or the little woman was cloaked in a dark garment of some kind."

Raine felt her heart leap. Dan had lived in that house and so knew it well. Remy St. Cyr would be a good friend for him to make at a time like this.

"Remy's got relatives up around Washington, D.C.," Rena said. "I think out in Maryland. I don't know their names."

"In Minden?" Raine asked.

"Could be. I'm not sure," Rena answered. "I could ask around. My friend down the street knows him better than I do. He was once friends with her son when they were in high school. Well, I swear, I thought something was amiss when I saw a man who reminds me of Dan Gibson—same build, but a big black moustache."

She turned to Raine, her face sad. "I've never forgotten or forgiven him for what he did to you, love. For a long time I couldn't stand the sight of that man, if you can call him that."

Lieutenant Davis took Rena's hand. "Mrs. Clark," he said, "you've put my brain into overdrive. I want to thank you."

"Please call me Rena," she said. "I'm a plain woman. Respect doesn't always have to have a title. Before you even ask, I'll keep my eyes open, and I'll ask questions on the block."

"I'm going to have to go," the detective said, "but you've got my card. Call me twenty-four hours a day, and I'll do the same for you if I hear anything. And another thing, Jordy, security is your line of work, so you know there's nothing too small to let me in on. You're going to stay at the bed-and-breakfast a few blocks away."

Rena Clark put her hands to her head in a dramatic gesture. "I won't hear of it. I've got three bedrooms here, and they're pretty and comfortable. Even if I wasn't lonely as can be, I'd want you to stay. But I am lonely, so I insist. Besides, this way, you're closer to Remy, if anything is going on."

Raine hugged her and looked at Jordy. "I'd like to stay here," she said. The bitter memories of Dan stayed for the moment on that side of the street.

When the sheriff's deputy saw the flyers of the missing Kym late that evening, he frowned, but thought little about it. When he saw a second photograph on TV that night, he let out a harsh sigh. The sweet little face looked familiar. But the flyer stated that the missing child had black hair. He thought almost immediately of the little girl who'd sat so primly on the backseat of Bennie Durham's car this afternoon. The deputy didn't know the other man with the big black moustache who was with Bennie on the front seat of the car. He was new around here to him. But Bennie was a bad one that he watched and waited to catch. If it was outside the law, Bennie Durham was in on it.

But the little girl sure as shooting had had clear brown, not black hair. Still, the face resembled that little girl's. The deputy had two little girls and two boys, and he was hell on anybody who messed with kids.

A gut wrench told him to call the number of the flyer lying on the couch beside him, as his own little ones hung over the couch and into his lap insisted he move with due speed.

After a couple of calls, he found himself talking to Lieutenant Davis.

"You know or you know now about Bennie Durham," he said to Lieutenant Davis, with whom he had collaborated on cases. "I'm glad I got you on this, Marty, because it's nagged at the corners of my mind all afternoon."

He told him about stopping the car and questioning Bennie that morning, just to keep him on his toes.

"I know Bennie Durham. You know I do," Lieutenant Davis answered.

"Well, today I stopped him, and there was this child on the backseat of his car and a man I don't know, when I thought I knew most everybody Bennie pals around with. She got on the boat with him and he was shepherding her closely."

Lieutenant Davis described Dan.

"No, this hombre had a fairly thick moustache."

"Could be a disguise. Fake ones are easy to come by."

"Yeah, and the kid could have had on a wig. It was all curly. I'd never know the difference. I don't forget faces, Marty. And this little face has haunted the hell out of me all day. You want us to haul Bennie Durham in, we can do it before you can bat your eyes."

Lieutenant Davis closed his eyes and saw Jordy and Raine's telephone number at Rena Clark's on a mental screen.

"I'll be forever grateful," he said, "if you'll do just that."

Before she and Jordy went to bed in Rena Clark's blue chenille-decorated bedroom, Raine looked outside at the floodlit backyard and the room-high scarlet poinsettia bushes growing near the back entrance. When she lived there, Rena had given her cuttings and she had planted them. Both women had filled their houses during the holidays with the beautiful blossoms.

She and Jordy had asked for separate rooms. Rena nodded and acquiesced. One thing, Raine thought dully, she knew that once this was over, she was free of Dan, but at what price?

In Rena's claw-foot tub, lying in the too hot water she had drawn, Raine's heart felt like lead, and fear was an icy monster at her throat. Drying off in the heavy towel, she remembered her body as she had carried Kym, remembered the pains of childbirth and the longing for Jordy.

In bed she grew agitated beyond bearing. Jordy came in and sat on the edge of the bed.

"Keep your chin up, Ray. We're going to find her."

Raine didn't answer what was in her heart: Yes, but how will she be when we find her? Was Dan crazy enough to hurt Kym? Kill her? With the last thought her heart nearly went out of control.

As she and Jordan clung to each other, Raine had a sudden thought.

"Jordy, I'm going to call Serafina. Give her this address and this number. She may have heard something else."

"That's a good idea, honey. Especially since the part of the McClure family she's staying with isn't that vicious."

She called information for the number and got it right away. Serafina answered on the second ring.

"Raine! What is going on?"

"Can you talk?" Raine asked.

"Yes. Only my son and I are here. Jenny and her children are at the movies."

Raine told her what little they'd found in New Orleans, and also told her, "I thought you might have heard something else that could help. What you've told me about Dan and Wayne talking about New Orleans could prove to be very useful, but we've found nothing yet."

"You know how sorry I am. I keep thinking of a couple of names I heard Dan and Wayne mention, but my mind goes blank."

"Names of people here in New Orleans?"

"Yes. Two names. One man I'm sure they never called his last name, but they did use the whole name of one of the men." She paused a long moment.

"Listen," Raine said, excited now at the hope the names might offer. "Please take this address and this telephone number, and call me collect when you think of it."

"You know I will," Serafina said, "the minute I think of it, no matter the hour. I call home late at night when it is cheaper. Jenny is a sweet woman: *dulce*. She will not mind, and I will pay her. I worked in Torremolinos a year at a resort, and I was paid well. I saved all the money to come to America and find Dan. Now . . ." She sighed and said no more.

"And you don't remember any names he spoke of from Philadelphia?" Raine asked.

"No. I listened carefully, because I thought he might be running away from me. He muttered once in his sleep that he would take you away. Raine, I am so sorry I did not tell you this, but it was only a few nights back, and I am afraid of Dan—but," she added, "not so afraid that I will let him take your child and do nothing about it. When I visited you, I lived with him and his mother, Vera. I was hungry the day I came to your house. My son was hungry. Vera refused to cook until we went to a cousin's, this cousin's house to stay. Believe me, I will do what I can to help you."

"Thank you, Serafina. And Jordan thanks you."

"The man you love so much."

"Yes."

Serafina laughed a little. "My prayers are with you, Raine. May God walk by your side."

"Thank you, and may He walk by your side."

"You, too, are *dulce:* sweet."

Raine thanked her again and hung up. Quickly she told Jordan' what Serafina had said about Dan and Wayne's mentioning names in New Orleans.

Jordy's face lit up. "Oh, Lord, let her remember," he said.

The phone rang, and after a minute Rena knocked and told Jordan the call was for him.

Answering, he covered the mouthpiece with his hand and whispered to her, "Martin Davis."

"I'm just checking with you to tell you what we've done,"

Lieutenant Davis said. He told him about the deputy sheriff who had seen a little girl on the backseat of a man named Bennie Durham and a man with this Bennie who could be Dan Gibson in disguise.

Thrills of hope ran down then up Jordan's spine. Watching him, Raine could see from his expression that something pleased him, and she waited with bated breath until he could tell her.

"We're getting search warrants for Remy St. Cyr's house, but the one for Bennie Durham will be more difficult. He's in a different parish, known to be buddies with some corrupt politicians who protect him. And he lives with a man who's in drugs all the way up to the Cali Cartel in Colombia.

"Fortunately the people have elected an honest sheriff who's willing to fight crime, so we're in luck."

"My God," Jordan exclaimed, "this deputy sheriff thinks it really could have been Kym."

"That's right. Now remember, we've got our work cut out for us. I don't think Dan would leave her over there in New Orleans, when Mrs. Clark lives on that block, and New Orleanians are famous for door-popping, or checking on their neighbors. Bennie Durham's place is an ideal hiding spot.

"Bennie's landlord and housemate is the notorious Jacques Duclair, who's led a charmed life as a drug baron. The new sheriff wants a piece of his hide, and I'm going to help him try for it. The sheriff has ten, you count them, ten kids, and he loves each one better than the other. You don't mess with kids where he's concerned. With him fighting, he's sent men to prison for child abuse who'd been getting away with it for ages."

"This sounds wonderful. Nothing panned out for Philadelphia, did it?"

"No, nothing. I'm pretty sure it's like you said. Philadelphia was a smokescreen so he could creep quietly down here with his buddies. Little Lafitte Island belongs to Jacques Duclair lock, stock, and barrel. He's in cocaine up to

STILL IN LOVE

his eyeballs, they're branching out into designer drugs and methamphetamine."

His voice husky, Jordan said, "I owe you, buddy. Forever."

Martin Davis chuckled. "One thing about New Orleans, we may have our faults, but we'll do anything to help a friend. The only trouble is the bad guys have friends they'll help, too."

The two men said good-bye, and Jordan replaced the phone in its cradle. He pulled Raine to him and hugged her fiercely.

"It looks," he said, "like we may be on the track of something."

Raine knew she waited for a call from Serafina that might never come or wouldn't have the information she sought if it did. English was a second language for Serafina and made remembering all the more difficult.

"That's wonderful," Raine said dully, "but Kym must be frightened to death. Thank heavens it's fairly warm down here. She was warmly dressed, but if he changed her clothes to make her less identifiable, I wonder if he dressed her warmly enough."

"We can only hope and pray."

"When can Lieutenant Davis get started on searching the house up the street? Remy St. Cyr's house."

"Tomorrow fairly early. And he's going to come by and pick us up."

"Oh, Jordy, that's wonderful. Sweetheart, I've been doing something constantly I want to tell you about."

"Okay."

"Every so often I hold the articles of Kym's that I threw in the suitcase: barrettes, a doll, a dress, a sweater. I concentrate on her. I talk to her. Tell her we love her and we'll find her, no matter how long it takes."

Her eyes misting, she held up a kelly green scarf of Kym's. Jordan gathered her in his arms, and she clung to him.

"I feel her presence, Jordy," Raine said, "and I know she feels ours. Oh, dear God, let her be safe!"

Jordan's cellular phone buzzed. He answered it and talked again for only a moment before he said to her, "Scott and Caroline."

Raine picked up the phone.

"We're praying," Caroline said. "Raine, is there nothing that bastard won't do?"

"I think this proves there isn't, except I'm praying he doesn't hurt or mistreat her in any way."

"He'd better not," Scott growled. "Dan wants to keep living if I read him right, and he isn't going to cut his own time short, which is precisely what he'll be doing if he hurts her."

"Yes," Raine breathed.

"With Miss Vi and Uncle Prince, I'm holding down the fort for you here, and Scott, as you know, is doing the same for Jordy. But if you need us, we can find others and we'll come down there on the double."

"Right now we can handle it," Raine said, "but you two know how much we appreciate your offer, and we will call if need be."

"Nothing about the Philadelphia trips Dan's been taking?" Scott asked.

"Nothing. Seems it was a ruse. Listen, Scott," Jordy said and broke off to give Scott Serafina's number. "Let her have money if she needs it and help her out. Check on her from time to time. It may be she'll be all the help in the world to us."

He told Scott about the names Serafina couldn't presently remember, and Scott promised to do what Jordan asked.

When he'd hung up, Jordy lay back and Raine lay across him.

"Let's sit up tonight, honey," Raine said. "Relax as best

we can, but one sleepless night isn't going to hurt. You know we're not going to sleep. I wonder if Kym can sleep."

They sat up in Raine's room all night, and after awhile Rena knocked softly and came in with a tray of hot chocolate.

"I heard you talking, and I know I couldn't sleep. If you don't mind," she said, setting the tray on a nightstand, "I'll turn on an all-night radio station in here, and we can listen to music and news."

They thought it was a great idea, and Rena fiddled with the dial until she got the station. Soothing music, classical, pops, a few spirituals poured out, enveloping them.

On the hour they heard the announcer's voice asking if anyone who'd seen a little girl—Kym—would call a number at police headquarters.

"And I want to say to the loved ones of this missing child, I wish her godspeed in coming back to you."

Raine's throat was too tight to cry.

Next morning Raine drank more chocolate but could eat nothing. Jordan ate a hard-boiled egg, some toast, and a grapefruit half.

Raine felt smothered in her own anxiety, but it was hopeful anxiety. She waited for Lieutenant Davis, and she waited for Serafina's possible call that may or may not have useful further information.

Lieutenant Davis came at ten, had a cup of coffee and chicory, and ate a coconut doughnut. He praised Rena's coffee and she blushed. "it's not often I get to serve a good-looking and nice detective," she said, flirting in the way of many New Orleans women, offering friendship only.

"You know we're moving in on your neighbor," the detective said to Rena.

"And not a minute too soon," Rena answered. "That

ex-cop devil. If there's a sin he hasn't committed, it's because the devil himself hasn't dreamed it up yet."

The detective questioned Rena more closely about what she'd seen the night she'd told them about.

"I guess it could have been a small man or boy," Lieutenant Davis said, striving to draw on reality as well as the hoped-for.

"I don't think so," Rena said. "No pants. The cloak came only halfway down the legs." She put a finger to her face. "Another thing is they were kind of urging or pushing her along—like she didn't want to go where they were taking her."

The detective was very quiet, thoughtful.

"Well, let's go," he said to Jordan and Raine. "I want you two to give Remy's house a thorough eye-check, and see if you see, hear, or smell anything connected to this."

"Maybe you ought to get a psychic," Rena said. "Oh, I know some folks don't believe in them, but . . ."

"We'll try everything," Raine said.

"Everything," Jordan echoed.

Rena put her arms around Raine and hugged her. "I'll be praying," she said, "every minute you're in that house."

SIXTEEN

Coming into the yard of the house she and Dan and Kym had lived in on Gentilly Boulevard depressed Raine with its memories. As they closed the tall iron gate behind them, Raine thought how much the place looked like a fortress.

From the front porch she could see the edge of the poinsettia bushes, and a lingering sadness swept over her. But the force of needing to know if Kym was in this house overwhelmed all else. Every movement seemed to take too long for her.

No one answered the doorbell. Lieutenant Davis walked around to the back edge of the large side porch and shook his head. "The garage door is open," he said. "No car inside. Remy drives an old Lincoln and a new Porsche. Neither one is there."

Raine and Jordan joined him where he stood and, in that spot, the poinsettias were in full bloom and full view. She began to tremble as if she might faint.

"Flashback?" Jordan asked quietly, "from the miscarriage?"

"Yes, I'm afraid so," Raine choked out. "I never wanted to see this house again."

Jordan took her in his arms and pressed her to him. "Cry, my darling, if you can."

But there were no tears, just the empty ache for the child that might have been.

With a slim-jim and other tools, the detective opened the

side door, and they were in the ornately decorated, musty house. Detective Davis and Jordan switched on the lights as they moved from the big living room, through the dining room and kitchen, then up the stairs to the three bedrooms.

Even with the lights on, the detective used his flashlight to search the corners. They had turned over cushions of the sofas and chairs downstairs, searched drawers and cabinets and closets.

Now on the second floor, they did the same.

"There's a crawl space to this house," Raine said.

"Let's look there before we finish here," Jordan said. "That's a likely hiding space."

The old panic and hysteria came back to Raine. Criminals used crawl spaces to hide bodies. Oh, damn you, Dan and Remy St. Cyr, if you've killed my child. Hell isn't going to be hot enough to hold you.

With her heart drumming, they went down the stairs. Jordan held her hand, his breath coming in spurts as they went outside and easily into the crawl space under the back porch. Lieutenant Davis shined the flashlight beam into every cobwebbed corner, and all three breathed a sigh of relief. There had been no one in here for some time.

"While we're out here, we might as well check the garage before we go back upstairs," the detective said.

The double garage yielded nothing, and they went back inside and upstairs. They were aware that Remy's neighbor had tracked their movements from first her front, then her back door.

Raine felt both happy that they hadn't found a hurt Kym and screaming with nerves that they'd still found no trace of her little daughter.

The master bedroom upstairs was expensively furnished with massive golden oak. The second room was nondescript and cluttered. They moved slowly, going over every possible inch. It was in the third, back bedroom that Raine gasped when she entered. She and Jordan both saw at once the black lacquered music box Jordan had bought Kym when he first came back. With trembling fingers, Raine picked it up and opened it to hear the strains of Londonderry Air. Turning it over she nearly dropped the box with excitement, as she read the inscription: To Kym, With love, from Jordan Clymer. Speechless, she held out the box to the two men.

Jordan took it first and read the inscription, his eyes misting over.

A search down the side of the cushions yielded a tortoiseshell barrette.

"Kym had two of these on when I left her," Raine said. "One on each side."

"Well, well, Remy," Detective Davis said, "I think you've got yourself into some real trouble. Now where the hell are you?"

As if in answer to this question, they could hear someone talking and cursing violently downstairs. The three of them met Remy St. Cyr on the stairs.

"What are you doing in my house, Davis?" Remy St. Cyr demanded.

"A nice, understanding judge gave me a search warrant, as if you didn't know." Lieutenant Davis held out the music box in a plastic bag, along with the barrette.

"Evidence—against you, St. Cyr. Or maybe you've adopted a kid lately."

Remy St. Cyr turned white. "I don't know what you're talking about. I have friends who visit with their kids. They leave things around."

"I don't want to hear your lies."

"You know you can't make this evidence stick," Remy St. Cyr howled. "Get out of my house."

Tiredly, Lieutenant Davis shook his head. "You're right. I can't. But if I run a few fingerprint checks, and the prints turn out to be Kym Gibson's . . . If anything has happened to her, we'll bake and fry you at the same time."

"Run the prints first," St. Cyr suddenly grinned, "then talk to me."

He was bluffing, but Jordan felt the man may have had a chance to wipe off the fingerprints—but maybe not. "I'll cross that bridge when I get to it."

Lieutenant Davis clenched his teeth, and Jordan felt the violent urge to knock the grin off Remy St. Cyr's face.

"How's your buddy, Bennie Durham?" Lieutenant Davis asked Remy.

"Aw, we're hardly friends, Loo," Remy said quickly, using the favored term "loo" for the lieutenant's title, as if he were close to him.

"Never mind snuggling up to me, St. Cyr," Lieutenant Davis grated. "It's a little late for that."

"Just said it to let you know that I'm about as close to you as I am to Bennie Durham."

"And Jacques Duclair?" Lieutenant Davis asked.

"Same. Know both of them same as you do. No connection."

"You're a liar and we both know it."

"Now, Lieutenant," Remy said softly. "Mind your manners. Haven't you heard about the new wave of community policing? I'm a fine upstanding member of the community."

"And I'm the king of England," Lieutenant Davis shot back.

"Come on. Let's get out of here," the detective said. "The place got a bad smell a few minutes back."

"Do come back when you're in a more social mood," Remy shot back. "Or when you've got some evidence you can make stick."

Outside at his police cruiser, the detective hit his car with the palm of his hand. "God forgive me for the thoughts racing through my mind," he said. "And thank you for helping me hold my temper."

* * *

STILL IN LOVE 217

Lieutenant Davis turned to Raine and Jordan when they got back to Rena's house.

"I'll drop you off here temporarily," he said, "but if I can put my ducks in a row, I'll be picking you up this afternoon, early. If I can get things going my way, I'll get a search warrant from a Parish judge, which isn't going to be easy, but with a good sheriff, it's possible."

"This time you're searching Bennie Durham's house?" Jordan asked.

"Bennie shares the digs of that super-scoundrel Jacques Duclair. I'm seeking a warrant for the whole damned Little Lafitte Island, especially Duclair's little palace."

"How do they get back and forth? Ferry?" Jordan asked.

The detective shook his head. "They've got speed boats, a helicopter, and a small yacht. You name it. These guys can buy and sell just about anything or anybody."

"What can go wrong?" Raine asked the detective. "You've got the barrette, the music box inscribed to her."

The detective nodded. "You heard what Remy said about friends. He'll have had time to warn them. They could be in Mexico in a few hours. I'm betting though on the scenario that Dan Gibson doesn't want to leave without you, Raine. I think that's going to save your daughter's life."

Raine closed her eyes as Jordan squeezed her cold hand. "I think we have an absolute and definite tie-in with the three of them: Bennie, Dan, and Remy St. Cyr," Jordan said.

"And don't leave out the kingpin, Jacques Duclair," the detective said. "He's been able to keep the state's whole police force at bay, with the help of a few powerful political friends. Maybe this time we can send him up for complicity in abduction."

Inside, Rena clucked over them both like a mother hen. She had coffee and chicory and red beans with rice and fine sausages. The food was spicily delicious, but it tasted like sawdust in Raine's and Jordan's mouth, and both ate very little.

Rena brought out scuppernong grape wine from the arbor in her backyard. "Unlike most liquor," she said, "I find this clears my mind."

They drank the delicious wine slowly, thinking of the house they'd just visited.

"I'm sure it brought back memories," Rena said, "but you had some happy ones, too. Don't grieve the past too much, love. Put it behind you and move on."

Quite grimly Jordan said, "That's what we were trying to do when this happened."

They talked quietly at the kitchen table. Rena wasn't surprised that Remy St. Cyr, whom she detested, was mixed up in this. And she was very pleased that they'd found evidence of Kym's presence in that house.

"Poor baby," Rena said, "I knew that dark cloak looked funny. It must have been Kym." She paused. "If I could be a witch right now, I'd ride my broom to Remy St. Clair's and sweep him off the face of the earth." She got up to answer the phone and came back to say it was Serafina for Raine, who got up hastily, nearly knocking the chair over.

"Yes, Serafina," Raine said, holding her breath.

"I remember the names, or a bit of them," Serafina said, excited to be able to help. "There was a man called *Rimmy*, but they didn't talk about him much."

"Yes."

"Bennie Durham," she said, drawing the name out. "They talked more about him than anybody. And they talked about a man named Jacques. If he had a last name, I don't remember, just as I only remember Rimmy" Rimmy, Raine thought, Remy St. Cyr.

"Rimmy and Bennie are McClure cousins on their mother's side. Raine, how are you? Will this help?"

"Yes. Oh, yes," Raine said. "It helps to put the pieces together faster. I thank you, Serafina, so much."

Raine's eyes were so heavy, she could hardly keep them open, and there were many hours to go.

"What have you heard about Dan?"

"Little so far." She told her about the music box and the barrette, as well as the flyers and radio and TV spots showing Kym's photo.

"Raine."

"Yes, Serafina."

"I'm going. . . ."—she paused a very long while—"oh, I am praying for you and the man you love. I have not stopped praying for Kym one minute. *Vaya con Dios.*"

"And with you also," Raine said, replacing the receiver in the cradle. What had Serafina been about to say when she began her sentence with "I'm going?" There had been a pregnant pause on her part, and Raine didn't think she had said what she started out to say.

They continued to discuss Serafina's call after they'd moved into the living room.

Jordan got up and paced the corridor of rooms and out into the hall.

Finally Rena sighed. "And you say, Jordan, that Dan has always been your enemy."

"It seems that way. We fought as children." He looked at Raine and smiled. "As teenagers we fought over Raine."

"And Dan lost."

"He married her through a major lack of communication between Raine and me."

"She talked about you with longing all the time," Rena told him. "And she felt so guilty."

Raine blushed. "I thought Jordy didn't want me anymore."

"That will never happen," Jordan said as he sat down from pacing.

Jordan's cellular phone rang and he picked it up.

"Hello, Jordan."

"Hello, Rita. How are you?" he asked pleasantly, unwilling to deal with his ex-wife at this juncture.

"Jordan, I just want you to know how sorry I am. I'd have called yesterday, but I had a small operation, and I was knocked out on painkillers."

"Thank you. Is everything better for you?"

"Jordy," she said slowly, "I'm doing okay. Let's not talk about me at all. Are they making any progress in finding your daughter?"

Jordan sighed heavily. "A little, but it's needless for me to go into it. We've heard nothing directly from Kym."

"Jordan, I'm sorry for the pain I've caused you. I seem to have a newer mental mirror in front of me now. Anything I can do for Kym, I will. But I think now I can best help by leaving you alone."

"Thank you, Rita, but let me know how you are. You're sure you're okay?"

"Better than okay, Jordy. I think I may be coming into a self I can like and respect."

When Jordan hung up, he said briefly, "That was Rita. She actually sounds like she might be changing. She wished us all the best in finding Kym."

Raine looked at him sharply. There was something different in his voice when he spoke of Rita, as if he admired her, liked her. Loved her? No matter, she thought narrowly. She was focused on Kym, of finding her precious child. Her battle with Rita would have to wait.

Raine and Jordan fell asleep from sheer weariness. Jordan came awake to his cellular phone ringing. It was Detective Davis. He glanced at his watch; one thirty in the afternoon.

"Things are in place," the detective said. "My boss has helped me kick some butt all the way up the line. The Parish gang has seen a lot of light lately, and we did get a search

STILL IN LOVE 221

warrant. So we're going to pay Jacques Duclair a visit tomorrow after I finish getting everything together."

"You know what we're risking," Jordan said. "It may be best to leave Raine behind. Will she be in danger, do you think?"

Lieutenant Davis thought a moment. "Frankly, I think Kym will be in far more danger if she doesn't go. I think she can quickly deflect Gibson with her presence."

With his hand over the phone, Jordan relayed the detective's message to Raine.

"There's no way you're going to leave here without me," she said. "No way at all!"

SEVENTEEN

"Mrs. Gibson?"

"Yes. Who's speaking?"

The male voice was low, guttural, and disguised. Raine strained to hear and understand the man.

"Worried about your little girl?"

"Who is this? And where is Kym?"

Jordy was with Lieutenant Davis at police headquarters.

"You look pretty this morning. You don't have to dress up to look pretty. Regular old housedresses become you. You look good, too, with your hair up."

Raine's nerves were on raw edge.

"Who is this?" she grated. This man was far too close for comfort.

"If you play your hand right and make old Jordan behave himself and not come on like gangbusters, you've got nothing to worry about—and you'll find out where Kym is."

"Who are you?"

"You're beginning to sound like a broken record. I am who I am."

"Dan?" Hardly breathing.

"Hell no! If I were in his shoes, you'd be a lot more afraid of me than you are of him. What have you got against him anyway? The man loves you, you know."

"Tell me where Kym is, or I'm going to hang up. This is Dan, I know it."

The man breathed heavily. "No, I'm not Dan, believe

STILL IN LOVE 223

me. You'd be in a lot more trouble if I were. And don't hang up, or you and your daughter will pay for it."

Raine wished for Jordy. Her head had begun to spin, then it cleared. She had to learn what was right to save Kym. Her heart squeezed nearly dry thinking of her little girl, and she was cold with fear.

"Would you like to talk to your little girl?"

"Yes. Oh, yes."

The man laughed, the ugliest sound she'd ever heard, she thought.

"I'll just bet you would. Well, maybe later if you play your cards right."

"Please," she said as steadily as she could. "Please let me talk with her."

"I said maybe later. And maybe she'll leave these shores without your seeing her again, if you don't play the cards right."

Half mad with fear, she breathed, "Damn you, Dan. Don't hurt Kym, and don't take her out of the country."

"You're tearing your pants with me, baby," the guttural voice growled. "I'm the one with the marked deck. Now you listen to me. This isn't Dan, believe me, but I'm calling the shots on this. It couldn't have happened at a better time."

When he was silent so long, Raine blamed herself for not having the courage to hang up. But this was a possible slender way to Kym, and she had to stay on the line, at this monster's mercy.

Remy St. Cyr's call was interrupted by loud knocks on his door. He recognized the two men: Jordan Clymer and Martin Davis. Slamming shut the cellular phone, he answered the door. Martin Davis leaned against the door frame.

"Mind answering a few questions, St. Cyr?" Detective Davis asked.

"Talk to my lawyer."

"Yeah, that'd be smart," the detective said. "He's a lot wiser than you are, and he's lasted a lot longer than you're going to last."

The two men went in. They were taller, but Remy St. Cyr was wider. All three of the men were trained law enforcement officers. But one now operated far outside the law and had told lies on Detective Davis that implicated him in graft and corruption.

"You're in this up to your teeth with Dan Gibson kidnapping this man's daughter, aren't you?"

Remy laughed in their faces. "You can't prove that. Besides, I didn't give a damn about Dan Gibson until you showed up as this man's friend." The last word was perjorative in his mouth.

Detective Davis ignored his last remark. "How well do you know Bennie Durham?"

"I could tell you again to talk to my lawyer, but I don't mind telling you. Yeah, I know Durham. How could I help it? He lives with Jacques Duclair, and Duclair and I go way back to childhood. Just because you law idiots are against him don't mean I'm ever going to turn on him."

Jordan listened, as the pieces began to fit better.

"Yeah," Lieutenant Davis said. "Your cop expertise and Duclair's drug-tainted millions go well together, don't they?"

"There've been stranger combinations in this world."

"Dan Gibson brought Kym Gibson here to this house, didn't he?"

"How do you figure that?"

"The music box and the tortoise shell barrette."

"You made that accusation yesterday. Don't you know when to quit? I told you I got lots of friends with kids. They come by."

"Tell me what you know, Remy, and I can make it go easier for you. The grand jury is already on your tail, breathing down your and Duclair's necks with an indictment. You know I can help you make it easier on yourself. Help us with this kidnapping."

Remy St. Cyr laughed derisively. "When it comes to friends," he drawled, "I'll take my old friend Jacques Duclair. I feel safer with him than I do with a dozen policemen."

He left them, held the door open, walked out on his front porch, and spat into the yard.

"This visit is over, Davis," he said. "Now I've answered all the questions I intend to. And don't come back unless you've got my lawyer with you."

Inside the house Raine had forced herself to relax. Rena fixed chamomile tea with orange slices and served it to her, massaged her shoulders and soothed her.

"And you didn't recognize the voice at all?" she asked.

"No. I'm sure it was disguised. You can get devices so cheap these days. You can make a child's voice sound like a man's if you push the right buttons."

"Oh, honey," Rena soothed. "This has to turn out right."

Jordan let himself in with the key Rena had given him and went to Raine's side. When she told him about the call, something flashed to his mind. The blinds had been open at Remy St. Cyr's house, and he had been on the phone with his back turned as they came up the walk. Probably a coincidence, but still . . .

"You say this character described you as wearing a housedress and having your hair up?"

"Yes. I've been out in the yard. That's the first thing I thought about. It was someone nearby."

"Yeah. St. Cyr's got an upstairs side porch. It would be a simple matter for him to take binoculars and scan over here. He'd know all about disguising his voice on the phone. We know he's in deep on this, Ray. We just don't know how deep."

Jordan explained to Raine and Rena the Parish police

plans for moving in on Jacques Duclair's house on his island. They had set up fishing and shrimp boats and helicopters would move in all at once.

The sheriff's deputy had seen a strange little girl getting into a boat with Bennie Durham, and had watched as they headed toward Little Lafitte Island, Jacques Duclair's island.

Fear blanketed Raine's spirit like a dark cloud. No one other than the sheriff's deputy had come forward to say they had seen Kym, or some other little girl who may have been here in this section, or may not have.

Raine and Jordan were in his room when the second call came around four o'clock that afternoon.

"Raine."

Unmistakably Dan's voice.

"Yes, Dan."

"So you recognize my voice. I wasn't sure you were going to admit you know me."

Raine started to ask him about the earlier call, but decided she wouldn't.

"Where is Kym, Dan?"

"I don't know. Isn't she with you?"

"You know she's not. What have you done with her?"

"Well, I'll tell you again, I don't know where Kym is—or what's it worth to you if I do?"

"You know I'd do anything to get her back."

"Then you and I may be able to talk turkey. Raine, I want you to come to me, and we'll go away together. You can take Kym with us if you want to."

Craftiness born of a bone-deep love for Kym began to seed itself heavily in Raine's mind.

"Tell me your plan, Dan. I won't take Kym with me. I'll leave her here with Jordy."

"You suit yourself. I'm giving you that choice. It's you I want, baby, and it's you I intend to have."

A violent shudder took Raine. Jordan had moved beside her as she sat on the bed, holding the phone a bit away from her so he could hear some of the conversation. Quickly he got a pad and a pen and held it.

"Tell me your plan," Raine repeated.

"My plan is to take you with me."

"You said that. I'm willing to go if you'll just set Kym free."

"Don't try to play me on this," Dan said, his voice lowering a couple of registers. "Kym's the one who pays if you try to mess me up. I'd hate to do it, but you leave me no choice."

Sobs choked Raine as she continued to talk, then a sudden calm took over. She had to be calm to save her child.

"What are your plans, Dan? You still haven't told me."

With a start, she realized she had gone too far. "Dammit," he roared, "I'm calling the shots now. You never have understood that a woman's not in a man's class when it comes to brains. Now you shut up and listen."

"Very well, I'm listening." Strange how in control she felt now, doing something to save Kym.

"Is Jordy with you?" he asked.

For a moment Raine wasn't sure whether to lie or tell the truth.

"Why do you ask?"

"Is he there?" Dan roared again.

"Yes, he's here."

"Put him on. Have you got a phone extension, more than one phone?"

"No, just one."

"I'm thinking both of you need to hear this, but he can tell you what I'm saying. Put him on."

Raine turned to Jordy. "He wants to talk with you."

She handed him the phone.

"Dan?" Jordy's voice was strained.

"It's me all right," he said, as Jordan held the phone a bit away so she could hear.

"Where is Kym, Dan?"

"Wouldn't you both like to know?"

"Don't play games, man. Don't take it out on Kym because you want to hurt Raine and me."

"Who said I'm taking anything out on Kym? Or that I know where she is?"

"Stop it, Dan," Jordan grated. He had been going to tell Dan that they knew where he was, but the less Dan knew that they knew, the better. Everything was nearly in place for the police to move in. A few more hours before, and it seemed like an eternity.

"Did you really think I was going to let you take Raine away from me?"

"You left Raine, Dan, joined the Army and she seldom heard from you. You married another woman who loved you enough to come looking for you. You have a son."

"I married Raine when you ran off to Canada—and I raised your daughter," he said, refusing to discuss Serafina and little Dan.

"Yes, and I'm grateful, but don't punish them now."

"I loved Kym, until you took over lately and back when we were kids." He sounded as if he were crying.

"Sometimes we can't help the blows fate deals us, Dan."

"Raine is coming with me, and we're going far away," Dan said. "Try that on for fate. I'm going to be fate, Jordy, and I'm sealing yours. You've always had the best of it. Now it's my turn."

"Dan, listen to me. You were the one who had the best of everything: parents who worshiped you, money, all the girls hanging on to you."

"Except the one I wanted. She dumped me for you."

"Because you were running around with a couple of other girls, Dan."

"It's the nature of a man to run, Jordy. I'm sure you've done plenty of it—you just kept it hidden."

"I like being committed to one woman."

"Then why in hell didn't you stay with your wife."

Jordan thought it best not to even try to answer Dan on that.

STILL IN LOVE

Dan drew a very deep breath before he said, "I'm leaving, Jordan, going a very long ways away, and even with Interpol's help you aren't likely to find me. I've got expert help at eluding the law. And I'm taking Raine with me!"

"You can't do that, Dan. You were raised to be law abiding."

"Don't talk like a fool, Jordy. Just your being a lawman turns me in the other direction."

"I'm sorry about that."

"Your being sorry doesn't matter to me, cousin. I'll call you tonight with my plans."

"Dan wait!" Jordan said. "Please let us speak to Kym."

"Who said I had Kym?"

"We saw the barrette and the music box at Remy St. Cyr's house. We know he's a friend of Duclair's and Durham's. And we know you're a friend of theirs and his."

Dan laughed. "Okay. You're so damned smart. You got all the answers. You tell me where Kym is."

Dan hung up then, and the sound of the humming dial seemed the emptiest and almost threatening sound in the world to Jordan. He was a lawman. Was his lawless cousin going to rob him of everything?

To give herself something to do, Raine helped Rena make shrimp and crab gumbo. She had to keep moving. When it was finally done, she hardly smelled the delicious wafting of the New Orleans specialty. But she and Jordan ate a little because they had to have strength.

They had all three done the dishes and sat disconsolately in the living-room when Detective Davis came by. Raine and Rena sat on the sofa. Jordan sat on the floor, his head in Raine's lap. Raine saw his car pull into the driveway and went to open the door.

"I've got a lot to tell you," he said to them. "Is that gumbo I smell?"

That was all Rena needed to go into the kitchen and

reheat the gumbo. She came back out in a few minutes with the bowl of hot gumbo and garlic-buttered French bread on a pretty floral wooden tray.

After he'd eaten the food and praised Rena and Raine, Detective Davis settled back.

"I've got everything lined up," he said. "Before daybreak tomorrow morning, cops will be the fishermen and shrimpers in that part of the Gulf. Now we've had to take over some of the boats and swear some of the fishermen and shrimpers to silence. Maybe it'll work, maybe not. Duclair's sharp, but he's gotten careless, and rumor has it he's into his own drugs, which is never good."

"And if it doesn't work," Raine began, then stopped. "Dear God," she said on a sob. "This has to work."

Raine and Dan told Lieutenant Davis about the calls. He looked thoughtful and disturbed as he listened closely to the tapes they had made of the calls.

"I think you're very probably right about St. Cyr and the binoculars," he said. "He's a piece of work. Since he got on the illegal side, he's got the money to buy powerful equipment. I'm thinking, too, about the first, disguised call, as well as the one you know was Dan."

"Do you think they'll really swap me for Kym?" Raine burst out.

Lieutenant Davis and Jordan looked startled at her question.

"We're not going to let them get away with that," the detective said.

"I know it's hard, Ray," Jordan soothed her, getting up to sit on the couch by her, "but stay as calm as you can. Dan and his friends are doing what they can to rattle us all."

They sat listening for a while to the Easter music, interspersed with pop music, classical, and spirituals. As near as anything could soothe Raine, the music did.

After a moment Lieutenant Davis cleared his throat. "I want to tell you a bit about our plans," he said.

"We've gotten the cooperation of a man who owns a fleet of fishing boats that operate off the little island where Dan is holed up. They have nothing to do with that island, but an occasional boat docks there if it's in trouble.

"Now before daylight tomorrow morning, as I told you, cops are going to be the fishermen manning those boats. We're going to surround the island, and we'll have helicopter support. We've also got an undercover man who's a plant with Duclair, and we're holding our breath."

They sat tensely nursing the warm scuppernong wine that Rena had brought them, awaiting the hours until early morning.

Jordan got up and began to pace.

"Thank God you're with us, Marty," he told Detective Davis.

The detective shrugged. "I couldn't be helping a better friend," he said. "I'll never forget the times you helped me, Jordy.

"Go over the conversation you had with Dan, Raine," the detective requested. "I've listened, sure, but I need your reactions. I want to memorize every word of it. Then tell me as much as you can about your reaction to the first call."

Raine nodded and told him her reaction to the calls. Jordan saw her fear, and his heart hurt for both of them.

"If he should call again, we're ready for him," Jordan said.

"I don't have to tell you we've got listening devices planted around Little Lafitte Island," Detective Davis said. "The only thing is, there's counter-surveillance as well as surveillance, and increasingly the bad guys are masters at it. But I do think we're ahead there."

"I keep wondering if Dan is capable of hurting Kym," Raine said. "I don't want her hurt. I'll kill him if he hurts her."

Jordan stroked her arm. "Calm down, sweetheart. I'm going to get you a tranquilizer."

As he started to get up, Raine pulled him back. "No," she said. "I want the sharpest possible mind. I know if I get too uptight, it interferes with my brain, but I can and I will calm down. I don't want to miss a trick in stopping Dan, Jordy. He's got to let Kym go. If I go with him, I can get away."

"Don't talk like that, Ray," Jordy said. "You're not going anywhere with that bastard."

"We need to get outside for some exercise," Lieutenant Davis said around seven that night. "Jogging maybe?"

They all agreed and jogged around the block several times. Outside the air was crisply cool and foggy.

"If this fog lasts into the morning hours, we'll be in luck," the detective said. "It'll be much harder to trace our movements once they know who some of us are."

Raine and Jordy said silent prayers for continuing morning fog.

"Do you think Dan will call again?" Raine asked.

"It's hard to say," Jordan answered. "I keep wondering if he has any idea of what's going down."

"Knowing Duclair's extensive inroads into this city's police department, I wouldn't be surprised," the detective said. "But I handled most of this myself, and I've got a few men I'd stake my life on. So we're ahead there."

The night air felt good to Raine, as good as anything could feel with the kidnapping weighing her very soul. And Jordan felt a sense of anger he had seldom felt. It was the Easter season, a time for love and sacrifice and good will toward our fellow humans—not treachery and lies and abducted little girls who must be frightened out of their wits.

They were out for a half hour. As soon as they got in, Raine checked the answering service for messages. There were none.

But as if he knew their movements well, Dan called as soon as they had met their personal needs and settled down.

STILL IN LOVE 233

Raine picked up the phone, said hello. Jordan and Lieutenant Davis had checked the electronic bug in the phone by them.

"Hello, Raine," Dan said as easily as if they were friends or lovers.

"Dan?"

"The same. Are you listening to me now? Is Jordy around?"

"Yes."

"I'm not sure I've got anything to say to him. My friends tell me I'm certain to be bugged since that's the business old Jordy is in. Well, you tell my cousin there're a hundred ways to skin one cat, and we're on to all of them."

Raine was silent, listening. Should she ask about Kym, or wait?

"Babe?"

Hesitantly, "Yes."

"I thought maybe you'd been foolish enough to hang up on me."

"No. I'm here." She wasn't going to wait when her heart said ask now.

"Where is Kym, Dan? And how is she?"

"Would you like to speak to her?"

Excitement rose in her breast. Was it a trap?

"You know I would. Please put her on."

"That's the trouble with you, sweetie. Bossy. If I wanted to put her on now, I'd have done so."

"Please, Dan!"

Jordan's and Detective Davis's eyes were on her, supportive, kind. Dan's voice was gloating, cruel.

"You're sweet when you're begging me." Dan chortled.

"All right, I'm begging you," she said sharply.

"Mom!" The tender young voice was choked with tears.

"Kym!" Raine fought to keep her voice controlled and clear. "How are you, honey? We love you—"

Dan's cold voice cut in. "You speak for yourself only.

You're the only one I'm interested in trying to please. Leave my damned cousin out of this."

"All right, Dan. Very well." Then to Kym, "How are you, darling?"

"I don't know, Mom. I'm so scared."

She heard a muffled sound, and Dan spoke clearly to Kym. "I told you no complaining, kid. If you can't stop complaining, I won't let you talk."

"Dan, please, wouldn't you be afraid?"

"Hell, no," he sputtered. "She knows I love her."

Pray God he remembered that love. She longed to tell him that he'd threatened to hurt Kym if it were necessary. But no, that had been St. Cyr. The conversations were jumbling in her head.

"Dan?"

"Yeah, baby."

"Be the man you can be and let her go. We'll meet you wherever you say and pick her up."

Dan's laugh was ugly. "You never really gave me credit for the brains I've got. Nobody ever did. It was always Jordan who was the brilliant one."

"No. I've always known you're smart. I've told you so."

He seemed temporarily mollified.

"Please let me speak to Kym again."

"Sure." Aside to Kym he said, "Now remember what I told you."

"Mom." This time the voice was full of tears.

"Yes, sweetheart. Try not to be so afraid. We're doing everything we can to get you back."

"Mr. Gibson says he'll let me go if you come here, but then he wants to take you away. Mom, can I go, too?"

"Darling," Raine said, hurting in every cell of her body. "We've got so much to get cleared up here. Try not to be so afraid, although I know you can't help it. Just know how much I love you with all my heart. Do you know that?"

"Sure I do, Mom. And I love you so much, and Dad—"

The phone was snatched away. "Damned kid just won't

do what she's told," Dan grated to Raine. "I told her not to bitch, because I'm treating her okay. I've told her she's got nothing to be afraid of. You told her not to be scared, but you didn't say she's got nothing to be scared of."

Outraged, Raine couldn't help fighting. "She's a child, Dan. Don't act like a bully.'

Dan's laugh was short, ugly. "Jordan's the gentleman in the family, Raine. Jordan's the class act. I'm the coach, a rough diamond. But hey, a diamond's a diamond, rough or otherwise. Don't you agree?"

"Yes." Her nerves were screaming. She didn't want to talk about his lifelong feud with Jordan—or whether Dan was smart. She didn't want to talk about whether he was a diamond. Anything about him. She wanted to talk to and about Kym.

"If you'll just put her back on, I'm sure she won't antagonize you again," Raine pleaded.

Without answering her, Dan said abruptly, "Put old Jordy on the line. I'll bet he's already on the line."

"Jordan," Raine said, "he wants to talk with you." She was denying the fact that Jordan had been on another line set up that afternoon by a special police operative.

"Jordy? I want Raine on the line, too."

"Okay."

"I'm happy to be the one to tell you, Jordy, your lucky streak's about to run out."

"Why, Dan? What did I ever do to you?"

"Be born in my family, I guess. Take away the only woman I ever loved."

"You have another wife, Dan, who loves you very much, and you haven't made any effort to get a divorce from her."

"Damn you. You know I had amnesia."

"We'll have you sent up for bigamy if you try to hold onto both women." Jordan drew a deep breath.

"Then you and Raine will be riding off into the sunset, I guess?"

"We haven't had time to make plans, but we love each other."

"Damn your love and your plans, Jordan. I'm messing up your plans. This time tomorrow night, we'll be somewhere else in this world—somewhere that you and the FBI and Interpol all combined can't find us. So much for law enforcement and the law you're so crazy about, Jordy. Do you read me clearly?"

"I think I do. Dan, please don't hurt Kym. Reconsider what you're doing. You've got a wonderful son, man, a child anyone would be proud of—and a woman who loves you with all her heart. Are you going to just throw all this away?"

Dan was silent a long moment before he said, "You always had all the answers, didn't you, Jordy? There's only one woman I want and that's Raine. And she is my wife, you know."

Jordan felt sad. Dan had done his homework well. And he was right. There were places he could go commandeered by drug renegades and no one would ever find him, given a bit of luck that he constantly denied ever having.

"No," Jordan said. "When you stayed married to the woman in Spain who's here now, you killed your chances of being married to Raine. She has grounds for divorce. She's told you that."

Again Dan was silent awhile.

"Would you let me speak to Kym, Dan?" Jordan asked.

"No, you can't speak to Kym. You got her like any animal, and you left. I raised her, supported her."

Jordan didn't want to unnecessarily antagonize Dan, but he felt he had to make him know the truth.

"I'll pay you back every penny you spent on her," Jordan said.

"And I guess you'll pay me back all the love I spent on her, too."

"I'm glad you loved her, Dan—"

"Love her, not past tense. I love her the way I love Raine. Can't I make you understand that?"

STILL IN LOVE 237

This time Jordan was silent. Was it love to curse a woman, push her through a rotten wooden rail so that she lost the child she was carrying for you? Was it love to leave her and go into the Army to get away and rarely come home? Was it loving her to marry again, then regain your memory after that accident in Spain and never let her know? What could he say to Dan?

"I know you love Raine and Kym," Jordan said. "And I'm glad. They needed your love, and I'm humble that you gave it to them."

"Cut it, Jordy. I'm the one who deserves Raine, and I'm the one who's going to have her."

Jordan had to keep trying. "You've got another wife, Dan. What about her and your son?"

At last a breakthrough, but it wasn't what Jordan sought.

"Where I'm going," Dan finally said, "a man can be a real man, have a dozen women if he can take care of them. Ten dozen children if he can take care of them. And I can."

"You're AWOL, Dan. Are you remembering that?"

"That's not a problem, cousin. I'll be beyond the reach of Uncle Sam."

"He's got long arms."

"And I've got fast legs. Let's get down to business, Jordan. This is what I want you to do."

Detective Davis had listened all along, but he relaxed and let Dan's words penetrate his brain along with Jordan's, getting words, impressions, psychic phenomena. He wrote on a pad swiftly. All sensory systems on go. Dan was a man they had to stop.

"You hear me, Jordy?"

"I hear you."

"I'm told at least one detective is noseying around, and that possibly means the whole damned force. But if you're smart, Jordy, you'll cut it close. It's been my experience that law people are some of the stupidest sonsabitches on earth. You agree?"

"You know I don't."

Dan laughed shortly. "You know where the pier is on the land side for Little Lafitte Island?"

"I can find out."

"I want you to bring Raine there at first dark tomorrow night. My folks and I'll be waiting with Kym. Like I said, as far as I'm concerned, you can keep Kym. Even if I do love her, it's Raine I want, and I'll swap you Kym for Raine. I know you'll fight twice as hard if I insist on taking them both. Are you smart enough to make this a deal?"

Detective Davis signaled that he was advising that Jordan pretend to take the proposed deal, and Jordan nodded to him.

"I don't see that I have any other choice, Dan. But you've got to be a man of your word."

"Count on me. See you at first dark tomorrow night."

Lieutenant Davis stood up.

"I'm not afraid," Raine said suddenly. "I would die for my child."

Jordan got up, pulled her to her feet and kissed her.

"I'll make more coffee," Rena said, her hands shaking. "Poor kid. This is a horrible mess."

Jordan found himself seething with anger, but along with a mild sense of helplessness, his brain felt charged, sharp, his senses working at their best.

"Tomorrow morning," Lieutenant Davis said, "between five and seven. We'll be there. We're not playing to his plan."

"How can I wait that long?" Raine said, her voice strained and tense.

Because, she thought, if the excuse for a man Dan had become let Kym get hurt, his own life was going to be worthless.

Jordan's arms were warmly comforting, and she felt electrical alertness begin to permeate her body. My darling Kym, she kept thinking, if only I could bear this pain in your place.

EIGHTEEN

By five the next morning, Raine, Jordan, and Lieutenant Davis were on the Gulf of Mexico, on a fishing boat that was part of seven boats set up by policemen that surrounded Little Lafitte Island. The weather was foggy, with visibility only fair.

Jordan and Lieutenant Davis huddled frequently to further refine their plan to rescue Kym. Raine was there, bundled against the unusually cold air.

Men working with the SWAT team, police, and sheriff's departments set out nets as if they fished and trawled for shrimp. A foghorn sounded in the distance, then another one nearby. Raine thought they sounded so mournful. Her body was unbearably tense with anxiety.

"I don't want anybody to forget that Duclair has a small army of henchmen as bloodthirsty as any you'll find. But he's played it smart so far and kept out of harm's way as far as the law is concerned.

"I'm frankly surprised he'd let himself be connected with a stupid caper like this. He was beginning to try for greater respectability.

"Just be very careful. The men you're up against, as you've been told, are well armed and very dangerous."

"Chin up, sweetheart. This is it," Jordan said softly.

"We'll go in on their private line."

In Jacques Duclair's big white stucco, red tile-roofed house, Jacques, Dan, and Bennie stood in an alcove in the front of the huge living room, with the blinds drawn. They had gotten up early to continue formulating plans for Dan and Bennie to leave with Raine. Dan picked up the ringing phone as servants scurried nervously back and forth.

Lieutenant Davis set up extensions so several of the lawpeople could hear as he dialed Jacques Duclair's number.

"Gibson, is this you?" Detective Davis asked.

"Yeah," Dan said. "You're early. I'm not going to let you screw me up. We can leave now. Is everything ready to roll? Is Raine on board?"

"Raine's aboard," Lieutenant Davis said quietly. "Bring the girl out."

"Not until I see Raine. And listen, we've got high-powered binoculars trained on you, so don't pull any stunts."

Jordan sighed. He and Lieutenant Davis had discussed what happened if Dan and Duclair used binoculars strong enough to tell them a police decoy was being sent and not Raine.

Raine hung up her extension and said to Jordan, "It's not a problem. I'll go, I tell you."

The boat bumped against the pier and the water. The fear made Raine's stomach queasy, but she pushed it aside, thinking only of Kym. Where was she?

"Where is my daughter?" Jordan asked Dan.

"She's here."

"Send her out."

"You take me for a fool, Cousin? Just use your eyes, and you'll see we've drawn two circles side by side in white lime in the middle of the yard. Now I want Raine to walk into the right circle facing you, and we'll spotlight her so we know it's her. Then we'll send Kym out to stand in the other circle. Don't try any tricks, Jordy."

"They're going to have to both be moving at the same time," Jordan said. "You can't expect me to trust you."

"Fair enough," Dan said, watching for Jacques Duclair's signals of approval or disapproval of what he said.

"I didn't expect Dan to be so up-to-date on our plans," Jordan said. "I don't want you to go out there, sweetheart. Too many things could go wrong."

"We have to trust in God and hope for the best," Raine told him. She was strangely calm, feeling that in just a few minutes she'd see Kym. "I've got to go, Jordy. You know I have to."

Jordan nodded, choking back tears. He had never been so scared in his life. His woman and his daughter's lives were in jeopardy, and he kept praying that he was wise enough, strong enough to pull them through.

"Okay," Dan yelled on the line. "What are you waiting for?"

"I want to see Kym come out into the yard, then Raine will get off the boat and walk up and into the circle," Jordan said, his voice hoarse with emotion.

Aside to Jacques Duclair, Dan said, "If Jordy shows his face to me, I'm going to be hard put not to shoot him." He fingered the AK47 assault weapon by his side.

"Don't talk like a damned fool, Dan," Jacques warned. "Bennie's got his hands full, keeping up with Kym, making sure she doesn't spoil things. And I'm in enough trouble with the law without getting into a shootout. You be careful, or I'll have to deal with you."

"Cool down," Dan grumbled, thinking Duclair was touchier than he'd ever have taken him for. Afraid of the law, was he? Well, Dan had found he liked this run-in. This kidnapping caper made him feel like a giant.

"Bring her out, Bennie!" Dan called.

Bennie brought Kym out bundled up in the thin black-hooded cloak he had bought for the kidnapping.

"Give me a kiss, kid," Dan growled.

"I don't want to kiss you, Mr. Gibson," Kym said.

"You're going to see your mother," he said, more than a little put off by Kym's refusal to kiss him.

"Are you really going to let me go?" Kym asked eagerly, her eyes shining.

"Isn't that what you want?" Dan asked, grinning. "You get what you want, and I get what I want."

"When am I going to see Mom?"

"Be patient. In just a few minutes."

Dan turned his binoculars onto the fishing boat. They sure as hell had set that up pretty. Law enforcement people were smart these days, but maybe he was smarter—smart enough that by this time tomorrow morning he and Raine would be settled on the rocky terrain of the godforsaken mountains of El Salvador. Let her try to get away from him there.

Raine's knees were shaking so badly she could hardly stand, but she willed steadiness into them. Jordan caught her to him fiercely and held her a moment.

"Be careful," he said. "We've got you covered."

But Jordan was sick with wondering could they cover her well enough?

Several police helicopters came in and hovered overhead.

The SWAT team was at the ready every second, and in his house Jacques Duclair knew he was beaten before he got started. He'd never have set up to help Dan with this if he hadn't had his own plans for using Dan in his drug operation. This was going to be a neat payoff, because Dan owed him his life. Too bad about the woman, Raine. He'd liked the photographs he'd seen of her.

Drawing her coat about her, Raine heard Dan bark, "Take off the scarf. I want to make sure it's you!"

Raine did as he asked, remembering his now repeated instructions.

"You go into the right circle, Raine. You go into the left circle, Kym."

But sighting each other as Raine went toward the yard and Kym stepped off the patio front porch, they went to each other in the middle of the yard, and Raine fell to her knees, crying and hugging Kym.

"Mom. I was so scared!" Kym wailed, as if the danger were over.

"Goddammit," Dan screamed from inside the open front door of the house. "I told you both to get into the circles!"

"Dan, please, " Raine begged. "She's just a child. She couldn't help coming to me."

Things were going sour, and he was losing control, Dan thought as he played with the assault rifle. Then he was screaming again, "Come back inside, Kym! Turn around and come back in!"

"No!" Raine cried. "I won't let you take her back."

On the boat Jordan stood on the deck, his own binoculars lifted in sighting. Was Dan mad? he wondered. He was surrounded. What did he hope to gain? The helicopters circled overhead. He tried to be cool, collected. But Raine and Kym were the hearts of his heart, and he was going to protect them or die trying.

"I want you both in this house!" Dan screamed. "Come on!"

Raine felt as if hell itself had opened up around her. She clutched Kym to her, stroking her back to calm her.

"Mom!" Kym said again. "I'm so scared!"

The child got up to try to go back into the house, but tripped over Raine's leg and went sprawling. Still on her knees, Raine bent to lift her up and held her tightly.

In the crazed depths of his mind, Dan felt his life turn against him and felt emptiness swallow him whole. In the haze a distance ahead of him, he saw a man who looked like Jordy, but his hands were trembling so bad he couldn't hold the binoculars steady. Jordan, he thought with fury—Jordan who had taken everything he, Dan, had. Well, if Jordy had won and he and his law buddies were going to keep Dan from having Raine as his own, Jordy wasn't going to have her, either!

Two of the helicopters had landed, and the SWAT team was closing in. Dan lifted the rifle and sighted Jordan.

"Dan, don't do it, man!" Bennie yelled.

"I can't let you do that, Dan," Jacques Duclair said coldly. "I told you I was in trouble enough with the law. I tried to help you, but I won't let you hurt me."

Through a bloodred haze, Dan could hear the sounds around him, but he couldn't distinguish between them. Jacques and Bennie became Jordan who was going to keep him from Raine. Coldly Jacques pointed his own .357 Magnum at Dan's head.

Bennie screamed, "Man, don't do it!" He knocked Jacques's arm upward, sending the shot wild. Then the shot ricocheted off a metal plate on the wall, and blood was seeping from Dan's head as he slowly went down.

Covered by the SWAT team, the sheriff's officers and the police from a larger island, Jordan sprinted to where Raine and Kym huddled and dropped to his knees, cradling them both. Like the others, he'd heard the shot and didn't know who it hit, but in a moment of searching he saw it was neither Raine nor Kym. They were fine.

The helicopters were landing, and police officers from them and from the boats streamed onto the beach and into Jacques Duclair's house.

"Oh, Jordy," Raine said, fighting back her own tears to see after Kym.

"Mom," Kym choked, then "Dad. It was so awful. I thought he was going to kill me."

Raine and Jordan comforted their child, making a circle of their love, and hot tears ran down Jordan's face as he said huskily, "Thank God, you're both okay!"

* * *

Back on the command boat, Jordan felt triumph fill him as he kept caressing both Raine and Kym.

Little Lafitte Island lay before them, swarming with police and the SWAT team. Lieutenant Davis came up, his face beatific.

"I'm so glad, Jordy, that we could put this one down as fast as we can. You don't know how long we've wanted to put Duclair's and especially Remy St. Cyr's game out of commission. We can't count the kids they've killed with drugs—buying and selling."

The two men shook hands gravely as they watched policemen bring Duclair, Bennie, and ten other men out in handcuffs and march them to a boat several boats over from the one Jordy, Raine, Kym, and Lieutenant Davis were on.

Something compelled Jordan to look up and into the malignant face of his cousin. With a look of searing hatred Dan gazed at Jordan for a brief moment before his captors pushed him on toward the boat.

Lieutenant Davis shook his head. "Even the Lafitte brothers, famous pirates though they were, had the good sense to go over to society's side before the end."

Without being prompted, Kym went to Lieutenant Davis and gravely told him, "Thank you for helping my dad save me."

"You're very welcome, honey," Lieutenant Davis said, bending to hug her. "I've got a son just your age. See that you and your parents come out to dinner before you leave New Orleans."

"Oh, yes," Kym said happily, then, "Can we do that Mom, Dad?"

Jordan and Raine nodded. "You bet we can," Jordan assured her.

As their boat first drifted, then sped from the shore, Raine looked at the white stucco rambler that had housed a wannabe drug kingpin. Quite casually this man, Jacques Duclair, had helped Dan Gibson kidnap her daughter. One more day and she, Raine, would have probably been in Dan's clutches, too, and on her way to either Mexico or El Salvador. She shuddered at the thought, then turned heavenward with a prayer of thanks before squeezing Kym's hand and bending to kiss her again.

Jordan, Raine, and Kym were in the news all day. They were on TV, and in a special edition of the paper because Jacques Duclair was so notorious.

Kym was like a little shadow. She couldn't bear for them to be out of her sight, and they didn't want her out of theirs.

Rena fretted over them all, crying happy tears. Filled with energy, she began to make more shrimp-crab gumbo.

"It's going to be the best year I've had since you left," Rena declared. "I'll let you rest, but after that we celebrate."

At Charity Hospital they operated on Dan for six hours to remove the bullet. Jordan was there when they finished because he would be one of the chief witnesses to testify against Dan.

Dan's brain surgeon was somber. His business was to save lives, not to make judgments, but he had hated Dan's kidnapping of Kym, thinking of his own children.

When Jordan talked with the doctor, the doctor said quietly, "In removing the bullet, we found a tumor in the hypothalamus that might have been long-standing, but it's growing, so another operation will be necessary. Do you know if he has suffered a serious head injury in the past that might have brought this on?"

Jordan told him about the automobile accident in Spain and that Dan was a coach and subject to injury.

"I remember, too," Jordan said, "someone saying that Dan had fallen and struck his head while coaching. Nobody

STILL IN LOVE

seems to have thought about subsequent damage. Magnetic resonance imaging wasn't widely used then."

The surgeon nodded. "I'd appreciate it if you'll get me all the information you can on his past injuries. What he has to say may not be too trustworthy. That tumor is spreading, and his judgment may not be reliable."

The surgeon let him see Dan, who lay high on his hospital bed. How different from the bully of that morning who had wanted to kill him. All our lives we've been enemies, Jordan thought, when we might have been friends.

When he went back to the waiting room, Serafina stood there.

"You are Jordan," she said. "I know from the photographs. How is he?"

"He'll live," Jordan said, and he told her what the surgeon had said about the brain tumor.

When he had finished, she nodded and her eyes filled with tears, but her small body steeled with determination.

"He will need me," she said, "as I need him."

Jordan pressed her shoulder. "Whatever I can do to help you, I will. How did you know about Dan? From the media?"

"You mean TV? Newscasts? Yes. When I heard about it this morning, I took a standby flight here. My heart is breaking for him. The Dan I first knew would never have done this thing. I am so sorry about your wi—love, and your daughter."

So she knew the whole story as the tabloid TV shows had laid it out. It was too wonderfully flamboyant not to broadcast. Dan was the aggrieved husband who had raised the child of a man who had abandoned her.

Yes, Jordan thought, and they had discovered the story of him and Rita as well. And that played with equal passion. He and those in his life had provided a field day for photographers, if not the paparazzi.

But he was happy. The worst part was over.

* * *

At Rena's home with Raine and Kym, they kept touching each other, and Rena kept touching all three.

He told Raine about Serafina and she was happy, but she said, "She deserves better, but she loves him so. Where is her son?"

"She said she left him with a woman she knows here in New Orleans."

"That's right, she would know at least a few people. She lived here when she came to this country. Look what good friends Rena and I still are."

Kym kept looking with anxious excitement from one to the other of them.

"Would he have hurt me, Mom?" she finally asked. "He had a gun. He said he'd shoot me if you didn't come, Mom."

Raine cradled her to her breast and felt the thin body's heart beating against hers as her child's heart had once beat inside her womb.

"Darling, I hope not," Raine said.

"But Dad and Dad's people stopped him, didn't they?"

"Yes."

"Is Mr. Gibson going to be all right. Will he go to jail?"

"Almost certainly yes on both counts," Jordan said softly.

Looking at each other across Kym's body that sat with shoulders hunched between them, they breathed a silent prayer of thanks as the joyful sounds of gospel music pealed from Rena's compact disc player, filling the room with aching wonder for all their hearts. Holding hands, Raine and Jordan fervently thanked God for His blessings so bountifully bestowed on them that day.

They lounged about, resting and sleeping when the telephone rang. Raine jumped with remembered terror for a moment. "Probably another reporter," Rena said. Then, "It's for you, Raine."

Picking up the phone, Raine thought it was probably Caroline.

"Hello, Raine." Rita's voice sounded sober, grave.

"Yes. How are you, Rita?"

"We'll get to how I am a little later. I'm sorry about what you've been through with Kym. I wanted to call when I first heard, but I was being prepped for yet another operation."

"Thank you. We're just glad it's over, and everything came out all right. Kym's young. Hopefully she'll be on the road to emotional recovery swiftly, but it will take me longer. Was your operation a success?"

"They can't tell yet. You know, my doctor thinks some of this may be in my mind. Psychosomatic . . . Not all, of course, or they wouldn't be operating."

"What do you think?"

"Anything is possible. Raine, I'm not going to play games when you've been through what you and your daughter and yes, Jordan, have been through. He's her father and should have been with you as he was."

This was leading somewhere, Raine thought. But where?

After a long pause, Rita said, "I'm changing. Growing up, I guess, belatedly. Losing Mike hurts like hell, but I've got a lot to go on for." She sounded then as if she were crying. "Tell Jordy hello for me, and I'll need to talk with him, and with you both, soon."

Rita hung up then, and Raine sat for a moment in silence.

"What is it, sweetheart?" Jordan asked. "I heard you say Rita's name."

"Rita asked me to tell you hello. She hasn't called about Kym's kidnapping because she's had another operation. She sounds down, Jordy. She mentioned Mike."

Jordan ran his tongue over dry lips. "Poor kid."

"No. She sounded more adult than I've ever heard her."

"That's good. I wonder what's going on with the operations."

"She doesn't know yet, but the doctor's told her he thinks it's at least in part in her mind."

Jordan sighed. "I hate feeling like a monster about this,

but we're all going to have to do something about this situation."

"You're not a monster. She stopped wanting you first."

"She never really wanted me. She got me on the rebound at Max's urging."

"And because you're a great catch."

Jordan smiled. "I'm glad you think so."

"Max has kept up with us where Kym was concerned," Raine said.

"Yeah. He's a helpful guy."

Raine sat wondering what Rita wanted to talk with Jordan and her about. Rita was ill and might be disabled for the rest of her life. Even if the doctor was right and a large part of Rita's illness was in her mind, what if she could never change, or didn't want to?

Raine reflected that she had always been happy during the entire Easter season, but this season was so filled with first the trauma, then the joy of getting Kym back.

That night, a well rested but media-worn Jordan, Raine, and Kym sat in Rena's living room surrounded by Lieutenant Davis and many of the law enforcement people who had rescued Kym.

Kym hugged each one of them tightly, her little face grave.

"Thank you for saving me," she said to each one, and many of them were crying with joy and release.

Friends of Rena's had come in to help her prepare White House eggnog, so rich a few sips was wondrously filling. There were fruitcakes that had been aged in brandy, bourbon, rum, and wine beginning back last summer, solid chocolate cakes, and delectable coconut cake, plus cheeses and hams and turkey and the potato salad that was Rena's specialty.

Raine bit into one of the crème de cacao chocolate chip cookies and savored the exquisite taste as Jordan fed her the morsel.

STILL IN LOVE

With the music and fellowship of this night eddying around them, she looked at Lieutenant Davis and took his hand.

"We will forever be in your debt," she said.

"It took all of us to pull this off," he said. "If you and Jordan hadn't been so strong, it could have failed."

Raine, Jordan, and his friend, Lieutenant Davis, sat at one of the card tables that had been set up.

"You've done the entire city a favor," Lieutenant Davis said. "St. Cyr, Durham, and Duclair were part of a criminal system that's getting out of hand. They've been lingering on the verge of becoming really big-time drug kingpins, and we've been trying to get something on them that will stick for a long time.

"Now, they're stupid enough to get involved in a kidnapping scheme. Durham's their weak link. He's talking. Of course, he and they were trying to do Gibson a favor out of Durham's kinship with him.

"They're bad guys, and we're happy to be able to take them down so soon. Ever since St. Cyr was fired from the police force, he's gone from bad to worse. With these three out of the way, we've put a big dent in drug crime in the city, and for that I thank you, and the city thanks you."

Lieutenant Davis stopped and smiled, his eyes nearly closed.

"You've got a great woman by your side, my friend," he said to Jordan. Then to Raine, "And you've got a great man by yours."

As Jordan's eyes met Raine's, he placed his hand over hers and pressed it lightly, and his touch sent small thrills through her.

Getting up, Raine and Jordan joined with Kym and Lieutenant Davis and they sang Creole love songs with Rena's pleasant mezzo soprano soaring above the rest.

"What're you thinking?" Jordan asked Raine.

"I guess about Rita's call. I'm clear now of Dan. I already

was pretty much clear of him. But Rita, Jordy—Rita's trying, I think, to grow up because she's realizing the sterling person you are and, having lost Mike, she wants you back."

Jordan looked miserable for a moment, then he drew a deep breath. "Ray, I've said it before, and I'll say it every hour on the hour if you need it. Rita would have to change more than I think she can change before I could get together with her again. We're fated to be together, my darling: you and I. Please don't forget that ever again."

He kissed the tip of her nose and squeezed her hand in reassurance, but the sadness was still there.

"It will take more time than I'd wished it would," he said, "but at some point Rita has to realize that our life together is no longer possible. Our divorce is truly final."

And for long moments of joy and revelry over having Kym back, it truly seemed to Raine that New Orleans lived up to its description as the city that care forgot!

NINETEEN

Raine felt it was wonderful to be back home again. Miss Vi and Caroline couldn't hug her and Kym enough, and Uncle Prince had never stopped beaming.

"Police've been asking them McClures plenty of questions and giving them hell," Uncle Prince said. "Wayne's got a hangdog look about him these days, and I suspect he's ashamed of himself. But now Vera, that ma of his, was one hundred percent behind Dan. She's never backed down."

Miss Vi bustled about the house, cooking dinner as Kym dusted and played with the big brown gingham-dressed doll Rena had given her. So many people had sent her gifts. Amazing. She and Raine were planning to share many of the gifts with children at Minden's hospital.

To save her, Raine couldn't stop glancing around at Kym, keeping her in sight. It had been a month since the kidnapping. School was out for two days to repair a major water main break, and Raine had set about finishing the portrait of Jordan.

"Well, that looks like Jordy, all right," Miss Vi complimented her. "You've done yourself proud, my girl."

"Do you think he'll like it?"

"No," Miss Vi said, "I think he'll love it."

"His birthday's next Saturday, and I'm giving it to him then—along with a special dinner at the same place he took me for a belated birthday."

Miss Vi laughed. "You two are like kids, in the good sense. It takes no more than one of you to light the other up."

Raine grew thoughtful. "Jordan and I go way back, as you know. Sometimes it seems to me I've always loved him, even when Dan and I were dating for a while."

Uncle Prince peeled an old stalk of sugarcane for Kym, then cut the joints into bite-size pieces. Raine got up and picked up a piece off the paper towel padding he used. The cane yielded juice that tasted delicious, and it brought back childhood memories of her own father cutting up her sugarcane and making cane syrup.

"So Dan's got a tumor on his brain," Uncle Prince said. "I guess that may explain some of the things he's done, but since he was a boy, he's always had a streak of evil."

"Spoiled he was," Miss Vi added. "It's just never been good to have a child thinking he's the be-all and end-all of everything. His folks never made him know the difference between right and wrong. He wanted it, he got it, whatever it was. That might work with things. But when it comes to people, they've got wishes we've got to respect."

"The woman that came from Spain seems to be a good sort. Maybe she can help straighten him out."

"If anyone can, she will," Raine said. "She worships him."

"It beats all how he came hankering after you," Uncle Prince said. "He left you, didn't he?"

"Yes," Raine said, "he went into the Army. We weren't getting along. . . ." Her voice drifted. It was strange how since the kidnapping, more of the pain that her miscarriage had left was disappearing. A lot of it had diminished when Jordan had taken her in his arms with tender compassion in Torremolinos, Spain.

"How's he doing?" Miss Vi asked, flipping a potato pancake.

"Jordan calls daily to check on him," Raine answered. "He says that the second operation will be done soon. He

STILL IN LOVE 255

sent word by Jordan that he's sorry, that he must have been out of his mind. I don't know, and Jordan says he doesn't know, if his apology is real, or if it's an act they'll use to get less time for the kidnapping."

Jordan's likeness looked back at Raine from the painting. Somehow she had mixed her colors to get the exact beautiful maple brown of his skin, the odd black brown of his eyes that had gold flecks in them sometimes and the big, perfect white teeth.

She had captured the wicked curve of Jordan's mouth that bespoke a controlled sensuality. Having painted him, she wanted to keep the portrait, but she would do another for herself.

A peal of door chimes, then Jordan let himself in with the key she had given him, bringing along Scott and Caroline.

There were hugs and kisses all around, with Jordan's kiss lingering on Raine's mouth.

"Well, it looks like we're just in time to eat you out of house and home," Scott said.

"Honey, there may not be enough for us," Caroline said. "We're unexpected guests."

"Then I'll go down to Popeye's and get more food," Scott said. "I'm in the mood for a big meal with friends."

"I've got enough here for you two and a couple more," Miss Vi said, eyeing the stack of golden-brown potato pancakes. She rattled off what she had cooking. "Mustard and turnip greens and ham hocks, fried chicken. The potato pancakes, of course, one of my specials. Big salad greens and tomatoes, and asparagus spears. And to top it off, the best bread pudding you've ever had with great big raisins and my extra tasty lemon sauce. Ready in a little while."

"Dad," Kym said.

"Yes, sweetheart."

"Nothing. I just wanted to say 'Dad,'" Kym told him.

Jordan bent to kiss the satiny brown cheek. "I'm glad you

just want to say 'Dad.' I've got all too little time with you before some rascal of a young man comes along asking for your hand."

Kym look puzzled. "What's he going to do with my hand?"

They all laughed. "Oh, Jordan," Raine said, "surely it's at least ten years, and with college, a good twelve-thirteen years."

His voice husky, Jordan took Raine's hand. "We should have gotten married when I wanted us to when we were in college," he said. "That was one of the biggest mistakes of my life."

Raine nodded, but looking back she knew how afraid she had been to face his mother's vitriolic temper and the fact that she wanted a life for her son that didn't include Raine.

Feeling the start of more frustration, Raine reflected that after all this time, she and Jordan still weren't joined in marriage. Kym loved Jordan now—openly and joyfully. To stop the fear she still felt, she focused on Scott who had changed so much. Where he had come to D.C. dour and defensive, clothed in an emotional turtle shell against others, he now flirted openly with Caroline.

"I'm going to do something Caroline's going to kill me for," he said now. Grinning, he dug into his sports jacket inner pocket and brought forth a black velvet ring box. Snapping it open, he displayed a set of clear white diamond rings that flashed their brilliance in the sunlight.

Thinking of her own rings that she wore in her bosom, Raine gasped with delight for her friend, and Caroline looked as if she would faint.

As Caroline sat down at the kitchen table, dizzy with joy, Scott knelt by her chair on one knee.

"My beloved," he said. "I won't ask you to marry me because I couldn't take it if you said no. I'm telling you you've got to marry me. I'm done for if you don't."

Caroline threw her arms around his neck. "Oh, you idiot. You don't have any doubts that I'll marry you. Yes! Yes!"

When the couple had been congratulated all around, Kym piped up, "Oh, goody, I get a chance to be a flower girl."

"First choice," Caroline said, hugging her.

"Will you have children like Mom and Dad have me?" Kym asked.

"Oh, yes," Scott said, expanding his chest. "Many children."

Caroline rolled her eyes and muttered, "Well, one anyway."

"Woman," Scott said to her. "We will discuss this over good wine and much love."

"Agreed," Caroline said, glowing like a star.

But Caroline saw the misery behind Raine's eyes and knew that as happy as her friend was for her, she suffered the pain of not getting over her own fear.

Jordan didn't miss one nuance of Raine's aching misery.

"Get your coat and walk outside with me," he told her and went to the hall coat closet with her for his own overcoat.

They walked slowly down the stone path and stood at the edge of the pond, with the weeping willows, furnishing a lovely contrast to the newly spring-leafed trees. Silently and friskily Ripley and Lilac, the hounds, padded behind them.

"Raine, my darling," he said. "I see how upset you are that Caroline and Scott are getting married but not us. Rita called last night. She wants to talk with us and asks if we can come up to New York this weekend. She wonders why we aren't married."

Raine felt her heart constrict. "I'm trying, Jordy. Really I am, to stop being afraid. Did she give any idea what she wants?"

"Well, she sounded upbeat, which knowing Rita, could mean anything." He frowned deeply. "She said she's making every effort to change, and she's succeeding. She talked more about that than anything. She said she now wants to be mature. She didn't have to tell me what it cost her to lose Mike. I just don't know, Ray. I don't know. We'll have to face that uncertainty when we see her. Are you willing to fly up?"

Inside Raine was crying: Why don't I get over my fear that I'll die if you leave me again?.

Gently, he turned to her and took her gloved hand. "It's going to be all right, Ray," he said. "I'm going to see that it's all right."

But could he see to it that it was all right? Hearts didn't always lend themselves to logic or reality. Slowly she began to try harder to overcome her fear, to move on in spite of it.

Rita was at home in the big apartment on Manhattan's East Side that she had shared with Jordan when they were in New York. The decor was stunning pastels and expensive furniture, Raine thought as Max let them in. A maid hovered in the background.

Max hugged Jordan and kissed Raine's cheek. "I hope you don't think I'm being too familiar," he said.

Raine shook her head. She couldn't read him. What was happening to the psychic power Miss Vi had assured her that everybody carried?

Rita was propped up in her lavishly appointed bedroom on many thick, cream, eyelet-edged bed pillows. She looked beautiful with her light brown hair spilling about her shoulders.

"Jordy!" she exclaimed and raised her arms to him. He bent and kissed her cheek, as her arms went around his neck. Did he tarry longer than necessary? Raine wondered.

"Raine, it was good of you to come," Rita murmured. Raine took the proffered hand that was exquisitely manicured with deep rose nails that matched her rose velvet bed jacket.

"I'm going to go out for a while," Max said. "I don't know how long you'll be staying, but please don't leave before I come back."

"Sure thing," Jordan replied, "but we do have several places to go and won't be staying long."

"I'm sorry to hear that," Rita said plaintively. "I'd thought you might stay awhile."

"Well, we're here now," Jordan said, settling in a chair by Raine's side next to Rita's bed.

Rita rang for the maid and offered them refreshments. They chose red-clover herbal tea and blueberry muffins.

"We're going out to dinner," Jordan told her.

Rita looked sad. "Those were the days for me," she said. "Dinner, dancing all night." Then, "Oh, well, I refuse to wallow in pity for myself. If I have my way, those days will come again."

Raine looked up suddenly and Jordan beamed. "You're certainly operating in the right frame of mind," he said.

The radiant look came back on Rita's face.

"Where to begin," she said softly. "Give me your hand, Jordy. Please push your chair closer."

He did as she asked. What was going on here? Raine wondered, her heart sinking.

Abruptly Rita began. "My accident and being afraid I was going to die set me thinking about my life."

Rita's face lost its radiance as she winced with pain and began to cough.

"Listen," Jordan said, rising with alarm. "You don't have to talk if it hurts you. We can come back." His voice was tender with concern.

"Sit down, Jordy," Rita said, forcing a smile. "Believe me, I am getting better, and this seems worse than it is." She paused, then continued. "Now is the time for me to talk with you both. Raine, when I heard about Kym, I couldn't stop crying. I had nightmares every night. For the first time in my life, I realized how short our time on this earth can be."

Again, she looked radiant, the way she'd looked when they'd entered the room.

"Thank you," Raine murmured, her heart in suspense.

Where was this leading? Raine wondered, and what was Jordan feeling? Was he falling in love all over again in spite of himself?

"I'm going to stop chasing you, Jordy," Rita said as Raine and Jordan reeled from wonderful shock. "Yes, I love Mike and he's gone, but not from my heart."

After the briefest of pauses, she went on. "I'm truly sorry for all the misery I caused you and Raine, Jordy. You were right. You were a good catch, but even when I married you, I married you because I couldn't have Mike.

"He always said I was too flighty, too immature. Well, lying here, I'm beginning to think he's right. But I am growing up. I'm determined, and I'm beginning to know the direction I want my life to take."

"Oh, God, Rita, thank you," Jordan said. He got up, bent and kissed her cheek again.

"We can wait until you're better," Raine offered, and Jordan looked at her gratefully.

Rita shook her head.

"No. I feel as if a powerful burden has been lifted from me. My own narrow meanness was dragging me down. Deep inside, a part of me isn't like this, but loving Mike and knowing he never loved me hurt. I had to keep proving something to him.

"It's always been Mike for me and not you, Jordy, but I don't think I hurt you by saying this because you've always known, haven't you? Besides we're even. I've always known, and you said in the beginning that you loved Raine before anyone else. Neither of us could help what we've felt. You've always known, haven't you?"

"Yes, the way you loved Mike. I knew."

Rita drew a very deep breath, and her eyes almost closed.

"For the first time in my life, I feel free. Can you both understand that?"

Raine and Jordan nodded their happy understanding.

Rita continued talking, her chin lifted. "I'm doing much better. I have all the hope in the world of getting well. And my heart is expanding now where it was squeezed shut.

"I know you won't be able to believe this, but I'm happy for you, the way I'm happy to have my own life free. I know I'll slip back from time to time, but I'll come out of it, too. This feels good. I'll find someone else who I can love and who loves me. I know that now."

"Rita, thank you so much," Raine murmured.

Looking at Raine, Rita smiled gently. "You're going to make a beautiful bride."

They stayed an hour longer, waiting for Max. Rita insisted that they were not tiring her. "This is a memorable day for me," she said, "the day that I took one of my longest steps toward being a first-class woman and not a spoiled brat."

With tears in his eyes, Jordan said, "You're already a first-class woman, Rita. You just never realized it."

"Well, well," Max boomed from the bedroom doorway. "Have I given you three enough time to thresh things out?"

"Yes, Dad," Rita said happily. "I think we're all going to be moving full speed ahead."

Raine and Jordan stood up awkwardly at Max's request. He squeezed Jordan's hand and kissed Raine's cheek.

"I want you to know," he said, "that I couldn't have chosen a finer husband for my daughter. But it was my choice—now she gets a chance to choose her own, with my blessing."

He turned to Raine, then to Jordan. "Jordy," he said, "next to my daughter here, you've chosen one of the world's finest women. I just wish she'd sell me that painting of Mr. Thomas that she calls A Prince."

Raine laughed delightedly. "Well, that painting now

hangs over the mantelpiece of the Prince himself, but you made another request that I can grant."

Max squinted. "You don't mean you'll really agree to do my portrait?"

"Well, it'll take time. I am painting and teaching, you know. But we could get started this summer."

"It's a deal. And price is no object."

Raine smiled. "In that case why can't it be my present to you?"

Max's laughter boomed throughout the apartment. He said to Jordan, "She makes an old bachelor codger like me want to marry again."

Jordan and Raine laughed and said they understood all too well. They left then, lingering a bit longer by Rita's bedside and wishing her well.

And Jordan thought it took forever for them to be back on the empty elevator where he could hungrily kiss Raine again.

TWENTY

Standing on board the *Sea Nymph* in the late July afternoon off Torremolinos, Malaga, Spain, Raine placed her hand on Jordy's arm, feeling the light seaspray on her face, reflecting that this July was the most glorious July she had ever known.

She and Jordan had been married in Las Vegas. Fear still knocked at her ribs, but Rita's courage had helped show her the way.

"No one was ever more in a hurry than we are," Jordan had teased her. Kym was their flower girl.

"How do you like her?" Jordan asked, speaking of the yacht they were on.

"She's perfect. Isn't that why they refer to ships—in the feminine gender?"

"Sexist," he teased.

"No way," she answered him. "Without you, my world would be sad indeed. We're equals. I like that about us, Jordy. We have—and we're going to have—a wonderful life."

"Mom! Dad!" Kym came running up to them, excited about a Spanish doll that one of the crew members had given her. "Isn't she beautiful?"

"Yes, honey, she is," Raine said.

"Well, she is at that," Jordan told his little girl. "But I know a certain young lady who's even more beautiful."

Kym giggled and hugged his side. "I'm so glad you brought me along," she said. "I'm enjoying this."

"Not half as much as we're enjoying having you here," he told her.

The *Sea Nymph* was a small yacht that belonged to one of Jordan's wealthier clients. Sleek and glistening white, it cut through the water effortlessly, often carrying the precious cargo of honeymooning couples.

A fiery sunset had just set, and the shadows of its rays clung to the horizons in a splendid array of reds and golds with a hint of grayed purple that reflected a coming rain.

They were on a two-week tour of Spain and would go to Madrid to visit the Prado and to other scenic spots. They would also go to Nevada Mountain, where they had gotten the information about Dan's marriage that had helped free Raine.

She now wore the engagement and wedding rings on her fingers that had lain so long in the valley between her breasts. Now Jordan lifted and kissed the hand the rings graced.

"You two hug and kiss so much," Kym said, teasing more than complaining.

"Ah, honey, a few more years and we'll have to caution you about seeing the light too soon."

"I don't understand what you're saying."

"Give yourself time," Jordan said. "You will."

They linked hands and went below to their stateroom and Kym's cabin which was a few doors down from them. The crew baby-sat her, and she had a special nanny, Anna, furnished by the company that ran the yacht. Now Anna came up the passageway.

"I wondered where my charge had gone," she greeted them. "Should we get ready for dinner now?" she asked.

"Oh yes," Kym said happily. "I'm going to wear my white organdy with the ruffled bolero."

Anna put her arms around her. "We know you're going

to look pretty whichever dress you choose," she told the child as she led her away.

In their stateroom Jordan pulled Raine close and kissed her thoroughly.

"Unzip me, please love?" she asked him, and his hands caressed the ivory linen and silk of the sheath she wore. She stepped out of her flat tan multi-strap sandals and pushed them near the bed.

"You're taking a chance," he said, "asking me to unzip you. We're only a couple of garments away from setting my heart on fire."

Raine shook her head, smiling.

"I've got you covered, mister. It's too close to dinnertime, and they've got your favorite rib roast and mango ice cream."

"You're my favorite dish."

He bent and cradled her face in his hands and kissed her so long her body began to slump against his, her heart drumming, tasting the honey of his mouth.

"Ray," he murmured. "I really ought to take you now."

Raine laughed merrily then. "You've got a one-track mind, my love."

"And how many tracks does yours run on?"

"Where you're concerned, the same track. Look, we're on the same wavelength—but if you'll remember, the skipper told us he was setting up something special and private for us on deck after dinner."

"Music," he said, "that we can dance to."

"And he's going to teach us to tango. Now we can't pass that up."

"I could."

"Don't do it, or I'll kiss you so hard your breath will stop," she said.

"I dare you."

But the supremely passionate mood had lessened. They

kissed again and began to move about the stateroom, dressing for dinner.

When Jordan was silent for so long, Raine told him, "Penny for your thoughts."

He sat down heavily on the bed, holding one black dress loafer.

"I'm thinking about my dad and how he would have loved having me married to you. He thought we were perfect for each other."

"He was a wonderful man, Jordy."

"Yeah. I'm thinking, too, of how he died with the community, or so many in the community, believing that he shot a kid in his custody. I'm going to make a special effort now to get to the bottom of this. Knowing the McClures, it isn't going to do any good to talk with them. Dad always said it was Wayne's father who shot the boy."

"That was a terrible time. The whole town was torn apart with it. Jordy, you know I'll do what I can to find the information we need."

Jordan nodded. "He wouldn't have wanted me to brood over this on our honeymoon."

Jordan didn't mention his mother at all. She'd told neighbors that the charges that led to his father's death were the major reason she was going back to her native Montreal.

Raine stood in front of him and drew his head against her body, stroking his hair.

"I remember how he loved you," Raine said, "and how good he was to me. Jordy, I'd like nothing better than to clear his name."

He hugged her to him. "My very own woman," he said. "Let's get back to a happier spirit."

Raine took a moment to enjoy their space.

"Jordy," she said, "it was wonderful for you to have the same flowers sent in that you sent me during my birthday week: green orchids, red roses, pale yellow roses, purple

STILL IN LOVE

orchids, carnations, peonies, a bird of paradise. Darling, you are a lover after my own heart."

As he sat on the edge of the bed, she went to him and kissed he top of his head, then sat beside him and touched the tip of is naked nipple with her tongue.

Jordan drew a startled breath and huskily told her, "You are one provocative woman. Keep it up, and I'll give you what you're asking for."

Raine laughed with delight. "Self-control is everything. Calm yourself now."

Jordan stood up. "Hurry up." He looked at her with a mocking leer. "We wouldn't want to miss the tango lessons," he said. "Man, after that, the glory of what we'll have tonight will make last night pale."

Raine shook her head, sudden tears misting her eyes. "No Jordy," she murmured. "Last night was beautiful. Perhaps tonight will be even more so, but I don't see how it could be."

"Trust me," he said levelly and quickly flashed her a kiss with his tongue in the corner of her mouth.

A long and leisurely dinner finished, the captain had the deck cleared and a dance floor set up on the starboard side, which was the right side of the yacht. Piped tango music greeted them as they went on deck. Raine felt romantic in her sheer blue linen dress with her high heeled dyed-to-match sandals. Her hair was banded in blue linen and pulled into a French twist.

"You look unusually beautiful," Jordan said as he lifted the golden stream of tiny-beaded necklace he had given her so long ago.

"And you look unusually handsome," she said, appraising his white linen jacket and dark pants and the starched, pleated white shirt. "Mr. Magazine Cover."

Kym came to bid them good night. "I wish I could stay for the dancing," she said wistfully.

"Leave something for later," Jordan said. "You've got a lot of living to do."

"Your father is right, you know," Raine said as the nanny came up to claim Kym, who kissed Jordan and Raine good night.

After Kym had left them, Raine went to the yacht rail and looked out on the sparkling blue Mediterranean lit by the full moon that hung in the star-spangled sky.

"Jordy," she said suddenly, "do you ever look at scenes like this and want to cry? Am I being maudlin?"

"You know you're not," he said gently. "Yes, Ray, I look at scenes like this and want to cry. But more than that, I look at you and my heart just fills up."

"A moment ago, seeing Kym, she's so much like you. I don't wonder that Dan had begun to be angry with her."

He placed a finger across her lips. "Don't talk about Dan now," he said. "Later, sure. But now there're just the three of us in our little universe. Yeah, we're a part of a greater world, but right now leave Dan out."

"Yes," she said. "I think you're right." She moved close to him and put her arms around his neck. "I love you so much," she whispered. "I never dreamed life could be this good."

"Same here," he whispered back. "And it gets better. I promise you that."

The captain came on deck, his ruddy face alive with merriment as the volume of the music increased. With one of the female crew members, he demonstrated the intricate, dazzling steps of the tango.

"It must come from the heart," he said. "Give yourself up to love, to life. The tango is a dance of the spirit, its movements as beautiful as any you will ever know."

Raine watched with awe and Jordan with narrowed learning eyes at the couple gliding through the passion of the tango. She squeezed close to Jordan's side, and he took her hand in his.

"How beautiful," she breathed. "I think I could do it just by watching them."

After so short a time, the captain bowed before Raine, requesting her as partner for his tango, and the woman offered her hand to Jordan. It was surprisingly easy for Raine to follow the captain's instructions. Expertly he led her up and down the deck in the dimmed pale-yellow light.

They paused, and the captain talked to her about the history of the tango, mentioning how its popularity waxed and waned, but never went out of style. As a dance, it was the epitome of romance. As music, it was the soul of love. Romantic love.

"And you, Senora Clymer," he said as they danced again, "are a natural. We seldom find that in those we teach."

Raine thanked him, wanting to get back to Jordan to exercise what she had learned. But the captain led her through two more sets before he told her she should take more lessons when she returned home. He said she had the talent for a master tango dancer.

Jordan watched Raine and the captain out of the corner of his eye. He had had a few tango lessons when he'd visited Argentina on business, and the woman he danced with was as expert as the captain.

"Senor," she said, "you know something about this dance."

"Not much, but some."

"You are fairly good already, but there is in you a little too much resistance. You need to let go and let your body flow with the music. Be one with your partner and the rhythm." She laughed.

"I have always said that the tango is the music of the gods. It is their gift to us."

To both Raine and Jordan, it seemed all too long before they were together with the entrancing tango. With her hands resting lightly on his shoulders and his hands on her hips, they moved with the magic of the music and the night, no less than their love.

Jordan's hands on her hips were making her dizzy with wanting him. The nearness of her body, fragrant with jasmine oil, was driving him crazy with desire.

The captain and the woman crew member left them, and they danced alone under the moon and stars accompanied by an unseen orchestra. Moving with elegant ease, dancing at last with abandonment to nature's passions, they seemed to themselves the essence of everything that was good on this earth.

They danced a long while, and as they began to tire, the music calmed and Luther Vandross' soothingly delicious voice touched them with its romantic splendor.

"How on earth . . ." Raine began, "would the captain guess that's a favorite of ours? Oh, Jordy, you had him play this song."

"Guilty as charged," he murmured.

She put her arms around his neck and drew him close, their bodies pressing into each other's until it seemed they would meld.

"Let's go in," she said. "I've had enough of the tango for tonight."

"Yes, let's," he told her. "I've got a different kind of tango in mind that we do well together."

Going below, they stopped by Kym's cabin, went in and kissed her good night.

"She looks like an angel lying there," Jordan said. "I get mad all over again when I think about what she's been through."

"She seems to be getting over it though," Raine said softly, closing her eyes for a moment, bringing a flashback of those awful days when Dan had held Kym as his prey.

"Jordy," Raine said, "we have so much to be thankful for."

STILL IN LOVE

Raine then Jordan kissed Kym, who stirred but did not awaken.

Back in their stateroom a sense of lassitude came over Raine when they entered.

Looking around them, Raine laughed. "All the flowers you sent and brought me during my birthday week repeated here. Darling, you're so extravagant. We'll raise our children in the poorhouse." Her breath caught when she said it, and she felt momentarily sad.

Jordan smiled. "A friend in Mexico ships me flowers at will at a nominal cost. He's a horticulturist." He stopped and cupped her face. "You said children, Ray. When we get back, let's bite the bullet and check to see if the damage you suffered falling through the rail can be repaired. I think I make a pretty good Dad. Might as well get a chance to prove it often."

Raine's spirits lifted. Maybe there was hope of more children for Jordan and her. "Three's the limit," she scoffed. "I'm the one who carries them nine months, not you."

"Make no mistake about it," Jordan said somberly. "I'll be carrying them right along with you. Oh, sweetheart..."

Raine went into her dressing room and slipped off her clothes. The night before they had made love in joyous haste, driven by naked hunger for each other for much too long. Now she felt relaxed sensuousness in every cell of her. She slipped into the dark rose silk gown with its snug and nearly backless bodice that was embroidered in an orchid pattern. She pulled on the exquisite dark rose chiffon wrap and went back to the stateroom.

Jordan stood at the porthole, looking out at the water. He wore the wine silk pajamas she had bought for him. Holding out his arms, he told her, "You're so beautiful," as she walked toward him, then into his waiting arms.

Barefoot, she stood beside him at the porthole as they looked out on the shimmering water. Blue cut diamonds. His hands stroked her bare back under the negligee. Silently he caressed her body. Languorously, deliciously his fingers massaged her scalp. Her supple body followed the outlines of his, and both were so full they could not speak.

Jordan lifted her as cool breezes swept over them. The moon's shadows followed them as he carried her across the room, putting her down by the side of the bed where he slowly and carefully stripped the wrap, then the gown from her glistening body.

Quickly and deftly she unfastened his pajama buttons and threw the top aside. Then she untied the string of his pajama bottoms. He stepped out of them, and both stood naked and still wild with hunger for each other.

He lifted her gently and put her on the bed where she drew him down on top of her. They traded kiss for kiss, both patterning circles of love. He loved to kiss her throat where the strong pulse beat, and she responded by sweeping her tongue up and down the large cords of his neck.

"Oh, my darling," she whispered after a long time. And hearing the magic of longing in her voice, he began to kiss her fervently, trailing kisses that began at her hairline, went into her hair, and traced her face and neck and arms.

His mouth found the tender brown mounds of her breasts and hungrily suckled first one nipple then the other, moaning in the back of his throat.

"Oh, Ray," he said softly after a moment, as her hands caressed his body in kind and found the tumescent splendor of his shaft that throbbed with near violence at her stroking.

He turned her over to poise above him, the wings of her soft hair brushing his face. His hard body pressed with aching tenderness against her soft flesh as she lay against him, half fainting.

"Now, sweetheart!" she whispered urgently.

He entered her smoothly, gently, his heart thundering in approbation of his movements, and he spread his fingers over her hips to press her further in on him. Raine gasped

STILL IN LOVE 273

with sheer delight as Jordan turned her over and arched above her, driving now with tender force that brought them both to the brink. Then he was still for long moments inside her.

"Right now, I'd like this to go on forever," he whispered.

"Oh, yes," Raine cried.

Leaning over her, he flipped on the switch of the compact disc player and the music of the tango poured into the room, surrounding them with the music of passion.

"Now," he said huskily, "I'll show you what else I know about the tango."

Raine's laughter pealed through the room. She was happy, and her heart was rife with love for him.

"And I'll show you what else I know about the tango," she challenged him.

He got off the bed, stood up, and pulled her to her feet. On the beige plush rug, they danced the tango, their naked bodies smooth against each other when they met. His hands on her hips seared her flesh with his touch. Her hands were on his shoulders, fingers pressing hard against him, pulling him in as if she were afraid of losing him.

Pausing in the middle of the floor, he drew her to him and kissed her ardently, their tongues alternately probing each other's.

"Bravo, tango!" he cheered as his hands stroked her hips.

"Jordy?" she said, suddenly serious.

"Yes, love."

"I love you in ways I'm not sure you know I do."

Jordan nodded. "Then we're even, Ray. The years I was away from you were the hardest I've ever known."

"Me, too," she murmured. "I was living in hell and couldn't bear knowing it."

"We're lucky," he said. "So many people never had what we've managed to get for ourselves."

"I know."

"I like the way we fit together: talking to each other, not

holding back—open, honest. Ray, if I had my choice of heaven, it would be to stay with you and Kym."

"I feel the same way, Jordy. I'm not afraid any longer."

"Good," he whispered, "I'm glad."

She pressed her mouth to his, then with the tip of her tongue slowly brushed along the outlines of his mouth, going inside where his tongue took hers. The tango ended, and a different song from Luther Vandross than the one they had played on deck came on. In his husky baritone, Jordan sang a bit of it to her.

"Shouldn't we be doing something about the fact that the tango is over and another kind of love song is on?" she asked wistfully.

He held her to him then, glorying in the feel of her softly firm body against his. They were even more intent with each other then, lost in their love and in their passion.

Inside the hot sheath of her body, Jordan felt delicious love flames take his body, felt her grip him as the entire length of her body shuddered with thrilling release. She cried out to him in love and wonder.

The world outside them was calm, glittering with stars, but they rode a wave of passion as turbulent as the ocean in the midst of a storm.

"Ray, my darling," he whispered to her. "This is what I mean when I keep telling you that I'm fated to love you. So much more than this, but so deeply this, too."

"Yes! Oh, yes!" she moaned in the back of her throat. As she lay beneath him, rushing to him in love, she heard herself call his name again and again as she spun into the depths of a vortex of passion, then came back to earth and lay there in blessed peace.

EPILOGUE

Sitting on their large screened back porch in late spring, Raine could hardly believe that two years had passed since she and Jordan were married. Smiling, Jordan looked directly at her belly enlarged with his child. She blushed.

Over a year ago doctors had been able to repair the damaged muscles of her womb that her miscarriage with Dan's baby had caused. The results of that operation had been one of the joyful moments of her life.

Oddly enough, another joyous moment had been when six months after she had had the terrible motorcycle accident, Rita had fallen in love with one of the doctors who treated her and two months later, they had married.

A short while back Raine and Jordan had gotten a letter from Rita. She wrote that she was happy the way she had never hoped to be and that she knew what mature love was for the first time. In her last paragraph, she added:

> When I am well—and my husband assures me that I will be well—there is at least one child in my future. With this kind of love in my heart, I can stop envying you, and I wish you only the best.
>
> Rita

Scott and Caroline's little girl sat on Scott's knee, as Caroline rolled her eyes. "He's going to make an impossible dad," Caroline said. "This poor little girl is already spoiled."

"Surely not my friend Scott," Jordan teased. "The man who took no love prisoners and was never going to let woman or child capture his heart again."

With a mock sigh, Scott said, "One and the same, I'm afraid. And believe it or not, I'm happy, really happy."

"It shows, Scott," Raine said gently.

Looking out on the expanse before them of heavily flowering pink and white wild plum, peach, and apple trees in the lower right quadrant of Challenger Farm, Jordan was happy that he and Raine had chosen to stay there instead of building elsewhere. His eyes lit up as he looked down at the pond with its weeping willows and stone benches where he and Raine had studied, argued, and sat rife with passion in their teenage years.

Biting his bottom lip, Jordan thought he nearly had it all. "You're awfully quiet," Raine said to Jordan as Miss Vi and Uncle Prince came onto the porch and sat down.

Jordan looked at his wife. "I'm thinking," he said, "about how we've run up against a brick wall, trying to clear my father's name. There's a great deal of feeling in the law segment of this town that the principals are all dead, so why keep pushing it?"

"It's a shame," Uncle Prince said. "Everybody knew Delman McClure was as mean a rascal as ever walked. I always figured his son Wayne just never had a chance with Delman and Vera raising him. Well, my advice to you, Jordy, is just keep looking to clear your daddy's name. He was about as fine a man as you could find."

Both Raine and Jordan nodded in agreement.

Miss Vi looked lost in thought for a moment, then she got up, took the baby from Scott, sat down and gently jounced her on her knee.

After a long moment of silence, Miss Vi turned to Jordy. "Son, I hate to get your hopes up, but I've got such a powerful feeling that something will break where you and your dad's concerned. Now, if I'm wrong, don't hold it against me, but I thought I ought to tell you what I'm feeling."

Jordan smiled a little glumly. "Thanks, Miss Vi. Yes, you tell me what you're feeling. If it takes me the rest of my life to clear Dad's name, and even if I don't succeed, I'll never stop trying."

Quite abruptly Miss Vi said, "I hear Vera McClure's in a bad way mentally. It seems she don't hardly know a soul anymore. I hate to speak ill of the dead or the mentally poorly off, but she's done enough dirt to people in her day."

They all nodded in agreement. No one had forgotten how Mrs. McClure had sided with Dan all the way through and said Jordan and Raine got no more than they deserved.

As if called by their thoughts, Kym came up with a spray of peach blossoms.

"I've been watching your progress over the farm today," Caroline said. "You're getting to be one lovely charmer, my girl."

Kym blushed. "Thank you. Your baby, Dana, is beautiful."

Caroline smiled. "Your world's about complete now, isn't it?" she said to Kym. "And you're growing up so fast. Eleven years old. How time passes."

Kym nodded and went to stand by Jordan. "I'm so happy my dad's with us now. And Mom's happy."

Kym frowned a moment and didn't tell them, but she had a brief flashback of the time she had stood on Jacques Duclair's lawn and in Raine's arms had heard the gunshot and been terrified—indeed, as she had been terrified from the time she had known she was being abducted by Mr. Gibson.

She came back to herself quickly. It was all right now. She and her mom and dad were together. Still, she couldn't stop the shudder than ran through her.

"What is it, darling?" Raine asked. "You look a little peaked."

Kym shook her head. "It's all right, Mom. Really, it is." she bent and hugged Jordan. "I love you and Mom, Dad," she said.

"And we love you," Jordan answered.

Miss Vi stirred. She was getting a vision, but it wasn't clear. When she went home, she'd brew fresh coffee and chicory in her old pot that left more coffee grounds for reading.

"Dan's served two of his fifteen years in a federal prison," Jordan said, "and all of his allies got just a few years less as accomplices. Duclair, St. Cyr, and Bennie Durham."

"Yes," Raine said, "and Serafina's moved close to the prison to be near him. She loves him so much, and he's accepted her and his son." Raine stopped, sighing, then continued. "He changed after the operation for the tumor on his brain."

"You reckon the tumor caused all that trouble?" Miss Vi asked. "You never said your feeling."

Raine thought about it. "The doctor said it wasn't likely that the tumor caused it all, but they couldn't tell how long that tumor had been growing. They don't think it grew from the time he was a child—and he could be, plenty mean then. The brain tumor, no doubt, made everything worse."

"Yeah," Jordan said. "We owe one hell of a lot to Martin Davis, our detective friend in New Orleans. But the whole New Orleans police force had wanted Duclair and St. Cyr's hides for a long, long time. There's nothing more rotten than a cop gone bad. St. Cyr had helped Duclair set up a drug empire that was on the verge of going really big-time."

"Now," Scott said grimly, "they're all in prison—federal prison for the interstate crime of kidnapping."

They talked around Kym because they knew she hadn't forgotten her ordeal, and they felt that letting her know that the men who had done this horrific thing to her were being punished was a good thing. And listening to them, Kym felt a little safer each day.

Raine remembered the discussion that day a few weeks later when Wayne McClure came up as they walked about the front yard pruning japonica bushes one morning that following June. School was out, and Raine was also working on a portrait of Dana, Scott and Caroline's baby. It was Friday.

"Like everything you do," Scott had said. "It has heart and even more, soul."

Kym had gone to spend the day with a friend. Raine and Jordan were alone in the yard, engrossed in the pruning, when they heard the gate open and someone's throat being cleared. They both looked up at once to hear Wayne McClure say, "Mornin'."

"Good morning," Jordan said stiffly.

Wayne stood twisting his old, dusty black hat in his hands. "I wonder if I could have a word with you all?" he asked.

Jordan had begun to refuse to talk to him. They had not spoken since Vera McClure had told him on the courthouse steps after Kym had been abducted, "For once in your life, Jordan Clymer, you got what was coming to you."

Somehow Wayne's demeanor was different, humble, something he'd never been before, and Jordan changed his mind.

"You don't have to invite me on the porch," Wayne said. "But I sure do need to set down. My legs ain't holding up too well lately. I got a lot to say I think you'll want to hear, especially you, Jordy."

There was something compelling about Wayne's tone. Raine signaled to Jordan her willingness to talk with Wayne. Grudgingly, they invited him onto the front porch and into the high-backed cane rocker. They sat near him on the porch swing.

"I'm gonna make this short," Wayne said. "But I got to explain a few things. I reckon everybody's heard how Ma's mind is going under. She don' even know me anymore." His eyes looked rheumy, and he looked full of despair.

"I'd of told you a long time ago, since my pa was dead. He told me on his deathbed to tell you and everybody, but Ma wouldn't hear about it—called me an ungrateful son. Said I was spittin' on my pa's grave, even if he told me to do it." He looked at them, his voice trembling. "I'll get to the point," he said.

"Pa killed that boy, Jordy. Your daddy didn't kill him. My pa was a man of strong with violent hatreds, and he couldn't stand being crossed. My ma couldn't, either. So it ain't always been easy for me. . . . The boy he killed threatened to sue him for beating him."

Jordan sat bolt upright. For a moment he felt lightheaded with joy, but then he thought, it still didn't clear his father's name. He couldn't expect Wayne to speak out.

"I reckon," Wayne said, "I can see your brain working. I'm telling you two. Ma don't know or care about me or nobody no more. I guess you're wondering what good's it gonna do, except you two know and that's got to help."

Jordan nodded. He started to ask if Wayne would be willing to speak out.

Wayne McClure anticipated him and nodded. "It ain't even gonna be no skin off my back anymore to tell whoever you think is necessary my pa did it. Like I said, Ma's out of it and Pa's gone on to heaven or hell or somewheres. That what you want to know, Jordy?"

Jordan nodded, his throat and chest too full to speak.

Wayne looked easier now, a little happier. "Course," he said, "there's members of my big family ain't gonna take it good. They'll blame me for telling family secrets. But I'm telling you all, since my own ma don't know me no more, I know what it's like to hurt. It's like the Lord's opened up a path for me that ain't been there before.

STILL IN LOVE

"I won't ask you to forgive me for knowing and never saying, Jordy. I even helped to keep it alive that your daddy done the deed. God forgive me."

Wayne McClure stood up then, tears in his eyes. "I reckon I'll just say good-bye now," he said.

"Wayne," Jordan said, "please don't go just yet. I do forgive you. You didn't have to ever say anything about this. Stay for a cup of coffee and something to eat. There're so many questions I want to ask you."

"Why, I'd be pleased to stay," Wayne said with alacrity. "And another thing I want you to know," he added. "Dan lied to me. He said he wouldn't keep the little girl more'n a day, just to scare you, Raine. I never held with hurtin' kids or frightening them too much. I'm sorry about that, too."

"Thank you," Raine told him. "And I forgive you, too."

Wayne sat up, the burden he had carried so long lifted from him.

"Let's go back to the kitchen," Raine said, remembering a day a couple of years back when Dan's wife, Serafina, had sat on this same porch with her son, then had come inside to break bread in friendship.

"Do you like pancakes or biscuits?" Raine asked, "or waffles?"

Wayne half closed his eyes, already smelling the food to come. "Oh ma'am," he said, "I like biscuits and pancakes, sure, but waffles is somethin' I love."

Jordan and Raine looked at each other, smiling, and both set out to prepare a worthy breakfast for their guest.

That night as Raine lay in Jordan's arms, the windows open and a growing moon peeking in their window, Raine ran her fingers over Jordan's beloved face.

"I still can't believe Wayne McClure came here and said the things he said," Raine told him.

"Neither can I," Jordan answered. "But I'm glad he did.

He's really in pain, sweetheart, and I feel sorry for him. He's right, you know. Some in his family are going to give him hell for telling this."

"I know. We'll have to do what we can to make it up to him."

"Raine, I can't wait to go with him to the Minden Police Department to start the ball rolling to clear my father's name. God, I hope he doesn't change his mind."

"I don't think he will," Raine said thoughtfully, "but we'll just have to wait and see. Hurry, Monday!"

"Yes," Jordan echoed her. "Hurry, Monday!"

Slowly Jordan drew her into the circle of his arms and pulled her across his chest, listening to her heart beating against his.

"Sweetheart, whatever happens," he said, "let's keep on believing what I've always said about us being fated for each other."

He caught her to him fiercely. "My darling, Ray," he told her, "no matter what, we will always be together." With tender hands, he cupped her face as he kissed her, tasting the honey of her mouth. She was his forever as he was hers. And together, they knew that they had all that heaven allowed. After all this time they were more than ever still in love.

Dear Readers:

Nothing is more poignant than love lost and regained. And nothing is more frightening and painful than a missing child. These are two primary elements of the story as Jordan Clymer, Raine Gibson, and Kym Gibson lived it. I enjoyed writing it, and hope you enjoyed reading it.

Your many letters pertaining to my other novels have brought me great pleasure, and I will be happy to hear from you again. I publish a biannual newsletter with tidbits about my book backgrounds and items of interest in the world of romance.

May your life be rich with romance, love, good fortune, and good health.

Cordially,

Francine Craft

Francine Craft

ABOUT THE AUTHOR

Francine Craft is the nom de plume of a Washington, D.C.-based writer who has enjoyed writing for many years. A native Mississippian, she has also lived in New Orleans and found it fascinating.

She has been a library searcher for a large nonprofit organization, an elementary school teacher, a business school instructor, and a federal government legal secretary. Her books have been highly praised by reviewers.

Francine's hobbies are prodigious reading, growing orchids, photography, and writing song lyrics. She presently lives with a family of friends, a "jungle-sized" cat, a cocker spaniel, and many goldfish.

COMING IN APRIL . . .

A TIME TO LOVE   (1-58314-008-5, $4.99/$6.50)
by Lynn Emery
To discover his roots, Chandler Macklin takes a job in Louisiana. He's interested in Neva Ross's insight on the history of Louisiana . . . and her charm. Neva's hesitant. Her past relationships failed—why would this one be any different? When his ex-wife wants to reconcile, Chandler's torn between giving his son a stable family and a true love with Neva.

ISLAND ROMANCE   (1-58314-009-3, $4.99/$6.50)
by Sonia Icilyn
Cara McIntyre, co-founder of a London advertising agency, is in Jamaica for her agency's first major international account. With business resolve, she meets with coffee plantation owner Cole Richmond. But she loses her poise in his presence, and Cole's set on proving he's the one for her . . . even when someone from his past threatens their chance at love.

LOST TO LOVE   (1-58314-010-7, $4.99/$6.50)
by Bridget Anderson
To start over after a painful divorce, family counselor Deirdre Stanley-Levine returns with her daughter to her hometown in Georgia. But after an article by journalist Robert Carmichael is featured in his newspaper, Deirdre becomes the target of a madman. Now, while falling in love, Robert must help save the woman who roused his burning passion.

SWEET HONESTY   (1-58314-011-5, $4.99/$6.50)
by Kayla Perrin
Samona Gray falls for the handsome writer who moved in next door. He's the first man in a very long time she feels she can trust. Then she learns that Derrick Lawson is really a Chicago cop on a special assignment: to get close to her and learn the whereabouts of a fortune in missing jewelry. Her faith in men is tested once more, and ultimately, her faith in love.

Available wherever paperbacks are sold, or order direct from the Publisher. Send cover price plus 50¢ per copy for mailing and handling to BET Books, c/o Kensington Publishing Corp., Consumer Orders, or call (toll free) 888-345-BOOK, to place your order using Mastercard or Visa. Residents of New York and Tennessee must include sales tax. DO NOT SEND CASH.

BOOK YOUR PLACE ON OUR WEBSITE AND MAKE THE ARABESQUE ROMANCE CONNECTION!

We've created a customized website just for our very special Arabesque readers, where you can get the inside scoop on everything that's going on with Arabesque romance novels.

When you come online, you'll have the exciting opportunity to:

- View covers of upcoming books
- Learn about our future publishing schedule (listed by publication month and author)
- Find out when your favorite authors will be visiting a city near you.
- Search for and order backlist books from our line catalog
- Check out author bios and background information
- Send e-mail to your favorite authors
- Join us in weekly chats with authors, readers and other guests
- Get writing guidelines
- AND MUCH MORE!

Visit our website at
http://www.arabesquebooks.com